The Green Line Runner

The Green Line Runner

A Novel of Cyprus

JOHN STEWART

McFarland & Company, Inc., Publishers

Jefferson, North Carolina

ISBN (print) 978-1-4766-7217-5

LIBRARY OF CONGRESS CATALOGUING DATA ARE AVAILABLE

British Library cataloguing data are available

Front cover: illustration of runner by Tithi Luadthong (iStock);
map detailing the UN buffer zone in Cyprus (United Nations)

Printed in the United States of America

*McFarland & Company, Inc., Publishers
Box 611, Jefferson, North Carolina 28640
www.mcfarlandpub.com*

"But I have dreamed a dreary dream
Beyond the Isle of Skye.
I saw a dead man win a fight,
And I think that man was I"
  —*Ancient Scotch poem attributed
  to the Earl of Douglas*

1954

Khlorakas, on the west coast of Cyprus. A cool night in November. A dinghy bobbed its way with resolve through the Mediterranean water lapping against the shore. It was within a few meters of the pebbly beach when a Greek voice with a rifle muttered from a rock, "Who goes there?"

"Grivas is here," came the soft response. The little man with the heavy moustache who stepped out of the little vessel was in his mid-fifties, quintessentially Hellenic. If it had not been for the high degree of secrecy which surrounded his landing, Colonel George Grivas, war hero and already almost a legend, might have been, from his appearance, a mild-mannered, cultivated businessman with little more important in his life than his grandchildren's birthdays. But his mission was bigger than that. He was here to kick the British out of his country.

1979

The Circle Line train jerked to a halt just before it got to High Street Ken. By that point most of the passengers had been disgorged and there were now only two left: John Reid and another man sitting across from him, a rangy, freckle-faced, sandy-haired fellow about Reid's age, sport coat, prominent Adam's apple, tan briefcase with "WW" monogrammed on it. Naturally, they had to talk.

"Could be worse. Could be in the dark."

The man with the briefcase laughed, not an attractive noise by any means. And not immediately identifiable as a laugh. More like a leprous

1

dog sneezing into its curlicue droppings. "Yeah. Could be the Black Hole of Calcutta, all over again. It's bloody hot enough."

Yorkshire accent. Stark. Uncompromising. Singularly unattractive. It always had that effect on Reid, as, of course, it does on most of the civilized world.

Then, the power cut off, and so did the dialogue.

Reid was always uncomfortable in tight public places when it suddenly goes dark. Didn't particularly relish the thought of a total stranger groping him, or trying to lift things out his back pocket, especially when he was sitting down. Nothing really paranoid here, it's just that this sort of thing happens a lot in blacked-out tubes. Always has done. Very English. Pubic transport. Mostly frotteurs when it's crowded and it's a hot day and everyone's standing, packed like Safeway's pilchards, sweat pouring out of them, every son of a bitch pervert out in force, the "Oops, sorry" bastards, the "Oh, dear, I must have dribbled yogurt down the front of my trousers" brigade. That's not so bad, but the occasional dip is what's truly upsetting, when, black as the ace of bloody spades in there and with nowhere to go and nothing to do except sniff undeodorized body parts, someone grabs your fucking nuts, and when the lights go on you look around for the likely suspect, and all you see is a thousand pretty women holding on to the overhead straps and grinning at you from their hairy armpits.

Needed to fix the guy's location, and keep it fixed. "Calcutta? Never been there. Have you?"

"No. Closest I ever got was Cyprus."

"Cyprus, eh? That's funny. I was there too. When were you there?"

"In the '50s." The disembodied voice was evidently not inching any closer. "My old man was Army."

"Mine too. Where were you?"

"Nicosia."

"What's your name?"

"Billy Wackett."

"Lala Mustafa Pasha Street?"

Reid heard the lad suck air. "What's your name?"

"John Reid."

Bullying his way through Billy's almost impenetrable dialect, Reid understood him to say, "I don't believe it. I don't bloody believe it."

Reid felt an almost uncontrollable urge to reach out in the blackness and throttle the guy, to press his thumbs against that gross Adam's apple until he heard it break.

Billy asked where Reid was getting out.

"Next stop, if we ever get there. High Street."

Billy suggested they go for a coffee.

Then the lights came on and the tube train started up again. The two grown men looked at each other with great interest, and shook hands. No marriage rings evident, but a dense patch of bristly ochre-colored hair covered the back of the Yorkshireman's middle finger like a mat. Odd, and singularly off-putting. Must have rubbed a lot of girls the wrong way. One would have thought he'd have gone to a professional to have that taken care of. They postponed whatever else they'd planned for the day and spent an hour yakking in a cheap cafe on Kensington Church Street, or at least as cheap as a cafe can be in that neck of the woods.

It so happened that after his time in the Army was up, Billy's dad had gone back to Sheffield and died soon afterwards. Something awful to do with his bowels. Pretty little Mrs. Wackett was still alive, and had married again, to the local postman of all things. Billy himself was now living in Bushey, Herts. Came to London a lot on business. Reid never did find out what his line was exactly. Billy didn't seem keen to tell him.

*   *   *

They swapped addresses and phone numbers and promised to keep in touch. The old eternal bond rubbish, the way you do.

Reid thought about the other old neighbors they'd been talking about. Just for the hell of it, and being a sentimental sort of bloke, and besides, there might be a book in it, that very afternoon, as he strolled back to his flat, he dropped into Kensington Library to see if he could track any of them down.

President Denktash he knew about; you couldn't escape the newspapers and TV. Despite their friendship in the '50s, Reid had never contacted him. Never even thought about it, really, until now. But it was the Zoffels he went for first. Partly because they were Americans, and American carried with it a sense of romance and mystery, at least in the movies and in one's memory of childhood. First people he'd ever heard speak through their nose, except that gossiping old bitch Mrs. Fond, who'd had a much-needed operation to remove her mouth.

3

Burt and Pam Zoffel. Burt had always been touchy, testy, ill-tempered. Reid had been particularly friendly with Tim, their older kid, who was his age. Joe was two years younger, and hadn't learned to talk. He had been merely a baby vegetable who sucked his toes.

The Zoffels left Cyprus in '58. No one seemed to know where they'd gone. Now, more than twenty years later, all Reid had to go on was that they were Americans. Nothing more. But, Zoffel must be a singular name. Not like Smith or Jones. The library had a battery of American phone books, and so Reid began trawling. Starting with New York City, of course, being the biggest, but nothing. So, it was truly then an uncommon name, very uncommon. Not a single Zoffel to be had in the world's largest city.

Then he tried Chicago. Bingo. George Zoffel. He took the number down, then pressed on through several more big city phone books: Washington, Cleveland, Seattle, Houston, before giving up. Couldn't find another Zoffel. This George in Chicago had to be related. Fifty million to one odds on.

Jerry and Helen Heditsian were next. Armenians. He knew they'd also left Cyprus in 1958, for Canada. Not a clue about the city. Luck was on his side, however, with the very first Canadian phone book he tried. Vancouver. Heditsian, J. So he took that number too. This was going to be fun.

The first call he made from his flat that evening was out of curiosity more than anything: Billy Wackett, or at least the number he'd given Reid earlier that day. Didn't look right. The code. And it wasn't right. It turned out to be Wang's Fish and Chips, in Harrogate, not even close to Bushey, Herts. The oriental who answered was of indeterminate gender, evidently had a growing queue of Yorkshiremen desperate for a big cod piece, and grew more and more disturbed when Reid kept repeating the word "Wackett." The phone eventually went dead.

Reid's mind went back to the cafe on Church Street, where he'd scrawled a phone number on a small decaying piece of yellow beer mat with stains on it that looked like a small scale map of the Outer Hebrides. With his thumb obscuring the isle of Benbecula, he'd handed it to Billy Wackett, saying, "Call me sometime." He felt quite certain that Billy would never put finger to hole. But you never know about these things. Reid smiled. A few months before, in the East End, he'd dropped into a public bog to take a leak, and on the wall, scrawled in purple crayon, some wag had reproduced last year's Who's Who entry for Beryl Cox-Ucker, high-class tart on the Isle of Dogs. It probably wasn't her real name, neither was the phone number, but you can't always tell when facts might come in handy. Who knows, maybe Billy might strike it lucky.

A little later that night John Reid made the first of two phone calls to North America.

"Is that Mr. Zoffel?"

"Yeah." He rasped. A file on metal. It was a voice out of an old black and white Al Capone flicker. George Zoffel was an old black and white man.

In the most friendly and open manner, John Reid explained his mission, but George had never heard of Burt Zoffel, or Pam. Cyprus meant nothing to him. So Reid thanked him and hung up.

*   *   *

George Zoffel set the phone down slowly, the corners of his thin, letter-box mouth working laboriously on the violet-flavored gum. He finally took it out, stuck it on the edge of the desk he was sitting at, thought some more about the gum, ripped it free with some savagery, and flung it in the trash can with a potent expletive.

After only a slight hesitation, he pulled out a soft pack from his top drawer, looked at it with total lack of expression for a good ten seconds, then all of a sudden shrugged his shoulders, and extracted a Camel with what almost amounted to gay abandon, ripped off the filter, and lit his first of the day. What was it the commercials used to say about walking a mile for one of these? His doctor had been telling him for years, "George, George, George," as if the diminuendo in the delivery would be more telling than the regular line of platitudinous bullshit. Maybe it had worked, to some degree. But hell, now was the time to inhale like crazy. The guy had sounded innocent enough, but you never know. He cleared his throat, and then dialed a number in North Carolina, let it ring twice, and hung up. He repeated the process and less than a minute later the reply came.

George Zoffel grabbed his phone on the first ring, and practically yelled into it, "Burt!"

"Yeah," replied Burt, not even bothering to tell the old man to keep calm or he might injure himself.

5

"Can you talk?" George was rapidly calming down of his own volition now the nicotine was getting into his bloodstream.

"Yeah."

"There's been a guy looking for you."

"Tell me everything," said Burt.

George got excited again. "Guy named John Reid. Ring a bell?"

"No."

"Cyprus. When you were there. Said he was a kid back then. Said he was just looking you up, for old time's sake."

"Yeah, I remember him. A Brit."

"Dangerous, Burt?"

"No, George. Don't worry about it."

"What if he calls again?"

"He won't," Burt said.

*   *   *

And that was that. But it was, indeed, something to worry about. More than Uncle George would ever know. But there was no point in agitating the old man any further. Burt knew how upset George could get and what that could lead to with the old man's digestive tract, his heart, his lungs, his colon, his damned testicles when he coughed. Burt didn't want to know about that, not at this point in his life.

He decided to keep this to himself. No reason to tell Pam. It would only lead to another long, drawn-out quarrel. He could see it now. The accusations, the recriminations. What a life. Burt slamming the phone down. Yeah. What a life. All the looking over one's shoulder. The triple locks on the doors. The things that go bump in the night.

For good reason the Carmine's Pizza boy sprang into his mind. No big deal, but it had set Pam off like you wouldn't believe. It was in D.C. They were renting an apartment for a week. One o'clock in the morning the doorbell rings. They both go to the door and Burt looks through the spy hole. It's a black guy. Burt throws open the door, grabs the guy and hauls him inside, fist cocked, ready to kill him.

"Carmine's Pizza! Carmine's Pizza!" Poor bastard. Been given a wrong address. The Zoffels picked the pizza up off the floor, paid for it, and ate it. It was pretty good. Had pineapple in it. But the following day Pam told him she'd had enough. Of the pizza and of Burt. She'd had it for

6

a quarter of a century. It was enough for Burt too. More even for Burt than for Pam.

Anyway, this Reid guy, dangerous or not, Burt knew he'd have to call Leo.

When you start turning over rocks that have remained unmoved for decades, you find things lurking there, breathing, breeding and palpitating, and they're rarely pretty. If they were, they'd be out in the sunshine, not lying buried, skulking under a rock. That's the way nature is, the way life is.

1958

The night of October 3, 1958, was a bad one in Cyprus. Particularly in the town of Famagusta. A bad night for everyone. Earlier that day Mrs. Margaret Cutliffe, wife of a British soldier, had been shot dead by unknown assailants while out shopping. News of the incident was broadcast early that evening.

Bitterness had been running high on both sides, the occupying forces and the Greek Cypriots. The emergency was now in its fourth year; the ethnarch, Archbishop Makarios, who had been exiled to the Seychelles in 1956, was now living in Athens, whence, from behind the scenes, he continued his struggle against Britain; and Colonel George Grivas, with his handful of EOKA guerrillas, was still free in the mountains of Cyprus, waging his David and Goliath war on the battlefield itself. EOKA execution squads were roaming the streets of the cities, blowing the heads off British soldiers. The government gallows were thudding with regularity as yet more batches of terrorists hung by the neck, and, to exacerbate the problem, intercommunal fighting had broken out between the Greeks and the Turks on the island. With an easy conscience the Turkish Cypriot minority found themselves pro–British. The Cutliffe killing was the spark that ignited the powder keg which exploded with an ugly bang that night.

Although the murderers of Margaret Cutliffe were never identified, the British immediately assumed the crime to be the work of Grivas's EOKA boys. Hordes of enraged squaddies swarmed armed into Famagee as the last wail of the old World War II air-raid siren died away to signal the curfew, and then the pogrom began, a feast of revenge and racial hatred.

Thousands of Greeks were the victims of the orgy that night, pulled out of their homes, beaten, kicked, raped, dragged off for interrogation in scenes reminiscent of some of the activities of the SS a decade before. The atrocities, by British standards anyway, were remarkable, and hundreds of Greek Cypriots were injured sufficiently to warrant hospitalization. Some died.

Soldiers combed the town in packs, looting and wrecking property, shops, houses, cars. It was carnage that night.

The alley was dark and led nowhere. The Cypriot should not have been there that night. To be alone, in an alleyway such as this, on a night like this night, was crazy, a bad choice. It was his fault for being there. But he had made a mistake, wandered in there, hoping to escape the violence of the streets.

The seven young soldiers were all privates. Most of them were in their early twenties, a couple were in their teens still. Some were from Lancashire, and a few from within the sound of Bow Bells, as could be judged from their accents, their broad, harsh accents. They were also extremely annoyed Englishmen, the sort of Englishmen who need only the slightest excuse to throw off fourteen centuries of civilization and revert to their true Anglo-Saxon barbarousness. Now they stood in his way, barring the nervous Cypriot's exit from this trap.

You'd never know it, the alley being dark, but the man's eyes were ice-blue, and, as everybody knows, fear and panic shine more wildly in ice-blue than in any other color. He made a dash toward the soldiers in an effort to get by them and back out to the safety of the dangerous streets. One of the Cockneys stuck out a uniformed leg and the Cypriot sprawled to the ground with a grunt, grazing the palms of his hands, and tearing his left trouser leg at the knee.

"Let's get the bugger," cried one, and a swift kick from a heavy boot connected with the body of the fallen Cypriot. He let out another gasp as another boot dug in savagely.

"No! No!" The voice was weak. "This is wrong. This is wrong." But the red had obscured the boys' eyes, the hot blood of vengeance throbbing in their heads deafening them.

The unfortunate Cypriot almost sang as a size-13 black Liverpool boot crashed sickeningly into his ribs, cracking several with that one blow, and he was down for good.

"Let's cut the bastard's balls off," suggested a skinny Londoner with ferocious glee. This kid was probably no more than seventeen. A large, evil flick-knife was produced with expert quickness, a click was heard and the long silver blade swept naked through the night air, glinting in the dull light from the distant street lamps.

"Get his fucking trousers down, then," yelled one of the Northerners, and the pack pounced on their helpless victim. They shuffled him roughly into a corner where it was darkest and most difficult to see from the street should anyone chance by, for they intended to commit a crime which was beyond the order even of that day. And it began.

"Hold his fucking legs still," ordered the ecstatic surgeon. His blade came down. "His knob's in the way. Hold his knob up."

From that wretched corner of the alley came a blood-curdling shriek, a despairingly bestial howl which could be heard for miles, and for years. And then it was all quiet.

"That'll teach the fucking cunt," yelled the knifeman, wiping his blade clean on the Cypriot, and slowly standing up. "He won't go round shooting innocent Englishwomen in the back any more." He plunged his toe-cap into the inert body on the ground. The group of soldiers stood up and gathered around the young surgeon.

"Anyone want an extra pair of pills?" he cried, throwing the contents of his bloodied hand into the air.

"It was easier than I thought it would be," said one of the boys, rather quietly, suddenly subdued by the force of the vicious events he had just witnessed, that he had just been part of. "I mean, I thought it would take a bit of time to do that."

"Not if you've got the knack," yelled the triumphant Cockney, folding the crimson blade and slipping it back into his pocket. He was still high.

One of the Lancs boys stooped down, and rummaged through the man's pockets. He stood up, looking at some papers. He walked toward a faint ray of orange light.

"Gimme a torch," he demanded, and a young hand passed him a flash-light. He shone it onto the documents, and his hand began to tremble violently.

"Fuck me, he's a bloody Turk. He's not even Greek. He's a fucking Turk."

"How do you know?" asked one of the others, the voice containing panic.

9

"'Cause I can fucking read, that's how I know," and the youngster jabbed afresh at the documents in his hand. Tears welled up in his eyes, and then wouldn't stop, streaming uncontrollably down his cheeks. The others crowded around to take a squint at the papers. Their faces were sober, and getting more so by the second. The youth dropped the documents and the flashlight, and stood shaking helplessly. No noise in the alley. The full realization of what they had done had come home to them. They had just castrated a friendly Turk.

"Get the fuck out of here, lads." The stern, deep voice came from behind them, and the seven spun around to see a tank-like figure blocking most of the dim light from the world outside, a world far away.

A short, shocked hiatus led of necessity to "Yes, Sergeant," the voice a skinny reed. The boys bolted anxiously past the big man.

"Get back to your barracks and stay there. You were not here, you understand?" And they were away, out onto the familiar street, where the comforting noises of the night could be heard and enjoyed once more.

The enormous sergeant walked over to the fallen articles and picked them up. He examined the papers then, without a glance at the body in the corner, he returned the way he had come. He lifted the lid off a metal garbage-can standing in the mouth of the alley, took out a silver cigarette lighter, set light to the papers and dropped them into the bin. And then he too was gone.

Two eyes burned wildly from the darkest recess of the alleyway, the eyes of a badly wounded animal. They burned a path of prodigious pain and hatred through the darkness, through the present, to a time that would surely come.

1979

Heditsian, J. This had to be old Jerry.

"Hello." Deep voice, almost your cartoon Bulgar.

"Is this Jerry Heditsian?" Reid asked in his most gregarious tone.

"Yeah." Very suspicious.

"Jerry. This is John Reid, in London. I just want to see if you're the Jerry Heditsian I used to know, who was my next door neighbor. Tell me, did you use to live in Cyprus?"

The answer was slow in coming. You could hear his brain working. "Yeah." Even more suspicious now.

"Did you use to live on Lala Mustafa Pasha Street?"

Finally, he answered. "Yeah. How old are you?"

A strange question, but it was the way Jerry's brain was grappling with this.

"I'm twenty-seven now, but I was a little kid back then."

Then, all of sudden, he was animated, for Jerry, anyway. "Okay, I know who you are. I don't believe it. How long has it been?"

"Twenty years, Jerry."

"Twenty years," he repeated. "I don't believe it. Helen won't believe this when she gets home."

After a while, Reid asked him if he ever heard from the Zoffels at all, Burt and Pam Zoffel.

"Used to. Not now. Not for years. Used to get a Christmas card from them every Chris—, every year."

"Where did they live, do you remember?"

"Nah. Don't remember. USA somewhere."

"So, they were definitely American then. Not Canadian."

To the untrained British ear, Americans and Canadians sound alike.

"Oh, yeah. American, okay. Can't remember the state."

"So, what are you doing now, Jerry?"

"Ships. Riveter. Rivet bolts onto ships in Vancouver. You know what that is?"

"Yeah, I know, Jerry."

Reid didn't have a clue what it was, but he didn't want Jerry to expatiate on the ins and outs of what sounded like the world's dullest occupation.

He gave Jerry his London number, and the Armenian promised to call. There are some moments you just can't recapture.

*   *   *

Jerry got off the phone, dumbfounded. But pleased. This was a good moment. You needed all the good moments you could get if you were a riveter. His heavy jowls seemed to recede back into his face, and for a few seconds he was the young Jerry Heditsian from the Cyprus days. Okay, wait till Helen hears about this. Then he started thinking about the Zoffels.

Somewhere there was still one of those old Christmas cards they'd sent. Somewhere. Okay, Helen would remember. She kept up with all that sort of thing.

When she got back that evening, she went straight to it. Yeah, it was in the photo album they'd made up years ago, for old time's sake, for the memories, the way other people do. There it was, envelope and all, address and everything. A 1971 address, actually a P.O. box in Washington, D.C. No phone number though.

It wasn't the last card the Zoffels had ever sent them, Helen reminded her husband, even though he couldn't really give a damn. The last one had been a couple of years later. "Burt and I are going our separate ways," it had said. "Will keep in touch." They never did. Helen had some more cards somewhere, in the junk closet. She'd dig them out some time.

Jerry reached for the phone. But Jerry was a cheapskate. It would be an international call. His last phone bill had been sixty bucks and he'd gone bloody nuts. Yak yak yak at eighty cents a minute. He took his hand off the phone, in order to avoid the low-level temptation. Okay, later, I'll send him a letter, he thought to himself, give him the Zoffels' address. But then Jerry was never much of a writer, not in English anyway. In fact not in any language. Neither was Helen. And besides, in order to get John Reid's address, they'd have to call him back. He'd left only his phone number.

*   *   *

Billy Wackett called his mum in Sheffield. This wasn't anything out of the ordinary, but in the course of the conversation he told her of his most bizarre encounter with John Reid, remember him? And she did. She was very interested. Thrilled even. Interested enough to mention it to Burt and Pam Zoffel when she sent her only piece of Yank mail that year.

Mrs. Wackett—she still thought of herself as Mrs. Wackett—could never grasp the new technologies that governed her world of the late 1970s: Airplanes, the speed of sound, the telephone. She was unable even to guess how long it took a letter to reach the USA. She only knew that America was a long, long way away. In the privacy of her uncluttered mind she pictured an English postman, a man looking very much like her new husband, but quite a bit younger, having to carry her piece of mail all the way to Washington by hand. It didn't seem fair, but it had to be done, she supposed. She didn't want the nice postman to have to hurry, which is why she mailed her Zoffel Christmas cards in June, or sometimes in May, or August, whenever the urge took her. As long as she gave the poor lad plenty of time to walk that awfully long way.

This curious intellectual deficiency on the part of Mrs. Wackett would have been surprising given that she'd once lived overseas, and especially now, considering her new husband's trade, if it wasn't for the sad fact that she'd had more than her fair share of admissions to institutions that attempt and usually fail miserably to treat idiosyncrasies of the mind.

Not knowing of her medical condition, the Zoffels used to be amused by Mrs. Wackett's eccentricity, that is before they'd split up. In those last, trying years, the Wackett Christmas card arriving in the summer had been one of the few occasions when Burt and Pam had laughed together. Not any longer, though.

The 1979 Wackett card was sent, with her husband's patient and kindly indulgence, on June 3.

*　*　*

It occurred to John Reid that the American Embassy might have something on the Zoffels. So he called. After a few delays and several oh so polite voices, he was able to put his inquiry to a soft-spoken Southern gentleman. Mr. Nash Stern took Reid's address and phone number and promised to get back to him.

*　*　*

A spy plane 50,000 feet up in the whateversphere taking a moving picture of London will pick Leo up as a hard-boiled egg bouncing on broad shoulders down Regent Street. When the aircraft descends, and we get out, there's chunky Leo coming toward us through the insane traffic in Piccadilly Circus, a finger of his right hand aloft in the eternal quest for a cab. He is, however, not to be confused with the graceful Eros, who also has a finger up. Our man is a Russian in the funnies, except in real life he's as American as a donut. If you were to see him in his office, with no one else around, and the spy plane unable to latch on to his billiard ball head, if you were to observe him closely with the black phone sticking out of his ear like a science fiction excrescence, you'd just know, from the way he sits, the way he looks at himself in an imaginary mirror, that his white balls had been poked a few times with a cue. Why not? you might say. There's room for all sorts in this fucked up world. And there is, even in the CIA.

"Burt. This is Leo. Thought you might like to know. Red flag."

"It's funny, old buddy, I was going to call you in the next few days. John Reid, right?"

"Nice to have old friends looking you up, Burt."

Burt was as sure of that as Leo was. "Is that what he told you? That's what he told my uncle in Chicago. You ran a check on him, of course."

"You think he's after you, Burt?"

"I don't know."

"Well, nothing on this guy," continued Leo. "He seems to be clean."

Burt was tense. "Well, he would be, wouldn't he."

Leo shook his head. Good old Burt. Nice guy, most of the time. But, paranoid. Hell. Always had been. He pressed on. "He's an aspiring writer, 27, votes Conservative. Lives alone in an apartment in Kensington."

"Aspiring writer?" said Burt. "Where did he get his money? That's not a cheap place to live."

"Don't know. Maybe he inherited. Maybe he's a high class gigolo on the side. Maybe the apartment's really a slum. I haven't had time to do any more on him, you know. Not unless you want me to."

There was a pregnant silence Stateside.

"Don't worry about it, Burt. Look, if he was after you, he wouldn't go about it this way. That's crazy."

"Leo, there is no way to go about it."

"Well, maybe he is what he says, Burt." Leo refrained from adding, "People usually are, in the real world." Instead, he said, "After all, he did live there. Cyprus, I mean."

Burt said, "But I only knew him as a kid. Didn't like him then. Don't like him now. And, I don't like coincidences, Leo."

"One swallow a summer does not make, Burt," replied Leo, trying, in a vague way, to lighten things up a little.

"Leo. Give me his address and phone number in London."

Leo hesitated for only a second, but gave Burt the information, which Burt wrote down in his address book. Burt was a very old friend. They had been recruited on that same day, long ago. A high-quality, full-length color movie of a couple of CIA agents in a house of the most ill fame possible, in Istanbul to boot, was a good incentive for recruitment. It meant good money on the side, but it also meant a hell of a prison sentence if they were found out. It's one way a bond is forged. A friendship of long standing.

"Burt. I'll head him off, if you want."

"How?"

"I'll reply to his inquiry officially. We've never heard of you. Okay? It should sidetrack him for good. If he's innocent, it'll sidetrack him, okay?"

"Okay, Leo. And, er, thanks"

"De nada, Pal."

* * *

The special courier-delivered registered letter was embossed and impressive, and so was the single page inside. It was from the U.S. Embassy in Grosvenor Square.

"Dear Mr. Reid. Your telephone inquiry of June 4 was passed on to me. I regret our records do not go back that far. As for our current personnel records, they are, as you must appreciate, governed by strict privacy rules. I'm sorry I cannot be of more help. Yours, Mrs. A. Vandersteen, Head of Records."

That wrapped it up for John Reid, as far as the Zoffels went. And really for this little project in its entirety. But it did kindle in him a desire to go back to Cyprus, more specifically to the old street. Money was starting to pose a problem these days. Not enough to prevent a trip to Cyprus, but enough to plan these things a bit more carefully than he previously might have. The bloody service charges in his apartment block alone were more than his income. Yeah, money was on his mind. Wouldn't want to have to sell the flat.

* * *

One of the things Pam had got in the divorce was the Washington P.O. box. They'd had it so long, and she wanted it. Besides, it wouldn't do Burt much good where he was.

Pam read Mrs. Wackett's Christmas card with great interest, and a little nervousness. She didn't know why she should be nervous, but she was. It didn't seem important, not really, it was just that it was something slightly out of the ordinary, and very much out of the past, that particular past. If Pam had been into metaphysics she might have experienced that

15

odd, tingly feeling that perhaps the future was casting a shadow on the present. But the occult wasn't her thing, and so she just felt unaccountably nervous. It might mean a phone call to Burt. She'd have to think about that. She would put off the decision until tomorrow.

*　*　*

John Reid just couldn't break the habit of looking in American phone books. That afternoon he was in Chelsea Library, waiting for Monica to get off at five. Monica was tall—willowy, as they say—and re-defined the word "stacks." What more could a library patron desire? Well, for one thing, that she'd agree to go to bed with him. And she'd been doing just that, for a couple of months now.

While Reid twiddled his thumbs he strolled into the reference section, and his eye fell on a phone book he'd never seen before. Northern Virginia. Kensington didn't have it, that's for sure, otherwise he'd have been on it. As he opened to the white pages he knew he'd get something, he just had that feeling. And there it was. J. Zoffel, in Manassas. His gut told him this was Joe, the baby vegetable.

He and Monica grabbed a quickie—a vegetarian crepe, that is, at Carlo's—and then went back to his flat. She liked the black and salmon bathroom. It complemented her complexion perfectly. Monica was at her best in the bathroom.

By eight o'clock Monica declared, "Got to go, love." It was still early, for lovers anyway, but Monica had this phobia about sleeping in any bed other than her own. She was also terrified of the noise of falling rain. Seemed odd for a librarian, to hide under bed covers whimpering at the sound of the elements, but it's what's in one's head that counts. Fortunately it rained all the time in London, and Monica was always so worked up after a good whimper.

*　*　*

Reid pulled out a Capstan full-strength, took a healthy drag, and dialed the Manassas number. A woman answered. He put it to her.

"Thought the "J" might have stood for my old friend Joe Zoffel."

"I'm Janet… I'm single… I live alone … no relation to any Joe Zoffel… No, sorry, never heard of George Zoffel in Chicago… Yes, it is an unusual name… Very sorry I can't help."

She sounded nice, and very genuine. She took Reid's number and promised to call if she found anything.

*   *   *

Susan Zoffel didn't even consult her asshole of a husband. He was spaced out anyway, watching reruns of George and Gracie and nursing a dented can of light, some of which had spilled down the front of his robin's-egg blue tee-shirt that announced "Kent State" in large white lettering. He'd picked it up at a flea market.

Joe was a mess. But Susie was a sharp girl. Her marriage to the toe-sucker wouldn't last, but while it did she was aware of her responsibilities. She dialed a number in Arlington, and left a message.

It wasn't long before she got a call back.

"Susie. What's up?"

"Pam. I got a call this afternoon from a John Reid. Said he was calling from London. He was looking for you and Burt."

She told Pam the entire conversation. Sure sounded like a nice guy. Real genuine.

Pam thanked her, and swore her to continued secrecy. Then, almost as an afterthought, "How's Joe?"

"Don't ask," said Susie.

Pam held the phone in her hand for several seconds. That's why she'd felt a little nervous after getting the Wackett Christmas card. Now it wasn't just nervousness, it was a warning bell. The future had cast its shadow.

She called a number in the Carolinas.

*   *   *

The front yard, which is what people saw, was perfect, just perfect enough and no more. The treey, leafy, neighborhood of Buena Vista, the best in Winston-Salem, automatically conferred upon him a set place in the hierarchy of this small Southern tobacco town, as any neighborhood tends to do in any community anywhere in the world. His house nailed him down even further. Richard B. Riley had money, but not too much. Retired from some business up north. But he was a quiet type, widowed or divorced it seemed, didn't socialize much, traveled often, had a stunningly beautiful daughter. Daughter? Yeah, right. Didn't look a bit like

17

him. After all, Mr. Riley was only 52. And, as the local Republican matrons would tell you after only a couple of glasses, very attractive.

"Richard Riley," he said when the phone rang. This was one of those nights when he felt like answering on the first ring, and not having to go through the damned code. He felt, almost, like a normal person.

Pam told him everything, in sequence as it had happened.

"Thanks for letting me know, doll. It's fine. He's just trying to find us to say hello. I've got it under control. I guess I'll call him."

Burt said it with such insouciance that she felt relieved. "It's a small world, though, isn't it?," she offered.

But Burt knew it was a damned big world. "How are the boys?" He always asked, as a matter of routine, but you could tell he didn't care. It was also a good way of getting off the conversation.

"The same. How's Vanessa?"

"Fine. She's doing fine, doll."

* * *

About an hour after his abortive call to Manassas, Reid was getting ready to get an early night when the phone rang.

"John Reid, please."

He recognized the voice immediately.

"Jerry. Nice to hear from you. What's the weather like in Vancouver?"

"Okay. I guess it's okay. Listen, Helen wants to say hello, okay?"

"Okay, Jerry. Good to hear from you, okay?" He was quite surprised to hear from his old Armenian neighbor.

Jerry, unaccustomed as he was to being gracious, tried, nonetheless, "Okay, yeah, good to…"

But, fortunately, before he made an ass of himself, Helen was on the line.

"Johng Reid. I don' believe it"

There were pleasantries, and Reid told her about Billy Wackett. Then he got down to business. "Helen. Do you know where the Zoffels went?"

Her English pronunciation was rather unusual, probably always had been, although the only thing he remembered about her from the old Nicosia days was her tits. What made it worse was that she hit her medial and terminal "r"s like an American from the Midwest, and her vocabulary

18

seemed to come from a 19th-century English-Armenian dictionary. A listener was titillated to a point almost beyond endurance, and you rapidly found yourself not only able to understand her without effort but starting to sound just like her.

"Jes. I hab seberal Chrisma cord from dem here. I keep everyting, Johng. I'm a pack rack. Every yaar they sent Chrisma cord, and we would send one to dem. Here is one from Tokyo, 1959. Dat was de fast yaar we was in Vancouver, Jerry an' me. The Zoffel leave Cypru same year we, I tink. Anyway, Washningtong, DC, 1960. Tripoli 1963. Longdong, 1965. Den nottink tilla 1971, from Washningtong again. But dere was some cord in between, as I said. I tink from Washningtong. I have dem songwhere."

"Helen, do you have a Washington address or phone number?"

"No phone nummer. Address jes." And she gave him the P.O. box in Washningtong from the 1971 card. "Now, it is eight yaar old. Maybe they don't hab box no more. Oh, yah, we got anoder cord from dem, maybe two yaar later. They was splitting up, Pam and Burt, you know? Hold ong, Johng."

She was back in a few seconds.

"1973. A cord. Not Chrisma cord, just cord."

The card was brief and she read it to him. It certainly sounded as if Burt and Pam were heading for the divorce court. Interestingly, the card still had the same P.O. box.

"Oh, incidentally, Helen, do you know what Burt Zoffel did for a living?"

"Jes. State Department. U.S. State Department."

* * *

The Armenian connection made Reid think again about old George Zoffel in Chicago, and the so-called Janet Zoffel in Manassas, Virginia. In truth, he'd already been suspicious of both of them for some time. Only two Zoffels listed in the entire USA that he could find, and they didn't know Burt and Pam? And he knew that Manassas was virtually a suburb of Washington, D.C. Two and two always make four. Don't ever let anyone tell you they don't. If they do, they're either very, very bad at arithmetic, or they're lying.

* * *

19

"Freddie. John Reid. Fine, thanks, you? Listen, you know a thing or two about the CIA and all that. A guy living in Cyprus in the '50s. American, yeah. Okay, claimed to be working for the U.S. State Department. Yeah, yeah, that's what I thought. Okay. Now, why would his family, all of his family, be so paranoid about him that they would deny any connection to him?"

Reid listened to his friend Freddie. He listened carefully. Freddie actually knew more than just a thing or two.

"Right. So, what are we saying?" Reid listened for a minute. "Yeah, but, as you say, he wouldn't have told them any of that, would he? No, no, better not do that. Not at this stage of the game, at least. Many thanks for the offer, though. By the way, how's your new novel coming on? September, eh? I'll order it now. No, can't seem to get an idea. Yeah, always fun. Cheers, Freddie."

*　*　*

Reid had normally never been a prankster, considering it unproductive. However, he was motivated now to perpetrate a practical joke that he honestly believed they all deserved.

After spending part of the day hatching his plot, and researching a map of Manassas, Virginia, in his most excellent atlas of the USA, he called the J. Zoffel number again. The same girl answered: Janet Zoffel, single, living alone.

Reid was good at accents and voices. Barney Rubble with a Southern accent ought to do it. That would confuse even Billy Bob Fucking Flintstone. "Hey, this is Barney down the street. I've got a package for Joe. Delivered to me by mistake. Some insurance company thing. You want me to bring it around? I'm just gonna walk the mutt anyways." With a smile on his face, he pronounced "thing" as "thang," and even stressed the first syllable of "insurance," just like he'd heard 'em do in the talkin' pick-chewers.

"Just a minute," she said, and Reid heard her say, "Joe. You expecting some insurance package?"

Reid didn't hear the reply, but the girl came back with "He doesn't know. He can't make the decision. Maybe. Yeah, could you bring it around? That's real nice of you. Which house are you in?"

Reid hung up.

*　*　*

Susan Zoffel looked into the buzzing phone, shrugged, and put the instrument down. A half hour later the helpful neighbor still hadn't arrived, and she asked Joe if he knew a Barney down the street. He wasn't sure. Susie called the phone company, and asked politely where the last incoming call had come from.

"There's a charge for this service, ma'am."

"Just whack it on the bill."

Two minutes later they got back to her. "From London, ma'am. Have a nice day."

Susie then called Pam, and Pam called Burt, the second time in two days. This time she was in a panic.

She told Burt about the latest development, and again, he brushed it off. "Persistent bastard. But it's okay, doll, I checked him out. He's clean as a whistle. I will call him, I promise. Don't worry."

There was a prolonged silence.

"How are the boys?," asked Burt.

"How's Vanessa?," Pam retorted.

Pam was wound up tight, and it didn't take an ex-husband to notice. She was about to blow. Burt knew that too. Maybe she'd better blow, get it over with.

"She still wants to join the Company," he said, slowly, lighting a cigarette.

Nothing from Pam.

"I'm still trying to talk her out of it," Burt continued, looking into the phone, expecting something.

"You'd better talk her out of it, Burt. Goddamned Company. Look what it did to us. Look what it did to everyone. Goddamn it, Burt. Just make it not happen, okay? Don't give her a fucking choice. Just take control. You're her father. Besides which, you can make it not happen. Okay?"

Burt took a deep drag of his cigarette, and as he exhaled slowly so did "Okay, doll." It was all he could think of to say.

Vanessa was twenty-one now, had finished college, early, in North Carolina. Ever since she was a kid she'd only had one ambition: To be a CIA operative, just like her dad. But she knew she'd be up against it, at least from her mother. Burt seemed ambivalent. There was no backup career plan, despite a fruitless month recently in New York City trying to break into the theatre world on her looks alone, so Vanessa just hung out at her father's place whenever she felt like it, spent his money, of course, and dated the occasional older, say thirties, attorney or race car driver. The last had been a fast Sardinian aristocrat, with violent mustachios and a well-developed addiction to speed. "Luigi, I'll see you later." She was bored now, straining at the leash. Any way you looked at it, Vanessa Riley's future was going to be full of adventure.

"John Reid. Is he a threat, really, Burt?"

Pam had calmed down a lot after the storm of the previous few minutes.

"How the hell would I know?" he snarled. Burt never snarled, or laughed, accidentally. No physical action or mental reaction without careful planning. It was all rehearsed. Always had been. He never, ever let his guard down. That had been another of the many things that had driven Pam crazy. "You don't know what spontaneous means," she had often yelled in despair, in several different countries.

So now, when he snarled, knowing him as well as she did, or not knowing him at all, she ignored his change in temperament. "You say you've checked him out. How well have you checked him out, Burt? It should be easy, right? I mean a good, real check. It should be easy enough." After some thought, she added, "He'd be Tim's age, wouldn't he?"

Burt shuddered involuntarily but noticeably at the mention of his elder son's name. This was one reaction he couldn't manipulate. The exception to the rule. He didn't want to hear his son's name at all. At that very moment Tim was in a rehab center in Washington. A real loser. A shithead since he was fifteen. A little part, perhaps a big part, of Burt Zoffel wished that this pathetic excuse for an offspring had perished out there in the Viet battlefields. "We're dreadfully sorry, Mr. Zoffel. Missing in action. A credit to his country." That's what Burt had really wanted to hear over the phone one bright, sunny morning. It would have solved the problem he knew would inevitably come his way: What to do with Tim when he got back from Asia. It would have solved the problem facing Burt yet again: What now for Tim?

Almost as if Pam were a new recruit at Langley, Burt gave her strict instructions that if John Reid or anyone like him or related to him, tried to contact her at any time, to let him know right away.

"Which is what I did, wasn't it?" she said hotly.

"Sorry, doll. You did right."

*   *   *

The devil had really got into John Reid. It had been the last few pages of Dostoyevsky's *The Idiot* that did it. That and what Freddie had told him about double agents. CIA. KGB. He put the book down on the coffee table, thought for a few minutes, smoked a cigarette, and then dashed off a card to the Zoffels at their P.O. box. He had no way of knowing if it was still in use. If it wasn't, then he'd lost nothing, except the cost of a pretty international stamp with a picture of the Queen. If it was, and it still belonged to the Zoffels, who could say? It might provoke an interesting reaction.

*   *   *

There was a message from Pam on the answering machine. She sounded frantic. Burt called her back as soon as he got in.

"Burt. Where the hell have you been?" she yelled.

"That's a real conversation stopper," replied Burt.

"Why don't you let me know where you are?"

"I can't, doll. You know the rules."

"He's found us," Pam said, some considerable alarm in her voice, almost a panic.

"What do you mean?" asked Burt, a little alarmed himself.

Burt had hoped this Reid thing would go away. Another couple of chats with Leo in London had almost put his mind at rest about the whole thing. Leo had ways of burning through the paranoia with a laser, to get to the rational Burt. Always had.

"John Reid. He's found us." Pam was on the edge.

"Pam. Just take a few deep breaths, and start at the beginning."

"I went to the P.O. box this morning, and there was a card, from John Reid, addressed to both of us."

"Do you have it? Can you read it to me?," asked Burt.

"Sure. I've got it in my hand."

"Read it, doll, read it."

"It's postmarked London. June 7," Pam began.

"And you got the card this morning? Did you go to the box yesterday?"

23

"Yeah"

"Okay, doll."

Pam coughed a little cough, as if rehearsing a speech. "This is what it says. You ready?"

"Yeah, I'm ready." Burt sounded flat. He was flat.

She read, "Burt, I know your secret, and I know where you are. John. P.S. Sorry about you and Pam. Do Svidanya."

After a moment's hesitation, Burt asked, "That's it?"

"That's it," said Pam. "What does he mean by 'Do Svidanya'?"

"It's Russian for 'I'll be seeing you.' I guess he knows some Russian."

As Burt Zoffel hung up he was deep in thought, with furrows not only on his brow but at the sides of his mouth. When Burt concentrated, his mouth turned down, making him appear miserable, which he was. He also tended to doodle; a bad habit. He ambled over to the john under the stairs.

Vanessa was truly stunning. Tall, athletic, long—almost black—hair, and a figure to stop traffic. Her almost square face could only be American, of German descent. Large eyes spaced far apart. Any closer together, they would have been too close. The Teutonic features overlaid with the American confidence; fine, determined jaw; good living; expert dental care; expensive soap; sunshine; freedom from disease, from care, from the ravages of war; and all the other little daily things that make Americans so, well, the 20th century's chosen people.

She walked casually over to the desk where Burt had recently stood, lifted the scribbling pad and read it. Written on it were John Reid's name and address. She memorized the information quickly, then walked quietly out of the room, as the downstairs commode flushed.

*　　*　　*

"Hi, Aunt Harriet."

Harriet wasn't her real name, and she wasn't Burt's aunt. In fact, Aunt Harriet wasn't a woman at all. But she was a she in the widest sense of the word, as a ship is a she, as Britannia is a she.

"This is Richard Riley. What's the weather like in Old London Town? Fog, I'll bet you."

She didn't answer. But, he didn't expect her to. She never said anything beyond the rather stern "Hullo" when she answered the phone. She merely connected him to a tall man in a gray suit in another office.

24

"Mr. Riley. How nice to hear from you again." Plummy accent. More specifically greengage, hanging ripe from a bough in an English country garden, a strange fruit belonging to the same genus as the odd testicle you see blowing gently in the wind in a nudist colony.

"How are you?," asked Burt, tentatively.

"How are you, Mr. Riley? Are you coming over?"

"Tomorrow. Are you available for lunch?"

"Certainly." There was absolutely no hesitation, despite the fact that you just knew the tall man would have to cancel luncheon with some cabinet minister, perhaps, the head of ICI, or a couple of successors to the Kray Twins. "Let's say tomorrow at noon? My office. Oh, and I've found an exceptional pub. Very quiet. Very discreet. Near the Temple. Wonderful steak and kidney pudding. My treat."

"I'll be there," Burt said, and hung up. He pictured the culinary delight proposed by the tall man, and shuddered. What the Brits saw in that shit he'd never know.

* * *

He was proud of her, the way she looked, the way guys stared. She took after her mother. When Burt had been younger, people had stared more at Pam, and at him only by association. But now he was older he was much more handsome, short hair graying at the temples in the classic Roman senator style. Pam had often told him, in their happier, much younger days, that he had a perfectly shaped head. And he did. Now people turned their imperfectly shaped heads at him and sighed inwardly. You couldn't hear the sighs most of the time, but you could always see them. Burt was not impervious to this. Now, these days, with Vanessa as a companion, the two of them could walk into a room and people just stopped talking.

But, it wasn't just the physical thing. Vanessa was very bright, very funny, and she was her daddy's girl. Always had been. He knew she'd die for him, if it came down to it. And she knew he'd die for her. There was never a doubt in the mind of either one of them. And until that time came, they could always live for each other. What's the difference?

On hearing that Burt was off to the capital of the British Commonwealth, Vanessa had asked to come with him. Shopping, friends, a couple of West End plays, maybe over to Paris afterwards for more shopping, more friends, a couple of diversions of some sort on the Rive Gauche.

"I've already booked two seats, Baby"

She knew that already. Knew he'd do it. But she was genuinely delighted nonetheless, and it showed. She was worried too. She'd actually heard two of the recent phone calls her father had had with Pam, or rather, one complete one and one partial one. They had rather alarmed her. It was evident that this John Reid was coming after Burt. It was equally evident that Burt was off to London to take care of that problem. She knew he could handle it by himself. He was quite capable, and had, after all, been trained to do things like this. What "handling it" entailed she had no idea. She had considered doing nothing to help him, fearing that she might get in the way somehow, screw up his plans. Yet, she knew how worried he was. Maybe he couldn't do it on his own, after all. Any help would be useful to him, provided it was all done very carefully. Finally she'd decided to be merely his intelligence gatherer. How harmful could that be? She wouldn't tell him, of course, because he'd forbid her to get involved. He wouldn't want to see her exposed to any sort of danger. That's when she conceived Operation Drei, as they were rushing for their plane in the States.

From the time she'd been a kid, Vanessa had been into ciphers and code-breaking, that sort of thing. Burt, who throughout the latter part of his career and travels with the "State Department" would often play code games with her, considering it a great form of mental exercise for the apple of his eye. It was during these interludes that Vanessa was happiest. To be with her father and to be playing mind games with him. She became very good at it very early on. She could very quickly construct an anagram from most words and names. If the words were short enough she could do it instantly, with no apparent thought. Reid was easy. For Operation Drei she wrote nothing down. It was all in her head. No paper trail. No one else knew about it. Her father had often told her, "If you want to keep a secret, don't tell anyone."

They made it into London early in the morning, right in the jet stream of a heat wave. They took a real London taxi to the Palace Hotel, where Burt had booked a small suite, which he always managed to get phenomenally cheap if it was available. Burt knew how to do these things, even when he was giving the airline only a day's notice.

Late that morning, as Burt made his way in a cab across London to Charing Cross, Vanessa, wearing sunglasses and a floppy hat as a disguise, took the Number 9 down Kensington High Street. She found John Reid's block of flats with ease, and about noon stationed herself in a bookstore on the other side of the High Street. This was her opening gambit in Operation Drei.

The store soon got boring. Not the fault of the store. It was a great place, innovatively laid out and full of fantastic bargains. She actually saw a massive book she wanted, *The New York Times Theatre Index*, going for three quid, but she knew it would have to wait. A tome that chunky would weigh her down if Operation Drei were suddenly to call for agile movement and fleet foot. She paid for it and got them to hold it for her.

Five minutes in the bookshop seemed like five hours, so she walked out and crossed the road to the apartment block. Patience is a CIA virtue.

It was a fine block, okay, one of many on the High Street, but newer than most: 1930s. The imposing entranceway leading directly into the central courtyard, guarded at all times by one of seven permanently pissed Irish porters, was flanked at ground level by two commercial enterprises bermed into the building: The Hwang-Ho Chinese Restaurant on the left, and on the right a Wac & Wave International hairdressers. Rising up along with the pretty brick facade were the windows of five floors of luxury apartments, with a duplex penthouse on top of that. Somewhere in this building lived John Reid.

Vanessa didn't have a plan. She didn't have his flat number, but she could walk in to the courtyard, chat up one of the tipsy porters, and get it. But what good would that do? It would be too much energy expended for too little result. She could wait until she caught a glimpse of him, but, again, what good would that do? While she stood outside Wac & Wave's big window she pondered giving it all up until a better plan came to her. This was one half-cocked venture, she suddenly concluded. There must be a better way.

As she came out of her reverie she found herself absently staring in the window, and was suddenly embarrassed. There was only one client in the hairdresser's at that moment, a man having his hair done in the middle one of a trio of chairs. For some reason the question flashed through Vanessa's mind: Did he pick the middle one, or did they place him there? Most people pick an end. But then the thought evaporated. The girl hairdresser with the torpedo tits and huge curly blonde hair who was rubbing his head with a towel and a shameful grin, spun his chair around until he

27

was looking out onto the High Street. He had a towel around the lower portion of his face. Big Tits was going to shave him too.

The man's eyes were too far away for Vanessa to see, but she knew he was looking right at her. He didn't have much choice. She was the dominant feature in the landscape. It was the way he had his legs apart, the way guys do when they're in the chair. She fantasized only momentarily, felt her cheeks getting very hot, then walked away back over to the book shop. She felt tired as hell.

*   *   *

"Can you find enough dope on a guy, a British guy, I mean, in, say, three days?"

The tall man looked intently at Burt across the booth table. The *Jacques de Molay* was lunched to the max, partly due to its reputation for burnt steak. And because it was busy it was discreet. The tall man had been right about that.

"Enough dope?"

"A good amount. Enough for me to be able to make a decision."

"I should think so, Mr. Riley. By the way, what do you think of the fish and chips?"

Burt didn't know how to answer, so he didn't try.

"They don't make 'em like they used to, do they?" continued the tall man, indulging himself in a sinister smile. "One ingredient they don't use anymore. Pity. Wish you'd followed my advice and gone with the steak and kidney. But, yes, provided he's not an unusual case."

"He may be," said Burt.

"Then we shall see, Mr. Riley. As you know, if anyone can, we can."

"I know," answered Burt. "What ingredient?"

"Sorry." The tall man looked vague.

"Fish and chips. Which ingredient don't they use anymore?"

"Oh, that," and the tall man allowed a subdued theatrical laugh. "They used to chop the potatoes up, dump 'em into a bathtub, usually upstairs or in the back room, fill the tub with water to soak 'em, then all the boys, and some of the girls too, would stand around the tub and pee into it."

"You're kidding." The American puritan emerging.

"Not at all," replied the tall man, smirking almost and taking a bite

28

of kidney, which he obviously relished as much as this tale. "Quite a visual, isn't it. Added brine to the flavor, and all the impurities were then removed when the chips were deep-fried. The Government health wallahs put a stop to all that in '64. Ruined fish and chips, I can tell you. Tell me what you know about this person."

And Burt did, which wasn't much. The tall man promised to get back to him at the Palace.

* * *

The Bog. By Spencer Godwin.

You just knew Spencer Godwin was the freak sitting at the back of the tiny theatre, wearing John Lennon glasses and smoking an imaginary joint, imaginary only because real smoking was not allowed in London theatres, fringe or otherwise, pot or otherwise. And this was very definitely fringe.

The actor finally got off the pot, pulled his wrinkled beige trousers up, and actually took a bow, as the play ended to faint applause. Well, actually, from the degenerate in the back row.

As they walked out of the theatre into the much-needed fresh air, Vanessa said, "What did you think, Dad?"

"I thought it was shit, baby."

Vanessa laughed. "You knew I was going to ask you that, didn't you? You've been working on that answer all evening."

He put his arm around her shoulders as they walked slowly through the night.

"I've never, ever, seen anything like it," he said. "I felt sorry for the poor bastard. I was wondering how he kept his thighs from going numb."

"Actors have tricks," she said. This was the life. Going to a really avant-garde play in the suburbs of London with the only man she had ever really loved, and feeling on top of the world.

"It's what they call a one-hander, isn't it?," Burt said.

It took a few seconds, but then Vanessa cracked up. She almost fell to the ground. Burt started too, and they couldn't stop. People were staring at them warily, and inching over on the sidewalk. Burt saw a cab and hailed it.

* * *

"Bit of a mystery man, this Reid of yours," exhaled the tall man, as they sat in St. James's Park. It was a glorious afternoon.

Burt was not amused at this opening sally. He didn't say "Well I'll be jiggered. What a surprise," but the tall man caught the look.

"I'm not saying he is deliberately so, mind you, that's for you to judge, Mr. Riley. All I'm saying is that he doesn't add up easily. Not comfortably, the way most people do. He's not a nine to five man, if you see what I mean. Doesn't work at Tesco's. But then, there are thousands like that. So, as I say, it's your decision, not mine. But you know that. I'll act in accordance with whatever instructions you give me, of course, but I have to say, and this will not be a surprise to you, we must move with extreme caution. Nothing rash. If you do decide to use our extended services, then I would ask you to spend some considerable time reflecting on your decision before giving me the green light."

He was long-winded, but he was right. Burt knew that and was comfortable with it. After all, if the tall man had been a merry madcap hit man, he wouldn't still be in business. And, furthermore, Burt knew the tall man was looking out for him too.

"So, what have you got?"

Without notes the tall man stretched back on the bench, ready to expound, but before he could release his breath a black lab bounded up to where they sat and demanded Burt's attention. "Fuck off," Burt snarled to it as its owner, a fat lady in a shockingly short summer skirt came up to claim her animal and put a leash on it.

"There's no need to talk like that to a dog," she reprimanded. She seemed quite upset.

"Yes there is," replied Burt, looking directly at her. "Fuck off."

The blown-up doll stared at him for several seconds, considering a retort, but she was warned off by Burt's eyes. It was the lab who pulled her away, though. He'd found a Peke coming his way, wanted to hump it. As the fat lady was dragged away by her drooling dog, she turned and yelled "Happy Waterloo Day, asshole."

The tall man found this all very amusing. "By Jove, she's right. It is Waterloo Day. It had completely slipped my mind."

Burt looked at him as if he'd lost his senses. The tall man apologized for the levity, but his smile remained for several seconds as he finally began his report.

"His father was Army, as you know. A psychiatrist, of all things."

"Yeah. Psychiatrist. I remember now," said Burt, clearing his head of cellulitic thighs and black Labradors, and trying to focus on the matter in hand.

"He was a captain when you knew him. Various Mediterranean postings. The occasional stint back home. The usual. Married. Two point two children. Well, two point zero, actually. They were back in Cyprus for three years, in the mid–'60s, during the civil war. Not Nicosia, however, that was then very much off limits to the British. They were in Larnaka, Famagusta, and then the British base of Dhekelia. Again, fairly usual stuff for a British serviceman. In 1968 he received his last promotion, to full colonel, with a cushy job at Netley, the joint services' psychiatric hospital near Southampton. He retired in 1974. That's all pretty much from his Army record, with a bit of supplementing from other sources. It's all fairly easy to obtain. Anyone can do it, if they know where to look."

The famous American impatience was evident.

"The good bit's yet to come." The just as famous British patience was evident. "But first, back to '68. The son, i.e., the Mr. Reid of your enquiry, left home and left school. He never went back to either."

"He was a high school dropout?"

Without any condescension in his voice at all—after all Burt was an American—the tall man informed his client, "We don't have high school in the United Kingdom, Mr. Riley. And we don't have dropouts. Reid was two years ahead, that's all. He took his A-Levels. Oh, and by the way, school children do not graduate in Britain, they just fade away, or go on to university."

The question "Are you familiar with our school system in any way at all, Mr. Riley?," went unasked, except for the slight raising of the tall man's left eyebrow.

"I know what A-Levels are, yeah," said Burt, without a trace of bad feeling.

"Well, he didn't go to University, which he could have done. Should have done, given his background. I'm not suggesting he was Cambridge material, or even Oxford, but Edinburgh, perhaps, or Manchester. Who knows? He would have found a nice niche."

"The good old ruling class." Burt sighed weightily.

"Precisely," said the tall man. "Our Mr. Reid left Britain in June 1968.

31

Went to France. We know that from the Passport Office. And then he disappears. We lose track of him for nine years. He just drops off the face of the planet, as they say, until 1977, when he re-surfaces in London, at the Kensington address. Word has it that he's a writer, but nothing published that I could find."

"So, what worries me is those nine years."

"It doesn't worry me very much, Mr. Riley. He certainly didn't work in Britain or any of the Commonwealth countries: Australia and so forth. And he wasn't employed by the British Government, or the Americans, or the Russians. You must remember he was only sixteen when he left England, and that's too young to get a work permit in European countries, under normal circumstances, anyway. And it was the late '60s, early '70s, with hippies swarming all over the globe. Very few records of these people. They came and went, in their perennial quest for cheap, exotic shit, from Morocco to Nepal, or, if you prefer things alphabetically, from Afghanistan to Zanzibar. My guess is he was one of them. It would fit. In which case, I'm not surprised at his long absence from Mother England."

"If he was a hippy," Burt mused, "then how did he get the money for this apartment in Kensington? It's not cheap."

"This is the interesting bit I promised you, Mr. Riley." The tall man gleamed like one of those old music-hall acts, the man with the waxed moustache and the ferret down the front of his trousers. "It is a good address, and he bought the flat. Outright. 100,000 cash. Pounds, of course. It's worth a lot more now. The Arab invasion has jumped up the price of a good London flat to figures no one in their right mind would have dreamt of two years ago."

Burt's lips had puckered into a silent whistle. "100,000 pounds is a lot of money." After a pause, he continued, "He's a hippy for nine years, comes back to England with enough of a pile to buy a flat for 100 pounds and calls himself a writer, although we can't find anything he's ever published."

The tall man cleared his throat. "Colonel Reid's Army List entry says he is deceased. From there it was just a matter of getting the newspaper cutting. Massive heart attack. Quite unexpected. He was a widower, was the colonel. Therefore, young Reid and his sister found themselves with quite a bit of money."

"I see. And the sister?"

32

"Living in Kent. Married to a salesman."

"What does he sell?," asked Burt.

"Fall-out shelters. To the Rumanians." Burt's eyes opened wide, and the tall man laughed. "Absolutely true. No joke."

"I don't buy the hippy thing," repeated Burt.

"Why not?"

"Because he votes Conservative."

*   *   *

Mike dropped his passenger off at the church. The garrulous cabby had never tried to stop convincing him, during the ride from the airport, that the Alexis, in downtown Larnaka was not only a great hotel, for a one-star joint that is, but for John Reid, and only for John Reid, it would be very cheap. Reid suspected the Alexis would be very cheap for anyone, but he didn't tell Mike that. The owner was Mike's cousin, of course. For a small, additional tip, Mike would give Reid the name of another cousin in Nicosia, who owned the Parthenon there. Reid gave him the tip. Mike gave him ten Parthenon business cards that sported an unflattering black and white line drawing of what Reid took to be a virgin.

"I only need one."

"Take ten. Give them to your friends."

And so Reid took all ten. What the hell. The Parthenon might come in useful when he eventually got to the capital.

But free is better than cheap any day, and here he was, standing in the dark outside the Anglican Church of Larnaka, guaranteed a better time than he'd have had at the Alexis, that is if his memories of his distant cousin had not been corrupted by the years. And it really was his cousin.

The entrance to the parsonage, or was it a rectory?—those terms were a blur, atheist that he was—was lit up as if it was expecting someone. And, indeed, it was: John Reid. He rang the bell and the door was opened by a bizarre human being.

Before he could fully take in the import of the creature who had opened the door, he was overwhelmed by the voice, which was followed almost immediately by the sheer physical presence, of Harry Blaikie Brownlow, live, not a motion picture, a fully deaconed and priested cler-gyman of the Church of England, and former captain in the Para Infantry during the EOKA days. This was Reid's father's second cousin. Mid-forties now, the faintest trace of Lowland Scots. Peebles, to be precise. Harry's grandmother had been a cousin of John Buchan, the guy who'd written *The Thirty-Nine Steps*.

"Reid, dear chap," he boomed. He shouldn't really have boomed because he wasn't particularly big. You've got to be over six three and weigh more than 250 pounds to boom, and you've got to have a beard. Harry was about Reid's height and shape, and he was clean-shaven. However, he was half a generation older than Reid, so if he felt like booming, it was bloody good to see him anyway.

"Cousin Harry, it's so kind of you to put me up at such short notice."

"Nonsense, dear boy, nonsense. Come and flop in a good chair. You'll need it after that flight." He made it sound as if Reid had just completed the long haul from Chungking over the Hump in a prop plane with Madame Chiang-Kai-Shek puking delicately into a paper cup by his side.

As the unusual-looking servant passed the living room entrance, Harry yelled something to him in a language Reid couldn't even identify, let alone understand. Not an unkind yell, certainly, more a yell reserved for the hard of hearing or slow-witted.

Harry glanced at Reid, and sensed that an explanation was necessary. No. It was more than that. He knew. He'd quite obviously been explaining this manservant for years.

"Gobbo, they call him, poor bastard. He's reached his pinnacle of achievement, caretaker of the only Anglican cemetery in Larnaka. Digs the graves, all by himself, puts the occasional flower on a forgotten soul's last resting place, waters said vegetation, that kind of thing. He is also the personal—paid, I might add—manservant to the prestigious local vicar, yours truly, Harry B. Brownlow."

They laughed at that, of course, as only Brits of their particular class and time could. "If Gobbo had been born in America he might have been a politician, perhaps one of national prominence. Certainly the movies would have sought him out. Horror films, of course. But this is Cyprus, and Gobbo has already lived longer than a Maltese hunchback should. No one knows how old he is, or even when he came to Cyprus, but he's over fifty, that's for sure. He remembers the War."

"Can he speak English?" Reid asked, with a trace of apprehension, in case the hunchback thought they were talking about him.

"After a fashion," Harry replied lightly. "It's not so much 'Can he speak English?' but 'Can he understand it?' His speech is pretty limited, even in Maltese."

"So that was Maltese you were speaking."

"Indeed it was. Strange lingo. Mixture of several languages, yet nothing like any one of them. You know I was there."

Reid did remember, now that Harry had reminded him.

"I didn't bring him here, though, as I think I mentioned. He was here when I arrived."

Gobbo came in with a whiskey for both of them. Then he left.

"In many ways Gobbo's a caricature," Harry said. "He's pretty when compared to Charles Laughton, but, then, who isn't. But he's still somewhat forbidding in appearance. It's his teeth when he smiles. That really gives you the willies. It wouldn't be good to have Protestant children exposed to that smile. He hasn't smiled at you yet, has he?"

Reid shook his head.

"However, one can only suppose he means well. And nothing really bad has ever been laid at Gobbo's door, as far as I know. The locals have always speculated about him, though. It's said that he bears a certain physical resemblance to Toulouse-Lautrec, if you get my drift, and it's kindly supposed that this is to compensate him for his rather obvious inadequacies. There is also speculation about whether Gobbo has ever had a woman, and if so, who she was, and how she could possibly have kept it a secret. The notoriety that would come with being the woman who'd indulged in more than just social intercourse with Gobbo would be payment indeed for being a social outcast, even for being stoned. But, no one's ever come forth and admitted it, so the chances are it's never happened."

Well, then, that explained Gobbo in a nutshell.

"And how about you, Harry?," Reid asked.

There was a comfortable pause as the two experienced club men, sons and grandsons of experienced club men, set about indulging their respective tobacco habits, Reid drawing on a fresh Capstan and the priest going through the long and necessarily ostentatious process of lighting a pipe.

"Nothing like a good shag, old man." Harry's eyes twinkled as he sucked on his briar.

"You're right about that."

35

The incumbent pulled on his pipe. "In truth, dear chap, I'm not exactly extended, professionally. Personally, perhaps, on occasion, but that never interferes with the execution of my few clerical duties. Of course, the head Diocesan boys in London know vaguely what's going on. But, hell, if someone has to man this decaying outpost of the Anglican Empire, then he might as well be allowed a certain latitude. And, it is 1979. If it had been twenty years ago, one would have gone bloody nuts, been dragged down screaming and very naked from the steeple, and finally been recalled. A sadly typical story. But now, thank God, the permissive age has come to Cyprus."

Reid stayed two nights with Harry. The cleric asked him if he couldn't stay another few days, as it was his birthday on Friday, but Reid couldn't stick around any longer. It had been a stimulating visit, but he sensed even another day would cause irk, and he wanted to remember his cousin sans irk. He wished him the best for the big day. Harry was taking the low road to Scotland for a five-day leave beginning Saturday, and would be back on the fourth of July. They agreed that if Reid was still in Cyprus then, hey, come back, visit again, celebrate America's independence, and all that. Get a couple of local girls in, have a big bang, perhaps. Reid suspected he meant "have a big bash," but, either way, it sounded like a good idea.

He hired a car, and drove to Nicosia.

* * *

"He's buggered off, Sir."

Newcome rubbed his nose. It wasn't that he had an itch, it was because he couldn't stomach the bloody perfume. It clobbered him like a brick, as he would tell Sandby, and he hated these interviews because of it. The tall man was clean and well-bathed, no question of that, but there was always this bloody perfume. Newcome couldn't tell whether it was expensive, or even good perfume. In fact, unlike sophisticated men of his age group, he never gave the question a thought. That wasn't in his line. All he knew was that it made him want to puke. If it had been on a woman he was going out with, he would have dragged her into the bathroom by her hair and shoved her head into the fucking toilet, but this was his boss, the tall man, and he had to put up with it. Sandby was totally immune.

The tall man looked astonished. Not really astonished, but that look of astonishment that the English mandarin cultivates as a means of putting an interlocutor on the defense. "What do you mean, Newcome, by 'buggered off'?"

"Well, Sir, he left for Cyprus two days ago."

"In that case, off you go, Newcome, you and Sandby. A little holiday for you both in the sun, perhaps."

*　*　*

The Greek half of Nicosia in the year of Orthodox grace 1979 was teeming with hotels. The Parthenon stood close to the Green Line. It was not one of the more salubrious. Tony, the hotelier, was a chubby, pasty-faced Greek in his late thirties, with small, mean eyes, a massive nose and weak, black hair that was neither tidy nor unkempt, but which kept harassing him as it collapsed over his eyes. It was clear, from his gut, that the only violent sporting activity Tony engaged in was at the backgammon table, a game the Greeks called "tavli."

John Reid found Tony wedged behind the bar doing his best to entertain a bunch of blonde Austrian bints, so obviously Austrians, who were resident there for the term of their contract with the Crazy Horse downtown. A cheap black and white television, one of the many riveting lobby features of a one-star hotel, sat high up in the corner behind the bar. A Greek musical comedy, one of the unsubtle kind, was playing to no viewers, as Tony regaled the girls with a joke, one of the subtle kind. They giggled. That was part of their job. If a laugh that has become hollow with constant money-grubbing meant any the less, Tony didn't think so, or if he did his skills were as well-practiced as theirs, and he was just playing the game. What the hell, false applause is better than none at all, if you wheel and deal in an entrepôt like Nicosia. Besides, he was the innkeeper, and these young ladies were staying at his inn, and if they sucked Tony's dick now and again, well, they got to get those little extras that the other guests would have to pay through the nose for. A budget is a budget, not only for touring performers. They all looked pretty chummy together and Reid couldn't help wondering, with some admiration but no envy, if Tony ever had a flaccid moment he could call his own.

The desk was abandoned, so Reid sauntered over to the bar. All seven blondes looked at him in unison, or rather looked him over, figured that as he wasn't dressed in a suit and tie he didn't have what it takes and, hey presto, returned to flattering the landlord with their plastic smiles.

37

A dump, but colorful. Reid signaled the corpulent Greek. Reluctantly the man broke off intercourse with the girls and pivoted his ample ass on the stool. The "Oh, fuck, you've caused me to pull a muscle in my buttock" approach to life.

"You Tony?"

He nodded, almost imperceptibly, in classic Greek style.

"Mike, the taxi driver in Larnaka, said you might have a room for me."

Without a word Tony tore himself unhappily away from the Austrians. The curse of business. He shuffled over to the desk and plucked a large, ponderous key from the wall-board. Reid noticed that the bulky Cypriot's forearms were extraordinarily white and completely hairless.

"Four Cyprus pounds, bed and breakfast," he said flatly. "Room 110."

Which meant one floor up, Room 10.

"I only have a double room tonight. How long do you stay?"

"Three weeks. Maybe four. I don't know exactly."

"Okay. From tomorrow I will have a single room with shower. Three pounds a night, bed and breakfast. Flit included."

"That's fine, Tony," Reid said, smiling. "You want my passport?"

The Greek shook his head. The transaction was completed.

Reid looked the room over. Not grand, but it would do. The twin beds, two feet apart, with plain blue counterpanes hiding who knew what secrets. That was all right. He'd try them both, if necessary. A couple of the walls boasted flowery prints of obscure Greek artists in shoddy wooden frames. An orange lay starkly in a wicker bowl on the dressing table. Funny how the quality and size of the traditional hotel donum are in direct proportion to the quality and size of the hotel. A bottle of Bollingers here, a reasonable Chablis there, a single red rose somewhere else, and in the Parthenon an orange that had seen better days. But this was just what he was looking for, inexpensive lodgings near the Green Line. It couldn't be better. And there was the can of Flit, as Tony had promised, complete with pump, just like in the old days. Mirmingia, the Greeks call them. We call them ants.

He undid his black grip, his only baggage—he always tried to travel light—found the toothpaste, and stepped into the bathroom. The taste of spearmint was gratifying after the long, hot, cigarette-strewn drive from Larnaka. He washed his face in the nineteenth-century washbasin, the type that has a blue-green stain where the water has dripped over the decades. The tiny mirror above was set at such an angle on the wall that it reflected the room, and in particular the bath. In the reflection he could see a brown cockroach inching its way up the white enamel on one side of the tub.

Cockroaches. He hated them. Had done all his life. Without hesitation, his right hand closed over the still-wrapped block of cheap hotel soap on the edge of the basin. Eyes glued to the mirror, he whipped the package over his left shoulder, splattering the filthy bastard into eternity. Lucky shot, no doubt. Not bad, though.

Looking around at his handiwork, he walked over to the bathtub and turned on the tap. Almost immediately the current picked up the pieces of bug and swept them down the hole.

1958

The summer of 1958 was hot. Almost 120 degrees in Cyprus. You only went out if it was necessary. The Reid family were off to Sussex the following week, for a month-long cool-down. The grandparents had finally moved down there from the land of the barbarians. Thinning blood. Everything was packed. They couldn't wait. Robins twittering merrily in the oak trees, the whistling milkman coming up the lane with his horse and cart, possibly dew on the grass in the early morning; although hopes of such precipitation were probably doomed given the season, they kept the family going through the unbearable Cypriot heat. Ah, the dew! Ah, the horse dung!

It was Captain Reid who arrived home one afternoon with the first alert of the impending invasion. In the next few hours the terrifying news was all over the radio. They were flying up from Egypt, millions of them, apparently, and there was nothing the British Army could do to stop them. The inhabitants of Cyprus would simply be overwhelmed.

The British government had considered evacuating the British on the island, but due to the lack of any useful advance warning, that had proved impossible logistically. So the Governor, quite rightly, didn't even try. The plan had to be one of defense and safeguards. Everyone on the island was given strict instructions. Soldiers came around, house to house, to let everyone know exactly what to do when the invading force landed. Families had to make sure they had enough food and water for a week; all windows and shutters were to be battened down, even if they lost fan power. That would make the heat in the house almost impossible to endure, but it was better than the alternative. Finally, they had to stay inside until the curfew sounded. Absolutely no one was to go out. Under any circumstances. The island prepared to grind to a halt, and everyone glued their ears to the wireless.

The EOKA war on the island, paling into insignificance for both sides, came to an abrupt cessation, just like that, as they all faced a common enemy, and Grivas's boys took refuge wherever they could, whatever cave was deep enough.

The next morning the radio announcer in trembling voice informed his listeners that the invasion force had already set out from the Egyptian coast, heading north, cruising at about a hundred feet above sea level. They should be landing on the island later in the day.

Despite the Army's instructions, the Reids had left a shutter or two cracked, and were looking out of the windows, eyes straining toward Egypt all day. Everyone on the island was doing the same thing, at least those who had a south-facing aspect. The radio gave constant updates. They would be able to continue broadcasting, but only up to a certain time, at which point communications might well have to cease, they said. Reinforcements were already on their way from England—several hundred had already arrived—to make what everyone knew was a hopeless attempt to stave off the menace. All one could do was wait, face Mecca, pray, and hope for the best.

The wireless reported the very moment the invading force hit the southern coast of Cyprus. Reports of the devastation followed immediately. This was not going to be pretty. Their next stop was Nicosia, where the Reid family was.

Young John Reid was the first in his family to see what looked like an enormous black cloud in the sky coming toward the capital. The biggest cloud he'd ever seen, and horribly black. The rest of the family were glued to the other window and could see it too. Captain Reid had his standard Webley, but a revolver would do no good against such an enemy. The family all knew that.

The cloud approached ever so slowly, getting bigger and bigger, until it was directly overhead. Then they started to land. It was a nightmare, almost from a science fiction novel. Captain and Mrs. Reid double-checked for the tenth time all possible entrances, then everyone waited, holding their breath.

Petrified, they heard them thudding down onto the street, in the yard, on the flat roof, on the tops of the few cars in the street; everywhere they could land. Millions was right. There were millions of the black bastards, all bent on one thing: Grabbing whatever they wanted.

Young John had never seen his father so pale. The gun was useless, and as strong and fit as the captain was, those physical attributes wouldn't cut it either. He had a wife to protect, and an eight-year-old daughter and a six-year-old son. Of course, the six-year-old son was John Reid. Because he was young, and had never actually seen an invading force close up, he was quite excited by the whole business. Scared shitless, but it was an adventure, after all.

Literally for several hours one could hear them landing. Then darkness fell. And comparative silence. The Reids didn't lose power, and the radio kept broadcasting. The captain and his wife didn't drink alcohol, but they sure did break out an orange juice from the fridge.

John's suggestion to open the front door and look outside was met with an icy contempt from everyone. He nixed that idea. But they all knew none of them would sleep that night. There were thousands of them outside, roaming the streets, pillaging. It was the tensest moment so far in John Reid's short life.

As morning broke and enough light came upon the Earth for them to do so, they all looked out the front window and through the tiny slits of the outside shutters onto the street. The sight was staggering, awesome. The bodies lying everywhere were so numerous it made the street look like a black carpet. Waterloo the morning after. The quince tree in the garden was bowed down with the sheer weight of the corpses caught in it, and was actually throbbing in slow rhythm with the final spasms of the dying. Fallen fruit lay on the ground, forming Picasso-like punctuation points to the dead.

As the little British family stared out onto this devastation, and the sun started to rise slowly, there was a stirring on the street, a movement as if those still living were awakening back into action at the same time. Slowly, almost painfully, they began to take off, like small black airplanes, using whatever they could as an airstrip: The road, the ditch, any flat surface, climbing and clambering over each other ruthlessly in order to become airborne. The departure lasted about an hour and then they were gone, heading north over the Nicosia streets.

What was left was a mess of such proportions that for the next two days the Army did nothing but sweep up cadavers. Families still had to stay inside, because of the threat of disease, but the real danger had passed. Lala Mustafa Pasha Street was systematically cleansed; swept, raked, and hosed down. Soldiers were up on the roofs, in yards, everywhere, one house at a time. The water bill alone must have been funded by the International Bank.

The Northeast African cockroach is about two inches long and dark brown. Every now and again summer in the Sudan becomes too excruciatingly hot, even for cockroaches. If it is going to be such a summer, the roaches see it coming, sooner than meteorologists do, and they begin a leisurely migration north to the Mediterranean coast of Egypt, or Palestine. Some even venture as far as Turkey and Bulgaria. Most of the Sudanese humans don't have the option of migration. They just die.

But this summer was hotter and more sudden than anything they'd experienced—human or insect—and the cockroaches panicked. Forming one big army they just lifted off the ground and headed north. Bug men would laugh at that, call it impossible, say it was fiction. But that's because the Sudanese cockroach, per se, doesn't rate an entry in the encyclopedias, so it can't exist. Yet, all you have to do is spend a little time in the Sudan and you'll find out what a North African cockroach can really do. They can't fly very far, so they hop on one another's backs, taking turns, until the distance is covered and the job's done. Even Egypt was too hot for them, and their internal computers told them that the rest of the Levant would be too. So, after a brief touchdown in Alex and Suez, they lifted off again, headed toward Europe. Two hundred miles due north, right in their path, was the island of Cyprus. The cockroach invasion helped put the EOKA war into some sort of perspective.

1979

Checkpoint Charlie, they called it. John Reid arrived there after a short walk from his hotel. He had returned the rental car because in Cyprus a vehicle might just be regarded as a show of wealth, and he didn't want that clouding a situation such as the one he was in now. Besides, he'd heard that you couldn't even approach the Green Line in a car. Keep it simple and humble. The foot is closer to the ground and the ground is where you form relationships with the earth and those on it. You don't get what you want from a car window. Lady Luck looks after the rest for you. She always does, as long as you remain her humble and obedient servant and don't take her for granted.

A sextet of well-nourished Greek policemen constituted the first line of defense. They cost Reid two Capstans. What the hell, cheap at half the price, but a very good cigarette is, of course, better than an actual bribe in Cyprus, indeed in any third-world country. That and a smile and a silver tongue. Buys you loyalty and friendship, which money can't do. They pointed him to a little hut at the side of the road.

The migrations minister studied the passport photograph carefully. He was trying to decide whether he could afford to underestimate the man in it. The official had some experience, you could tell that by the way he held documents. He looked up and carefully matched the applicant with the description on Page 2.

Profession: Writer. Surely there must be something more, something undisclosed. Writer means bugger all. But, if he says he's a writer, then he is a writer. Passports don't lie.

"So, you're a writer, Mr. Reid. What do you write?"

"I'm working on my autobiography at the moment." A lie.

"I shall be interested to read it when it is finished." The truth.

"I'll make sure you get an autographed copy." A lie.

The minister smiled.

Lieu de naissance: Aberfeldy, Perthshire

Date de naissance: 5 March 1952

Résidence: England

"Whereabouts in England do you live, Mr. Reid?"

"London."

"I also lived in London," the man said, with a spectacular surge of interest. "I attended the University of London for two years. Do you know it?"

"Yes." A lie. Reid didn't know much about universities, but he thought he'd heard of that one. "I know the University of London. Did you enjoy it?"

"Greatly. More than anything I would like to go back to London. But, the money, you know."

Reid laughed compassionately. "I know, my friend, don't worry."

"My name is Nearchos Papanicholaou."

"Nearchos." Reid shook the minister's hand. "Call me John. My friends do."

"John. Thank you. Do you know Newcastle?"

Ah, something's coming.

"No. Not really. I've been through there several times, though."

Nearchos continued to study the photo in the passport. He glanced again at the written description.

Taille: 1.88.

"You were a boxer, John?"

"Yes. How the devil did you know that?" Reid was genuinely impressed.

Nearchos merely smiled. But it was a gratified smile.

"I wish I could let you through, John. But you must have a guard in order to go through."

"Why, Nearchos?"

"Hmmm," he replied. "Nobody goes through unless they have a guard."

"So, people do go through, then."

"Yes. But only special cases."

"I'm a special case, Nearchos. Look here." He pulled out an orange folder and put it on the counter of the wooden hut that served as the Migrations Office.

"Take a look through these, Nearchos."

Nearchos opened the folder, and thumbed slowly through a batch of old black and white photos.

"This is you, huh?" He was looking at a little blond crew cut sitting astride a donkey.

"Yeah, that's me. In Nicosia. Turkish Nicosia. In 1957. You see, Nearchos, I must get over into the Turkish side to see all the places I grew up in as a kid. You understand that."

Nearchos looked sad. "I am from Famagusta. I know how you feel, John. When the Turks invaded I was forced to leave my home."

Reid grabbed the photos and selected one of himself as a boy standing in front of a smart looking house.

"This is Famagusta, Nearchos. Which suburb of Famagusta do you come from?"

"Kato Varosha," he replied. His answer didn't surprise Reid in the least. Famagusta had had only a few suburbs back in the old days, three maybe, and most of the Greeks—the more affluent ones, anyway—had lived in Kato Varosha. At least it always seemed that way to him.

"Do you remember the Marathon Taxi Office?," he asked the minister, and he could feel his adrenalin starting to pump. This was the sales presentation. He had the prospect interested. Now it was just a matter of closing. "Calvas Street. This is Calvas Street in 1963."

Reid pushed the black and white into Nearchos' hand. The Greek studied it wistfully for a while and handed it back.

"John, my friend, you must have an official reason. The only people who pass through are special workers. They do jobs over there that the Turks cannot do. But they have a guard when they leave here, and a Turkish guard when they are on the other side. They leave here early in the morning and return before six o'clock at night."

"Do any other people go through, aside from the special workers?"

"Some European businessmen have been going through recently, British mostly, but they too have a guard. And an official reason." Nearchos stressed this last phrase. Then he added, "Would you like a Coca-Cola, John?"

He stepped out of the rear of the little wooden hut, walked over to a machine, and returned with a couple of ice-cold bottles. Reid accepted gratefully, as it was already hotting up, despite the early hour. And besides, Coke in an ice-cold bottle—there's nothing like it.

From his pocket Nearchos pulled out a photo of his own, a picture of himself as a younger man, and handed it to his visitor. Unless Reid was off track, this was a big buying signal, as they say in the sales business. Nearchos was about to ask a favor. When you get back to England, John …

Oh, an ex-girlfriend? Sure, I'll look her up. Bladon? Never heard of it. Near Newcastle, eh? Let her know that Nearchos Papanicholaou is still interested? Sure. Ten years is a long time, and she may well be married now. Try it anyway? And give her this photo to remind her? Why, but of course. But what's in it for me, old chum? How about a pass to cross the Green Line, Nearchos? I'll chance my luck on the other side. One condition? Name it, Nearchos. To report back on conditions in Turkish Cyprus? If I succeed in getting through the Turkish barrier? Why, nothing would please me more.

Reid was a man of his word, sometimes. Nearchos could tell that, instinctively. He wrote busily into a logbook.

"Aren't you going to stamp it?," Reid asked.

The Greek looked at him, an enigmatic smile on his thin, clean-shaven face. "My friend, a stamp would say that you have been through the Green Line."

"Nearchos, if this is all so unofficial, tell me, why are you taking down the passport particulars?"

Nearchos looked at his watch, inserting the time in his ledger, as if he did this sort of thing every minute of every day.

"Thursday, 28 June, 1979, 8:14 a.m.," he said to himself, but aloud. "Which hotel are you staying at in Nicosia, John?"

"The Parthenon."

"Ah, good choice."

He finished writing with an exaggerated flourish, and handed the passport back to Reid.

"This is in case you do not come back. Your embassy can then have the information. It is better than nothing."

"And if I don't come back? What will my embassy do then?"

Nearchos Papanicholaou grinned. "Nothing."

Reid smiled as broadly as he could, which at that moment was pretty broad, and prepared to set out.

"John," said the Greek. "Be back before six o'clock this evening, no matter what happens. I cannot re-admit you after that time."

"You mean, I'd be stuck over there?"

"Something like that," Nearchos replied. "To be honest, I don't really know." Then he laughed. He was having a fun morning, for once. So was Reid.

"Don't worry, Nearchos."

"Oh, I am not worried, really. I will almost certainly see you again in a few minutes. I do not expect that the Turks will allow you through into their zone. What will you do if their migrations minister does not have an old girlfriend in England, eh?"

Reid leaned over the counter, formed his fingers into the shape of a pistol, put them to Nearchos's head, and pulled the trigger.

*　　*　　*

So, this was the Green Line. A romantic name for an ugly excrescence. The Turks called it the Attila Line, after Operation Attila, the evil deed that started it all, the operation in turn being named for a fat midget rapist and pillager in the fifth century.

Like the Berlin Wall, the Green Line snaked its foul, divisive course across not only a country but also the frontiers of common sense and decency, yet another stupid blot on the face of humanity in a century when the decision makers have yet again failed to learn from history.

To cross the Green Line means death! Since the Line went up, 342 Greeks had been shot in the effort to get back to their old homes, just to see the old place, or perhaps to retrieve something they'd left behind. Maybe just to die. There was no record of how many Turks had suffered a similar fate. Being smart lads, probably none.

Well, he was in it now, right in it. Alone. Not accompanied by guards. Walking carefully and deliberately through the no-man's-land between the Greek and Turkish checkpoints.

It was fortified. No doubt about that. Sullen Greek sentries stood idly in the forks of trees and in bombed-out buildings to his right. They eyed him with maximum suspicion.

"Hi, fellas," he shouted, but not very loud. There was no response. No warmth here on the Green Line. Rifles ready, new, clean. Because these soldiers were stationed at the only checkpoint on the whole island their aim was probably quite good.

The Ledra Palace Hotel reared up on Reid's left as he walked the couple of hundred yards along the dusty tarmac toward whatever fate the Turks cared to dole out to him. The Ledra Palace. Formerly the most genteel building in town. That magnificent residence which had long ago been turned into a five-star hotel. He remembered the grounds well. Every month, when he had been a little kid, his old man would bring him here to get his hair cut. At the conclusion of the operation, the barber would always ask if there was anything else. The little nipper never knew what he meant, at least not until he got a lot older, and always politely said "no." Times gone by. He felt sad. The sort of sadness a Cypriot feels. Now the Palace was the HQ for the Quebec contingent of the United Nations "peacekeeping force," and was barred from the road by a high, barbed-wire fence. An impressive number of Canadian soldiers patrolled inside the grounds, where, presumably, they were doing the most good.

Reid's left wrist had started itching early that morning under the metal, so he raised his right hand to glance at his watch. Almost 8:30.

Plenty of time. This was easy. And pleasant too. What memories here. The old novelty shop, opposite the Palace. It had had the novelty bombed out of it, but it was still there. Good memories. Small plastic airplanes, the color of your choice, a piaster a piece, from Mama or Papa, whoever happened to be behind the counter. Now new memories to take away: Soldiers, younger than he was, but tough as nails, possibly hand-picked. Probably hand-picked.

Farther on, just behind the sentries, rose a stone parapet to a height of about three feet. On the other side of this was a sheer drop of fifty feet or so to the old British parade ground below. From this parapet John Reid had often stood as a boy watching and listening to the magical processions of the Highland regiments. For old times sake he ventured across the gravel. He could hear the pipes. Not just any bagpipes. Those bagpipes. The Argyll and Sutherland lads. After almost a quarter of a century. Scotland the Brave. The Skye Boat Song.

"Hey," barked a dog-soldier, his rifle pointed directly at Reid's left testicle. Just ten feet from the parapet… But no. The timing was wrong. Definitely wrong. The guard waved him back to the road with no show of emotion. A curt, friendly nod from the retreating tourist did little to reassure the impassive soldier.

Greek troops made way for a few UN troops who in turn yielded the road to Turks. The healthy red placard at the Ottoman barrier welcomed visitors. A good sign, surely. Ironic, but good. He stepped past it into Turkish Cyprus.

Wooden huts abound in the Levant. One such became his target. The sergeant inside grinned as Reid fought his way through hordes of uniforms. It had been a long time since they'd seen an unaccompanied, plain-clothes European, if at all, and they were curious as hell.

The sergeant was a nice, easygoing sort, who, even as he talked was studying a girlie mag and running his middle finger up between the girl's thighs. He directed his most unusual visitor to the minister's office, another hundred yards farther on.

Another damned minister.

The building was next to the Radio Broadcasting Office. This was definitely Turkish territory now. At the top of three marble steps he turned right into a modern, air-conditioned office. Behind a large shittim-wood desk stood a lean man in his mid-thirties, berating a red-faced, middle-aged Englishman dressed in a pinstripe suit and carrying a briefcase. Soldiers stood around idly.

The minister—he was so obviously the minister—looked up sharply as Reid approached, and told him brusquely to wait until he was finished. Better than "piss orf," though. The minister was being harried for a pass. That the English gent was getting no joy became apparent, for he finally stormed out of the building, accompanied by a UN guard. "This is an outrage. I am a subject of Her Britannic Majesty. You haven't heard the last of this."

"Thanks for the rehearsal, pal," Reid muttered to the man as he went by. The blusterer jerked his head to the right, nostrils akimbo, and stared at him, as only a red-faced Englishman in a pinstripe can do. Dr. Watson, I presume. And a lot younger than he had first appeared.

"Next," growled the minister, exasperated. He sat down, wiping the sweat from his face with the back of his hand. A grizzled old Turk, who must have been ninety, appeared, as if by magic, from the woodwork, and beat Reid to the punch. There was nothing for it but to retreat into the other room.

A young, squat, jolly-faced lackey came up and introduced himself as Mahmoud, immediately declaring himself to be Reid's servant. He ran off to get a Coke and returned in short order, carrying instead a Turkish coffee and a tall glass of water.

"This is the life," thought Reid, as he sat smoking, and drinking his favorite coffee. Mahmoud hovered, awaiting his master's every pleasure, over the moon to be so closely associated with a foreign explorer. Of course, he was on the make. He wanted something. They all do. Reid did.

The minister appeared at the door after a brief while. "You," he said sternly, pointing right at Reid.

He followed the ill-tempered official into the main room and sat down at the receiving end of his desk.

"What do you want?" asked the minister, getting right to the point.

Out came the photos again, the smiles, the big black passport which had eased passage through many a sticky frontier crossing. Reid praised the locals, with utmost sincerity. The role he continued to play was the man back to visit the haunts of his childhood. Without the ado he'd been expecting the minister handed him a long duplicate form and told him to go over to a stout wooden table and fill it out. This took twenty minutes.

49

Then back with the official. He took a long time studying the application, not looking at Reid once. Reid, on the other hand, observed the minister closely. The features were good, regular, but cruel. Made even more sinister by a neat white scar the shape of a sideways W that ran the length of the left cheek. Wonder where he got that. The blue shadow over his face indicated two shaves a day. But he hadn't got that scar from a shaving accident.

Finally the minister looked up. "Okay."

"Incidentally, Minister," Reid said, coolly, delighted at this unexpected good fortune, but not missing a beat, "I want to go down to Famagusta on Saturday."

The minister could have simply thrown him out for pushing his luck, but it was all or nothing. Reid was prepared to gamble. He had to go to Famagusta sooner or later, to see his old home there if nothing else, and something told him he might need a separate pass to venture that far into Turkish territory. Crossing the border and wandering around the capital for a day was one thing, but Famagusta! He knew he'd better ask now, in case there was a delay.

"If you wish to spend so much time in our country, why did you not come in from Istanbul, instead of landing in Larnaka and helping the Greek economy by spending all your money there?"

The minister had blurted this out, with a suspicion of emotion, of frustration. A good man born on the wrong side of the tracks. His W seemed to become whiter for a moment.

"I didn't know the situation." Partial lie. "In Britain we don't know this is possible, but when I get back I'll make sure everyone knows they can fly in from Istanbul. After all, all the great tourist attractions are here, aren't they? And I grew up here. I feel that Turkish Cyprus is my country. I regret having landed on the Greek side at all, but I just didn't know."

"We welcome tourists here," responded the minister, with less hostility in his voice now, "but all we have is a few Germans in the north, in Kyrenia. You can have a day-pass to Famagusta. You must fill in another application form, so that your pass will be ready for you on Saturday when you come through. If the Greeks will allow you through at all a second time. They are not as co-operative as we."

"But I want to be in Famagusta for a week, at least," Reid protested, disappointed.

"Impossible," stated the minister, flatly. "This I cannot do."

"But I have so much to see there, and so much to do. Besides, isn't it better to have a tourist in your country for a week than to have that money being spent to the benefit of the Greek community?"

"This has never happened before," the minister said. Reid said nothing. The official stared at him for a long twenty seconds.

"You are a lucky man, Mr. Reid." If he didn't manifest a smile on his actual face, he may have thought one. It had been a boring morning so far. Admit, refuse, admit, refuse. Statistics. Characters without faces. Faces without character. Finally here was a real person. You could see him thinking it. Young, perhaps, but the way they used to make 'em in the old days. Almost good enough to be a Turk. Maybe.

"One week. If you can come back Saturday, your pass will be waiting. Don't worry about completing this form. I can do it for you. Just sign here. And here. And here."

*　　*　　*

He was in. He'd made it. The first unaccompanied human being to cross the Green Line. It had all been so ridiculously easy. The Greeks had certainly overplayed the danger here. So had the international press. Perhaps anybody could do it, if they had the desire, and the charm. You've got to have both.

The sun was bright and strong. The ground was hard and dry. Just the right combination to bring you well and truly alive early in the morning. Reid was glad of his running shoes and loose-fitting Chino trousers. Made him feel free and easy, at least below the waist. The Venetian walls of Old Nicosia loomed up on his right. He jumped off the road and strode across the dirt and the fallen pine needles. Curious how the walls didn't seem so big now. But then everything is larger to a seven year old. He'd experienced this phenomenon numerous times on return visits to old haunts. Everybody has. Perspective warps throughout the years.

No troops here. No one around at all. Reid studied his map and turned left at the dusty crossroads. A bum was sleeping it off, snoring generously, at the side of the road, not even having availed himself of the decency of the ditch. A large silver and gray bird pecking at the bum's chest eyed Reid cautiously as he passed by, croaked out what sounded like "What are you doing here?," and reluctantly launched himself into a

51

nearby tree. You certainly wouldn't see this sort of disgrace on the Greek side of the island. There, employment was virtually total. Prosperity and self-improvement were the burning ambitions of most Greeks. Crime was practically nonexistent, and, given the limitations of the state budget the five-year old refugee problem was being dealt with in a high-powered, professional manner by the government under Spiros Kyprianou, successor to the late and possibly lamented Archbishop Makarios. At least that was the propaganda handed out by the Greeks.

Yet these ill-kept Turkish roads, and the bum and the bird, pointed up the romance again—the charm, if that word can be used without hesitation—of the old days, the pre–British days, of course, when one could actually sniff Ottoman decay in the air. That is, if what one reads is true. Walking through the modern streets of, say, Greek Nicosia was like walking through any other civilized place; clean, neat, the people reasonably affluent, the old barbarian customs gradually dying out to make way for more acceptable, Western, manners. It had been somewhat disinfected, it was on the way to becoming sterile now. In Turkish Cyprus, however, progress had had little impact. Change, on the other hand, the inevitable change, had occurred, as everywhere else. Houses had sprung up in the twenty years since Reid has last been here, where only barren space had existed before. Fresh trees had grown in, people and animals had died to be replaced by new ones. Change is change. Progress is progress. One does not necessarily equal the other but, for sure, romance is shortchanged by progress.

His map proved quite useless and the street names had changed beyond recognition since the occupation by John Turk. Several bicycles passed and the riders almost fell off in disbelief at seeing this European wandering alone in their country. He asked a few people the way to Lala Mustafa Pasha Street, but nobody was able to provide any information. They just stared at him, some with mouths open, some not. He then asked for Osman Pasha Caddesi, one of Nicosia's arterial avenues, off which his old street lay. Surely such a huge highway would elicit some sort of enthusiastic response. But not so. Nobody seemed to know. The Turkish colonial malaise.

A few yards farther on he spotted a clear street sign. Osman Pasha Caddesi. It could be that they didn't refer to streets by name anymore. Maybe they couldn't read now that the good old British influence had gone. Perhaps both. No, it's not that. Got to remember, should have remembered, Turks, and similar peoples, had always been this way. Most of them didn't even known the name of the road they lived on, let alone other street names. As a good many of them never received mail, or bills, they would go to the grave blissfully unaware of many of the minor irritants which send Westerners so early to theirs.

Osman Pasha had been called Nelson Street when Reid had been a kid. All they'd done is switch one hero for another. Who the hell remembers Osman Pasha today? Reid wondered if Lala Mustafa Pasha had also changed its name. Unlikely. It was a Turkish name anyway, honoring the leader of the 1570 Invasion force. So it was probably still so named. And it was, for sure. Reid was at the entrance. His surprise was as great as the changes that had been wrought in the whole area.

Twenty years. The street had altered somewhat, but not a great deal. There was enough left of the old landmarks to make him feel elated as he approached Number 15 on his right. Mr. Zakis's ancient little house directly opposite was still there. Mr. Zakis might be too; he'd be about ninety-eight now. Maybe his dachshund Strudel was there as well. But no, Strudel had belonged to the owners of the next house down, the Armenian couple, Johnny and Alice. Besides, Strudel had been run over by a Ford Prefect. John Reid had seen the whole thing. Squashed sausage-dog. Sausage patty. Sorry owner of Prefect. Distraught Armenian lady. That very day a nail-bomb had exploded beneath the wheels of a British Landrover, killing three soldiers and blinding another. It was Meadows. Mr. Zakis had owned a woolly white sheepdog named Meadows.

The old bungalow which had once been No. 15, with the quince tree in front and the fig tree in the back, had gone. Much to Reid's dismay it had been superseded by a monstrous three-story apartment house gasping for an architectural soul.

There was really nothing to hold Reid to the old street, and so he went exploring. Finally, at the end of the day he passed by the deserted Minister's office on his way back to the Turkish barrier. The guards looked at him amicably, in recognition, and he just walked through, without let or hindrance. No search, either way. That was good. Bloody brilliant. On the Green Line itself were the usual guards of three flavors, but he encountered no opposition and simply walked the length of the Ledra Palace Hotel until he arrived back at the Greek checkpoint. He was amazed that it was this easy to cross, but then his earlier adventure must have caused such a stir that he'd become a cause célèbre on the Line. Simply everyone must have known who he was, and that he'd be returning. Nearchos Papanicholaou had gone for the day and Reid had a little explaining to do to the Greek soldiers at the barrier, but there was no problem, and he arrived back at the Parthenon at six, to take up his new room there, a single room with shower and no ants, just as Tony had promised.

"Are the streets clean?," was the most common question. Most of the Greeks had the idea that everything on the Turkish side was in ruins, trashed, that the streets were filled with garbage, and that riots were going on. They'd gone five years without an accurate report. When the Turks had invaded, tens of thousands of Greeks had had to flee, and now came someone who could give them a detailed account of life in their old quarters. When Reid mentioned that he was off again on Saturday to Famagusta for a week, the interest among the Greeks at the Parthenon became intense, for a large number of them had fled from the Famagusta area. Moreover, that city, being so psychologically deep in the heart of enemy territory, had taken on an air of mystique over the last half decade, amounting almost to legend. And this is not such a bad thing if it keeps alive the dream that one day the Greeks will go back.

Some of them simply wouldn't believe he'd crossed the Green Line at all, but this doubt was quickly dispelled by the majority. Word had spread from the checkpoint in that swift and efficient grapevine manner typified so well by the Greek people.

The Parthenon turned out to be the local focal point for evening society, the veranda attracting the neighborhood philosophers, and that means all Greek Cypriot men, who gathered to mingle with the guests and expound on their theories and discuss international affairs. Despite the fact that it was only a one-star hotel it had turned out to be a good choice, just as Nearchos Papanicholaou had said.

There were several Arabs staying at the hotel. Cyprus had become a cheap vacation ground for tourists from most of the Muslim states. A Jordanian engineer was there with two Saudi buddies from Dhahran, where they all worked for ARAMCO. A Bahraini maniac named Ali, who would screw anything female: Woman, cow, camel. He couldn't speak a word of English and asked Reid's help in translating from the Arabic a certain phrase which he was keen to try upon any European woman who passed within his range of vision. He wasn't very adept socially, this lad, and although "Hello, may I fuck you?" got him a lot of hostile response it provided a lot of amusement to a lot of wags. An Armenian goldsmith from Dubai who was actually staying at the classier Kennedy Hotel downtown but who was drawn, unavoidably, to the earthy internationalism and bonhomie of the Parthenon's porch. Many Lebanese were there. A Kuwaiti with alarmingly ferocious features. A Palestinian and his family, enormously genteel people, now residents of Egypt. A brace of remarkably black, remarkably homosexual Mussulmans from a non–Arab African country, who filled their days and nights fondling each other in public. All of these went in and out.

However, the guest who interested Reid the most was a tall, stocky Sudanese Christian merchant from Atbara. Mufid Habib Basta was in his early forties, a Nilotic Negro, with a strong character and an even stronger sense of humor which readily crossed cultures. His English, which was very good, had been taught him largely by his pretty wife Nellie, whose grandmother had been Welsh. Ahmad, the son, was a delightful personality of thirteen, who looked at least twenty, and who back home was a disco dancing champion. Ahmad immediately set about helping Reid brush up on his cruder Arabic vocabulary, much to Mufid's dismay. Marianne was their comely eight-year-old daughter. They were all enjoying a well-earned holiday, and took to Reid straight away.

Already latched onto the family Mufid was a London-Irishman named Bob Holmes, a wiry fellow who claimed to be the trainer of a Greek Cypriot Olympic boxing contender in London, but no one had heard of either Holmes or his fighter. Holmes was suspicious of Reid from the first, quizzing him about his background, about the Green Line, and about what he was doing in Cyprus. At one point Holmes grabbed Reid's triceps.

"Hard as a rock," he declared, triumphantly. "I thought so." He turned to Mufid and exclaimed, "This man is dangerous. I know. Stay out of his way. You'll be asking for trouble if you don't."

Reid laughed uncomfortably.

"You can laugh. But I know what I'm talking about. There's more to you than meets the eye, mate. And I'm sure I've seen you somewhere before. It'll come to me. But I know what I'm talking about. I'm a boxing trainer. The average man's triceps are flabby. They never get used. But yours! Hard as a rock. There's something you're not telling us, mate." He looked again at the Sudanese. "I'm warning you, Mufid, me old mate, don't get tied up with this man."

Reid glared at Holmes. What did he mean by "I've seen you somewhere before?" Did he recognize him from his amateur days in the ring, or possibly, highly unlikely, from the two professional bouts? Or did he know him from somewhere else? He began contemplating severe action against this fellow.

Hey, hold on, you mad bastard. You can't go around wiping people out just because they think they've seen you before. It might have been a bloody pub in Islington, for Pete's sake. It might have been on a train somewhere. Maybe this bloody Holmes character has one of those memories. After all, he wouldn't be the only one, would he. So what, anyway, if he does recognize you? You didn't leave your address anywhere that he could find it. You didn't have to hand your passport in. You only put London in the Parthenon register. They feel comfortable with London, these foreign desk clerks. They expect it. So, he goes to the register. He sees John Reid, London. There are hundreds of John Reids in London. Still, better be careful. He looks like a prying little shit. Liable to go through one's baggage.

"When are you going back to London, Holmes?"

"Tomorrow. Why?"

"Nothing. Just wondered."

Mufid diverted Holmes's attention and Reid turned to a group of very interested Greeks at a neighboring table.

*   *   *

To anyone watching, and no one was watching, Newcome and Sandby strolled almost by accident into the graveyard of the Holy Trinity Church. It was the largest cemetery in Cyprus, so it was said. They saw a figure bending over one of the tombstones about thirty yards away, and threaded their way delicately, almost reverently, through the plots.

It was a typical Cypriot late June afternoon: Hot, sunny, not a cloud in the sky. Very Mediterranean. Gobbo had plenty to do, even though he was hardly what you would call worked to the bone. Aside from his servant role in the parsonage, his job consisted merely in tending the enormous graveyard, and getting around to it whenever he could. The gravestones themselves he neglected. Gobbo felt, as did the Reverend Brownlow, that it was somehow sacrilegious to tamper with the monuments. So, the resting places went inexorably to seed and took on an aspect that only the French can describe perfectly, and the older inscriptions became increasingly illegible. Nobody ever wanted to read them anyway. If Gobbo was bored, and it would be difficult to determine the state of mind of a creature such as the Maltese hunchback, then things were about to change. Gobbo was about to participate in the most stimulating experience available to mankind.

The two men looked respectable enough. British. Gobbo had seen enough of them over the years. But, with these two he recognized that the respectability was only part of their job, not of their character. Although they wore good suits, they were obviously hard men. Gentleman thugs is what this type is called. Since the War the British government has used them to great advantage. They're well educated, very tough, and especially amoral. Something has gone wrong in their childhood. They make good junior officers, in time of war.

Gobbo muttered something in response to their "good morning," but his English wasn't good, and his mouth was suddenly dry, very dry. The two men appeared affable enough, but this was Gobbo's last afternoon on Earth, and he knew it.

Inspired by the moment, a man in a black robe flashed through the dim memories of those unfortunate early days in Malta, a kind man, the first person ever to impart to young Gobbo the startling information that in the celestial hereafter he would be just like other boys. Although he couldn't really grasp the concept of life after death—after all, Gobbo was little more than an animal in that regard—the natural attraction of an eternal reward had had an enormous impact on the little hunchback, and that, as for all other unfortunates over the ages, was what had always kept him going through a lousy vale of tears, especially as, over time, that attraction had hardened into a certainty. So, it wasn't the fear of death that worried Gobbo, it just seemed strange to be in the moment after all these years of waiting, hoping.

"We're looking for the incumbent," said Sandby. He spoke very clearly, and slowly, and to the point, yet his message wasn't getting through. "The minister." It was only the word "minister" that rang a bell through the confused haze wrapping itself around the hunchback's brain. But that was enough. Silently, because there was nothing to say, he pointed his gnarled index finger toward the edge of the graveyard, where stood the church and the residence of the Rev. Harry Blaikie Brownlow.

"He's in there?"

The two men glanced at each other. They had been lucky all day, ever since arriving at the airport when they'd found Mike the taxi driver within five minutes. Money talks. Their luck was still holding as they made a beeline for the building that constituted the principal and most lively component of Holy Trinity Church.

"Can I help you?," called out the Reverend Brownlow jovially, as the two men came in the door. Today was Harry's birthday, and he'd been celebrating the occasion since he woke up, although the casual observer wouldn't have noticed. He held his booze well, did Harry Blaikie Brownlow.

Newcome, the intellectual, offered, "I hope so, Father. We're here to meet John Reid."

From the moment his visitors stepped in, Brownlow's attention had been somewhat desultory, owing to the considerable intake of the confusing substance throughout the course of the day, and he was now alternating between "Come on, Harry, focus" and "Fuck it." But suddenly his concentration became fixed, and he adjusted his eyes, one at a time, to study his two visitors closely. He, too, had seen men like this. He had known them in both of the professions he had held in life.

"Gone, I'm afraid."

"Gone?," Newcome said. Overcoming his disappointment he continued, "We arranged to meet here, you see. We all met on the plane coming over."

Harry relaxed, but not much. "He was here. Spent a night or two, as a matter of fact. I tried to persuade him to stay longer—my birthday, today, you see—but he moved on. Let me see, it was on Monday morning."

"Well, Father, we'd certainly like to get together. Where did he go, do you know?"

"Hmmm. I've got to think for a second." Harry scratched his head. "Wait a minute, lads, he did leave an address. It's in my drawer in the vestry. Just a moment. I'll go and dig it out."

And he went into the neighboring room. When he emerged he was holding an automatic in his hand, medium caliber, black.

"Sometimes I feel naked without this," he said, smiling. "Do sit down, gentlemen, please. If I'm wrong about you two, I'll apologize."

It was at this point that things began to veer out of control. It should never have happened, but, of course, when there are human beings involved, it probably will happen. When booze enters the picture, it's going to happen, for sure.

With a nonchalance that might have suggested that this sort of thing happened to them every day—certainly didn't faze them in the slightest—Newcome and Sandby sat down in the easy chairs indicated by the incumbent, both covered by the field of fire.

"This is a joke, isn't it, Father?," said Newcome. "Please tell me it's a joke. Toy gun? Roy Rogers? Bang bang, you're dead?"

"No joke, my lad. Never been more serious in my life. And this pistol is very real." Harry was dying for action. He had stagnated too long. However, he was wondering if he wasn't making a complete ass of himself. He'd never have pulled this gun trick if he'd been sober. He knew that, drunk as he was. Stupid thing to do.

"May I inquire as to your names? If he calls, or comes by, I'll be glad to let him know you're looking for him. Your names, please."

"Tweedledum and Tweedledee," said Sandby, with more than an undertone of menace, at which Newcome gave him a disapproving glance.

"Is that Mr. Dum and Mr. Dee?," asked Harry, shifting his body weight, but maintaining his pleasant smile. "And you'd be Mr. Dum," he added, nodding toward Sandby, who took this, quite rightly, as a personal insult.

Newcome came in as diplomat. "Look, Father, he told us he'd be staying here. Told us to drop by, and we'd get together for a drink."

"Gentlemen, I'm devastated that I can't be more helpful. I'll tell you what, though. I'm going to call the Larnaka Police. They'd probably run him down for you."

Harry walked toward the phone, but he never got there.

Gobbo, stupid bastard, chose that very moment to make his entrance through the vestry door. It was his final mistake. Like all other self-centered fuckwits, in his mad rush to meet his destiny, the thought that he might be imperiling others never crossed his mind. It was all about Gobbo. Me, me, me. Newcome, the more cerebral of the two Englishmen, slid off his chair and went into a crouch so fast it was as if the move hadn't been executed, and all within the same blurring motion he let a knife go underarm with such force that it pushed Gobbo momentarily up against the heavy

59

door. What was so astonishing was not so much the speed of the delivery, or the power, but the fact that the blade entered Gobbo's head right in the middle of his one eyebrow. The hunchback immediately and without any ado "flew to Heaven," as the old Venetian Catholics on the island used to say. Volò al cielo.

Harry might, just might, have been able to make a slightly better initial showing if he hadn't been so bloody drunk, but even if he'd been in the best form of his life, Newcome and Sandby had been a team for a long time, and they were good. In the split second that Newcome was administering the last rites to the hunchback, Sandby had moved very fast toward Harry, and with textbook economy of movement had kicked the gun from his hand. Harry backed up against the fireplace, and, as Sandby lunged toward him again, the priest was ready for him. He moved with great agility to one side, and Sandby ran headlong into the fireplace. He wasn't hurt, but he yelled at Newcome, "Grab him."

Harry Blaikie Brownlow lifted his foot a few feet within the vertical, and it caught Newcome in the shin. Newcome went down on one knee, panting, but otherwise silent. Sandby came in from behind, and Brownlow back-elbowed him in the chest, and sent him staggering back against the fireplace again. Harry then grabbed a poker from the fireplace and wielding it in front of him, yelled "Come on, lads. Let's be having you." It had been a long time since he'd seen good, first-class action. It was such a shame that it had to be now, when his reflexes were dulled and he could feel the stoutness in his legs fast diminishing. But, regardless of all that, he was going to have a jolly good time, no matter what.

However, one against two, and two trained thugs at that, and with Harry smashed, it was just a question of the old pincer movement and Sandby it was who got him on the back of the neck with a vicious karate chop, and the priest went down. Newcome stomped on his face and Brownlow blacked out.

When he came to, his brain was considerably clearer. He was tied up, and sitting on a hard chair. His mouth was issuing blood from the left side. He didn't look great. You never do when you sober up so fast.

"Where did he go, Father?," asked Newcome, almost soothingly.

"Don't know, old boy, sorry."

Newcome, who had his knife back in his hand, waggled it at the priest. "Let me tell you this, Sunshine. We don't have much time. I'm going to count up to ten, then, if you haven't talked, I'm going to cut your left ear off. Then your right one. Then your nose. I'm going to leave your tongue in, 'cause I want you to talk. Then I'm going to proceed in a southerly direction, as they say, toward your toes, missing nothing out along the way. 10–9–8–7..."

"All right, I'll sing," said the priest.

The boys relaxed their hold on him. Sometimes it's not this easy.

And Harry began to sing, "Jesus loves me, this I know, for the Bible tells me so. Little ones to him be..."

"What the hell!," cried Sandby.

"Maybe he really doesn't know," said Newcome.

"Bollocks," uttered Sandby, the less cerebral of the two. "He knows he's going to die, whether he talks or not. And he's pissed as a newt. I mean, he's been drinking, a man of the bloody cloth has been bloody drinking. We've really botched this one, John."

"Yeah, I think you're right," replied Newcome, fatalistically, but with a touch of sadness in his voice.

"Finish him off, John," suggested Sandby.

Newcome was reluctant. He knew things had gone horribly wrong with this interview, but it wasn't often he got to torture an Anglican incumbent. But Sandby was right. They had to kill him now. He probably wasn't going to talk, time was against them, and if they let him live he would warn Reid and they, Newcome and Sandby, might be in trouble. Newcome's fist connected hard with his victim's jaw, and Harry passed out again, the way you do. With his left arm locked around Brownlow's throat, Newcome was just about to do the dirty when they heard the front door open and an Englishman's voice called out, "Hello. Harry. Anyone home? It's me, George."

Newcome froze. But only for a split second. Within that very brief space of time his eye was caught by a small stack of white business cards lying on a side table and proclaiming the virtues of a hotel in Nicosia. His left hand made a grab for them, and then he stuck the knife very definitively into the priest's chest and turned the handle. The two gentleman thugs rushed out through the side door, and, as if to mark their passing, a glass that had been balanced precariously on the edge of the desk fell and shattered, spilling the vicar's faithful Scotch companion into the cracks of the stone floor.

* * *

61

The Turkish sergeant apologized. "I have no such permit." He seemed genuinely sorry.

Not half as sorry as Reid. "I'll tell you what. How about if I go to the minister's office, and bring it directly to you."

"The minister does not work today."

Bollocks. Without that pass, no Famagusta. Maybe the minister had forgotten to process it. Maybe he'd been unable to swing it. Maybe anything. It was bloody annoying. Aside from anything else Reid had temporarily checked out of the Parthenon that morning. No one likes to be thwarted at the final hurdle.

"But he said it would be ready today. Could you have another look, please?"

Suddenly, in the far recesses of the tiny hut, the sergeant exhaled with a mildly orgasmic "Ah!," and turned exultantly toward his visitor, flourishing a color magazine open to a page sporting a smiling ash blonde with a well-developed bust, well-brushed teeth and an air-brushed pudendum. Although Reid appreciated the aesthetics, given his taut situation right now he couldn't get as worked up about them as the sergeant. But it wasn't over. The Turk snapped shut the mag, and the cover revealed that it was Danish, dated 1963. For a big man, the sergeant was moving his hands fast. Practice, obviously. He re-opened the naughty little periodical to a different page, a sticky one, and, this time, a monumentally triumphant "Ah!"

Now Reid was able to share the Turk's enthusiasm. He walked lightly through into the Turkish zone.

A taxi-driver hailed him. The man seemed to be waiting for business. But there was no business to be had on the Green Line, for a cabby anyway.

"You go to Famagusta?"

Reid leaned into the window. The interior of the old hack smelled like a burst intestine. He tried to narrow his eyes to steely slits, like Lee Van Cleef used to do in those Italian westerns. It frightened the cab driver into an attack of verbal diarrhea.

"They say an Englishman comes this morning. They say he goes to Famagusta. You are carrying a bag. You look like an Englishman. I mean only to help you. You want to go to Famagusta? You want to change money?"

At the left corner of his mouth the man had what looked like an enormous raspberry seed which cracked open every time he spoke, oozing a thin, pink liquid that trickled down diagonally into the stubble of his chin. It was this more than anything that swung him in Reid's favor. He'd always been partial to raspberries.

Reid climbed in, next to the driver. They pulled away and headed around the walls toward the Kemal Ataturk Gate.

"Who told you I'd be coming across?" His voice contained little pleasantness.

"Migration. I have a cousin who works in the office. He tells me you come today." The man was nervous. But he was scared. It sounded feasible. And the raspberry liquid was fairly cascading down the front of his shirt.

"You're bleeding," observed Reid, but he was dying to know.

"Syphilis," the cabbie said, with a wistful smile, as if it were nothing more than a bad cold.

It may have been a Turkish joke, but Reid made a mental note not to shake the guy's hand. Aside from the words of advice from an old flame of his, "Don't sit on public toilet seats," he didn't know much about the physical manifestations of venereal diseases, and this wasn't the moment to find out. "Take me to the Itimat Taxi office here in Nicosia."

"You do not want to go to Famagusta?," he asked, more than surprised. Disappointed. Missing out on a good fare? For a few dollars more?

Not all the way to Famagusta with that bloody raspberry, let me tell you that, Pal. "Itimat. Nicosia. This town."

The car coughed and squirmed its way through the Gate into the old walled part of the Capital. Reid got out, handed the man the appropriate coin of the realm, and refrained from making one of the three clap cracks he had come up with. He watched while the taxi disappeared down the series of little side streets, and then he ambled up to a respectable looking man loitering on a corner and sporting a badly fitting eye. As the lira was absolutely useless outside Turkish Cyprus, the ubiquitous Black Market offered a better deal than the banks in this nationwide obsession to acquire foreign currencies at any cost.

The small variegated group of Turks eyed him with the greatest curiosity, and before long a huge black Mercedes rolled up. Reid climbed in with the other sardines.

The Itimat Taxi Service was a company of collective cabs which plied from Kyrenia in the north through Nicosia to Famagusta in the south, serving all the major villages in between. A trip from Nicosia to Famagusta cost 300 lirasi, or about 40 English pence, which was ludicrously cheap. Most hot countries in the world have this sort of service. In Latin America they call them colectivos. The Middle and Near East, including the Greek part of Cyprus, call them service taxis. Israel has the sherut. In Turkish Cyprus they call them Itimat.

The only other form of public transportation was the bus, but that was not only uncomfortable, it took ages to reach its destination. Although Reid had considered hiring a car, or a motorcycle, he'd decided that a car would only impede him, and, a guy his size, he'd look a little silly on a tiny putt-putt Simpson. Besides, one goes slowly and innocently into the unknown.

During the uneventful ride to Famagusta, Reid made friends with one of his fellow passengers, a student home from Turkey for the holidays. When they arrived at the Itimat Taxi Office in Old Famagusta, he and the young Turk got out and stretched their legs by walking a couple of blocks to the student's car, which by well-developed routine he always parked in the walled city to await his periodic return from the mainland.

"I take you to Plambitch."

It was an offer Reid found hard to refuse, but he had some questions first, notably "What is Plambitch?"

"Hotel. Good hotel. Correct hotel for you."

"Where is it?"

"In new city, outside the walls. On bitch."

"Bitch?"

"Yah, Golden Sands Bitch."

"Palm Beach Hotel?"

"Yah, Plambitch."

But, in the end, Reid declined the offer, said he'd rather find somewhere in the old walled city. There are certain times in life, especially when one is traveling alone, when the inexpensive pervasive odor of antiquity is preferable to exorbitant bullshit. Ian Fleming used to rail against the standardized strip of paper American hotel housekeeping crews used to spread over the toilet seat after they'd finished cleaning it. "Sanitized."

Reid and his young scholar friend parted with a stiff unmasonic handshake and what in the old days would have passed as salaams. While the young Turk drove off amid belching fumes and engine flatulence, Reid swung his grip onto his shoulders and started walking.

The Altun Tabya was a quaint little caravanserai. Pleasant, comfortable, looking out over the tiny medieval street in which bustled dogs, scruffy kids and Olde Worlde Mussulmans amid the inimitable scents of the Near East. The true Mohammedan magic, unchanged for centuries, was what had brought travelers to this walled city since the days of Othello.

The name translated as the Golden Bastion. Reid went inside to investigate the accommodations, which were satisfactory. Two pounds a night, bed and breakfast, or at least that equivalent in Turkish lirasi. The manager was a Turk from the mainland, one of the many thousands resettled here after the Invasion. About thirty-five, friendly enough, his right eye was considerably closer to his mouth than his left eye was. He was stupid, oh, so wondrously stupid, and totally, absolutely totally ignorant of the English language. His two flunkies were also from Turkey. Teenage scum. Rude and shifty.

Reid grabbed a quick shower, then went out for a jaunt in the city. Strolling through the winding, tiny streets he pondered how little it must have changed since the 16th century. Only the nationality of the rulers had varied over the years.

He changed some more Sterling into lirasi through a cabby, and later that afternoon, with difficulty, he succeeded in finding his old home. Although the roads leading out of town had changed their face beyond recognition, and the look of Kato Varosha had altered quite considerably, the very street and house remained exactly as he remembered. He took out the old photo. No change. He knew that for him, at that moment, time stood still.

The first half of the next day was spent relaxing on the beach, reading Dennis Wheatley's *Mayhem in Greece,* and for the rest of the day he bit the bullet of indignity and hired a little Simpson motorbike, on which he explored the city and suburbs until he'd completely re-familiarized himself with the place. He had a strong feeling—no, he knew—that this knowledge would be indispensable in the not too distant future.

By the end of four days he was beginning to get a little bored. The people were just not relaxed, which wasn't surprising as there were well over fifty thousand troops in the Turkish zone, guarding the Green Line, the highways and the seafront. Too many troops. Tense civilians. Galloping inflation. Unemployment out of sight. The brain drain to Istanbul. The émigrés from Turkey taking over local businesses and homes. The lack of contact with the outside world. Barbed wire, oil drums stacked two-high, submachine guns everywhere he walked. But above all the uncertainty. No wonder the natives weren't relaxed. Moreover, the old place seemed devoid of all its character now the Greeks had gone. In pre–Invasion days Famagusta had comprised two towns : The old walled city which was Turkish, and the modern town just down the road, which the Greeks called Varosha. Varosha had been mixed, but predominantly Greek. It had been the nerve center of the area, and with the great harbor had to some extent been the pulse of Cyprus itself. It was here that all the foreign businesses had set up shop. It was here that fun could be obtained, free or for a price. Varosha had been the thriving metropolis. Now, though, there were no more bustling market stalls, no more one-way streets which had seemed to go both ways despite the one-way street warnings. No more teenage girls bending over and hiking up their cotton dresses. "Hey, George!" They called all Englishmen George, out of respect for the late kings. "You want jig-a-jig? Only ten shilling." No more anything any more in Varosha. No more Varosha. A mysterious barricade had gone up around a large part of the town since the Invasion. It was now forbidden. Forbidding. Not a soul inside. Heavily patrolled on the outside. A ghost town.

He was glad to get back to Greek Nicosia, among friendly folk, where things were happening, and where the free integration of races made things pop.

*   *   *

It was the afternoon of July 3 that John Reid checked back in to the Parthenon. There were only a few old faces left. That's the way it is in these hotels.

He strolled out at dusk into one of the little side streets, walked into what had rapidly become his regular hole in the wall, and grabbed a pocket kebab from the elderly ray of sunshine whose campaign slogan was "Yanni, you came to the right place." The kebab man was right, though. The best meal in the world at only 600 mils. That was the man's pitch, and it was true. Reid's kebab was out of this world. That and a couple of glasses of triantaphilo, the rose water cordial found at vending machines on every street corner in Cyprus, followed by an hour's conversation with some of the locals, and he was ready for anything.

About nine o'clock he headed back to the hotel, where the conversation was heating up on the porch. The familiars were around by now, and all hailed Reid as he came up the steps. His Greek was almost back to being perfect, so they launched into a philosophical discussion in that discipline's original language.

When she sauntered uncertainly out of the hotel lobby with a drink in her hand, he knew he'd seen her before. She was alone, so he stood up, introduced himself, and invited Vanessa Riley to join the group.

She apologized for not speaking their language. Reid smiled. It didn't matter. Everyone spoke English.

She sat down and listened as they all chatted. Reid tried to include her in the conversation, but she was clearly preoccupied.

"May I get you another drink?," he asked.

"Yes, please. Ouzo."

"Ouzo? Is that what you're drinking?"

He felt like asking whether she'd had much experience with this stuff that had put the Greeks where they are today. Instead he got up, went inside, ordered, and came back out. As they resumed their introductory chatter, she and Reid subtly detached themselves from the philosophers and became just a boy and girl shooting the breeze on a hotel porch. The Greek lads had noticed Reid's move, of course, but accepted it without a whimper. One philosophy above all others is that there is only one thing better than philosophizing, and that's scoring. And they all knew that that was on his mind, even though it wasn't. At least, he didn't think so. Maybe they knew better than he did.

"So, Vanessa, you're American."

"You've got a good ear. And you're English."

"You've got nice ears. I'm Scotch."

"Ooops," she apologized, taking a slurp of ouzo, a small portion of which didn't quite make her mouth. She tittered gaily. Nice titters.

"Don't worry about it," he said. "So, where are you from in the USA?"

"North Carolina," she replied. "Do you know the United States at all?"

"No. Never been there. Everything I know is from the movies."

"Ah." She laughed. "You can't believe any of that."

"The Carolinas. That's in the South, isn't it? You don't have a Southern accent."

She looked at him almost coyly. "You're notorious, you know."

Reid was just a bit taken aback by that, but, fortunately, before it started to gnaw, she expanded. "Your reputation in Nicosia is growing. The Green Line Runner, they call you."

"They do?"

"So how do you do it?"

"Do what?"

"How do you get across the Green Line?"

But, of course, it was niggling him. "You know, you look awfully familiar. Have we met?"

She laughed, and it was very pleasant, like rain tinkling down a drainpipe and hitting a frog at the bottom. "I'm just twenty-one, and even I've heard that line a thousand times. Mostly in movies. American movies."

Reid looked at her more closely, as closely as he could without appearing to be either gross or exceptionally near-sighted. "London? Have you ever been to London?"

She seemed flustered. "Of course. Many times. But we've never met. I would have remembered. Sorry. I just broke up with my boyfriend."

It was Reid's turn to apologize, or rather to express his condolences. But he didn't. Picking his nose would have been a more meaningful gesture, but he didn't do that either. The girl looked like she was on the point of a minor nervous breakdown, one that would have escaped the casual observer, kind of like a mild stroke. But she was acting. A diversion. You didn't need a fifty-dollar psychiatrist to figure that out. "Mum! Mum! A wasp!" Boy, that one used to get him out from under a lot of looming black clouds as a kid.

"What do you do? Are you an actress? Someone famous? Could that be where I've seen you?"

She re-laughed. That old drainpipe feeling came over Reid again. She had moved on, past the boyfriend now.

"No. I did think about being an actress, but it sounded too much like being a waiter."

"A waiter?"

"Yeah. Waiting for roles. Waiting tables in New York City."

"Ah, I see." And he did. Not the life for her. Waitress, there's something in my fly. All those old sodden fine-dining jokes. Or maybe the star attraction in a cheap hamburger joint in Queens. "So, what do you do?"

"I've got a rich father."

Reid sighed. "Nice."

Then she went on the attack. "What do you do? Aside from running the Green Line."

His turn to laugh, so he did. "I'm a writer. At least that's what it says on my passport."

A mystifying look passed across her green eyes for a second. "You're kidding. Have I heard of you?"

"Why, of course." He laughed again. He could do things on cue, if the pressure was on.

"What name do you go under?"

His delivery was slow and strung out so she wouldn't miss it. "William Shakespeare."

She suspected he was joking, you could tell, and she half-laughed. It was more of a hiccup.

"So," Reid asked, as if it were purely for conversation, which it partly was, "what are you doing in Cyprus?"

"Just a tourist. After the boyfriend I needed something different."

"You realize this is a one-star hotel," he said. "Not a dump exactly, but one star down is zero star. And that would be a dump. I would have thought you'd be staying at, say, the Kennedy."

She smiled an enigmatic smile. The Mona Lisa of the song rather than the painting. "I like character."

"Me too."

She changed the subject again. "What are you doing in Cyprus?"

"I'm the Green Line Runner."

She smiled again, and took a drink. God, that smile. God, that drink. "No, really. I mean, what brought you here?"

But Reid couldn't shift from his mind a vague image he had of her, somewhere, half-buried among more recent, vivid memories. "I have seen you before. It's just a matter of time before I get it."

After a pause, not a word between them spoken, he added, "I came here for old time's sake. A journey back into my past."

She looked at him hard, and he could see the stuff was really starting to get to her. In fact, she was quite pissed. She stated, quite emphatically, but with a distinct slur, "You're not really Scottish."

This sort of amused Reid, and sort of didn't. It wasn't the first time he'd heard that. He'd heard German, Jewish, Norwegian, even fucking Chinese on the occasional dark night. "Oh? What makes you say that?"

"You said Scotch. No Scotsman ever says Scotch. He says Scottish. Scotch is the drink. I thought everyone knew that."

Reid lit a Capstan and looked at her again, with some considerable interest, and in a different light. Not necessarily a kinder light, but definitely one that shines prismatically through the bottom of a glass of ouzo.

"My dear Miss Riley," he said, as patronizingly as he could under the circumstances, "a little learning is a dangerous thing. A wee Scotchman once gave me some great advice: When you climb the ladder of success, keep one foot on the ground at all times."

She missed the funny, as any normal person would have done, but she was truly excited. You could see that. She was anybody's. "You see, you said it again: Scotch."

Reid felt a lecture coming on, and he indulged himself. Why not? A lecture for intellectual peasants or for very young well-meaning people who hadn't yet had the necessary time on Earth in which to sift the truth from the very full bucket of bullshit loosely called History. After all, his lecture was well rehearsed, and he had nothing better to do, and certainly nothing to look forward to this evening except an American girl hugging the porcelain, puking her guts up, and moaning for God.

"Scotch is older, better, sturdier linguistically, and it just happens to be the word I sometimes use. Not always, but often. In that regard, I'm no different from Sir Walter Scott, Byron, John Knox, John Buchan, and many other wee Scotchmen you care to mention. As long as they've been dead for over thirty years."

"So, it's an affectation," she observed, rather astutely. Booze obviously brought out the best in her, as well as the worst.

Reid smiled appreciatively. "Yes, it is. But no more than any other affectation when you bear in mind that everything we say is an affectation."

She appeared thoughtful, or as thoughtful as she could, given that she was now desperately tanked.

Reid hadn't quite had enough of the Scotch history lesson. "Besides, you have Scotch tape over in the States, don't you?"

"Yes, but that's different. That's just a brand name."

"Well, in Britain we call Scotch tape Cellotape, did you know that?"

She replied, with a mild, open and sunny sense of triumph, that she did.

"Well, did you know that in Australia they used to call it Durex?"

She laughed, giggled on the verge of hysteria. "Durex? Durex is a condom."

It must have been contagious, because Reid felt himself starting to crack up. "Yeah, gotta be careful these days. Things could get a bit sticky."

"You know what they call a condom in North Carolina?" Her turn to ask technical questions about rubber johnnies.

He didn't, so she told him. "A Trojan."

"No kidding?"

"No kidding."

Of course, he could see the classical image, and it was truly funny. "You mean, like the Siege of Troy? Achilles. Priam loose and all that?"

"Yes," she answered, "but they're only used by Homer-sexuals."

This girl had looks, and a sense of humor. She'd set him up, drunk as she was. But, he'd seen her before, somewhere. And that worried him.

* * *

"Reid's back, Sir, from his little trip across the Line."

"Lion?" The tall man's puzzlement was clear. "As in the Lion of Judah?"

"No, Sir. Line as in the Green Line."

"What's he doing tripping across the Green Line? I may be out of touch, John, but I thought that was somewhat difficult."

"It is, Sir. For everyone but Reid. He seems to go across whenever he wants, no problem. He just got back after three or four days in Famagusta. They're calling him the Green Line Runner."

"Are they indeed? Where is he now?"

"He's upstairs in his room."

"He doesn't know you're on to him?"

"No. No way. We're in the same hotel, but he doesn't suspect a thing. No reason."

"Don't be so confident, Newcome. My guess is he's pretty good."

"So are we, Sir, and there are two of us."

71

"Good man, John. Good man. Mathematics always was your strong point at Cambridge, wasn't it? Before you got sent down."

"Yes, well, we don't want to go into that, do we, Sir." Newcome seemed genuinely embarrassed. "Uh-oh, here he comes now. It's breakfast time at the zoo."

The scene in the dining room was something out of a 1940s black and white British movie, one that never got made but which, if it had, would have starred Celia Johnson and a young Trevor Howard. Seven o'clock was too early for most guests, and there were only two men in the room, both so obviously English. They were sitting by the big window, noshing on their fruit plates. The older one, mid-fifties, destroyed by years of Attlee and postwar rationing, had his elbows in at precisely the correct British angle. He was just the sort who would have grown up touching his forelock to the local squire. The much younger one, a crude and stocky specimen with long blond hair, was strewn all over the table. A slob. Would have been perfectly at home in the twelfth century. Right down to the unsightly blemish on his left cheek, an unfortunate defect caused not by the pox, as one might suspect, but by an air-gun accident in his youth. Stupid bastard had slipped on a piece of dog shit while trying to impress a cheap tart, and shot himself. The pock blossomed from his face like an ugly lily, and would have severely limited his ability to pull girls, even cheap tarts.

The older man looked up nervously as Reid entered the room. Then, as an immediate reflex action, he looked down again at his grapes. Wouldn't do to be rude and stare, would it? The youngster didn't feel that way, however, liberated as he was by the New Age, and fixed his eye malevolently on Reid, who took in the look with passing interest.

"Hi, guys, how ya doin'?," Reid said loudly, in an effort to break the ice that he knew would frost his breakfast if allowed to remain unthawed.

The older man looked up sharply, somewhat unbelieving, as if he had been kicked in the balls. He nodded, that's all, and his mate continued to stare at Reid.

"What's for breakfast?"

"Fruit and Greek walnuts to start," came the nervous reply.

"Where you from?," Reid asked, in a friendly, casual tone.

This direct question, aimed at two people who come from a society where one still backs away from the monarch rather than show your bum to a royal, had a galvanizing effect on the older man. It was as if he'd never been put on the spot like that before, and perhaps he hadn't. You could see, by the way his hand went to his crotch, that he'd just been the surprise victim of a wee spasm of incontinence.

"Leicester," he blurted out.

"You're a long way from home." Reid stated the obvious, but only in order to keep the flow of meaningless dialogue going.

"We're on a job. We're plumbers."

Reid couldn't help smiling. The man had actually volunteered information, and what he'd said had sounded so reasonable.

The younger man, the slob with the pock mark, revved himself up into a new gear, a scowl he'd been itching to get into. "Stickin' your bloody nose in a bit far, aren't you, mate?"

Reid smiled again, almost beatifically. "Just making polite conversation, that's all. Better than sitting in this little room, ignoring each other over breakfast, right?"

"Wrong."

The slob's pal, the one who'd pissed himself, looked a little nervous, in fact more than a little. "Leave it out, Fred," he said, but the young man didn't take any notice.

"I think you're being very rude," said the young man, now grinning, and trying to imitate Reid's cultured accent. "You bloody queers are all the same. Putting something where it don't belong."

Reid raised an unappreciative right eyebrow. At that moment he noticed that two other men had assumed seats at the other end of the dining room. Hard looking fellows. British, probably. Suits. He nodded in their direction, and they nodded back. Friendly enough. One of them looked at the other and raised his eyebrow too. A lot of eyebrow raising going on in the dining room. That's because everyone could sense a bit of early morning fun with their breakfast. The young plumber ignored the new arrivals or, if he was aware that they'd come in, perhaps felt that his act might go off better with a bigger audience.

"Not here, Fred," counseled the older, and wiser, of the two plumbers, but his advice fell on deaf ears.

"Cyril," announced the slob to his mate, and as he did so he leaned back on the two rear legs of his chair, "we've got a raging queen here, and I don't like having breakfast with raging queens."

73

His mate looked very uncomfortable, but made no further effort to stop the young man, who then turned to Reid, and ratcheted up the ante. "You fuckin' poofters. Bleedin' fairies. Ought to be fuckin' shot."

Reid said, calmly, "I think I'd better leave." He hadn't slept well that night, and he was tired, too tired for this. He stood up, preparing to make his way to the door.

"Oh no you don't," said the young plumber, rising to his feet. "You've put me off my Greek walnuts, you fuckin' queer. And I don't like queers puttin' me off my walnuts. I reckon you've cheated me out of a couple of quid, and I want it back. Now."

Reid was almost at the door, but young Fred rushed over, blocking his exit. "Not so fast," ordered Fred, smirking. Fortunately there was no one else around except the two hard men in suits. The staff were probably all in the kitchen, stirring eggs. Fred made the mistake of moving close in toward Reid, and suddenly the young plumber's grin had expanded to the point of What do you think of the melon seeds infesting the spaces between my bared teeth? How do you rate the halitosis coming in short gasps? It was so subtle that it almost hadn't happened, but Reid's hand had shot out and grabbed the young plumber's testicles in an iron grip, and he was squeezing. There was no change of expression on Reid's face, or even in the position of his body. It was just something he was doing, something that required little more effort than just standing in the doorway. But the boy was demoralized, you could see that, and the pain was getting worse. Cyril, the older plumber, positioned as he was, couldn't see what was going on, and he was genuinely puzzled at the unnatural hiatus in the action.

Young Fred started to fold, a classic case of plumber's droop, and seconds later sagged to the floor, mildly unconscious and making small mewing noises. At that point, the older plumber looked at Reid and said, quite calmly, "What happened?"

"His nuts went down the wrong way," Reid said, smiling benignly. "Is this your last day at this hotel?"

"No, we've got three days left," replied Cyril the plumber.

"A really good idea would be to settle up with the landlord right now, pay him whatever he asks, no questions, and find another hotel as far away from here as you can." That was Reid's suggestion.

"Good idea," agreed Cyril. As Reid passed the two hard men they nodded again, he nodded in return, and he was on his way up to his room.

The lad was coming to, wondering what time of day it was. He looked around him in a daze, eyes glazed, and then he saw his mate.

"Cyril, I think I'm going to be sick."

"Serves you right, you thick arsehole."

Cyril walked over, helped his young friend to his feet, and with a glance toward Sandby and Newcome, they set out in search of a good-sized toilet.

"I admire good craftsmanship, don't you, John?," said Newcome to Sandby, grinning. They went to the phone.

"We just witnessed an interesting spectacle," said Newcome into the mouthpiece, once he'd been connected. "You were right about our man Reid. He's good." And he described briefly for the benefit of the tall man the episode of a few moments before.

"I see," said London. "Look, Newcome, how sure are you that he's not on to you?"

"Impossible, Sir," said Newcome, a little put out.

"Improbable, perhaps, John, but not impossible. If it had been impossible I wouldn't have said it, would I?"

"No Sir," replied Newcome, "I suppose you wouldn't. It's just that we haven't done anything to tip our hand."

"All right, but be careful."

The tall man frowned for a few minutes, then inserted his index finger in the dial. Within seconds he was talking to Burt Zoffel.

* * *

Lashed to the giant, neon crucifix, and naked but for the awesomely casual G-string which did well to hide her bladder, Fräulein Lise had been entertaining enough, if a trifle bizarre. And the energetic, if rather unsophisticated, obligatory simulated lesbian act between Fräulein Helen and Fräulein Margarethe had gone down well. But the highlight of the evening so far was Mufid Habib Basta, shirt open down to the navel, ripping it up on the stage with seven topless danseuses, in the most frenzied jig of the night.

The Sudanese clambered, sweating and panting, down from the thrust-stage to rejoin Vanessa and Reid at the ringside table. Reid grabbed the microphone from the compère, who had been standing within inches of Mufid, waiting to introduce the next routine and, amid thunderous applause from the audience, yelled, "Ladies and gentlemen, Mufid the Great!" The cheers and whistles were deafening, as a pretty blonde hostess, Australian, from Brisbane, apparently, brought the three of them a beer each on the house.

The Crazy Horse was by far and away the best of the leading Nicosia cabarets, the other two being the Ambassador and the Miami. All were in, or around, Regaena Street, Nicosia's traditional red-light district, just within the walled city. All clubs charged one Cyprus pound admission, which got you a table and a beer for the evening. At the Crazy Horse subsequent beers cost two pounds each, while a bottle of whiskey went for a staggering thirty-six pounds; around fifty Sterling. The girls who worked here were of various nationalities. Some danced and stripped. Others performed … other acts. A few merely hosted. However, most of them had interchangeable roles, each function being an integral part of their repertoires. Blondes were in high demand, naturally, as this was the Near East, but none of the rich, swarthy, rich, five-o'clock-shadow-ridden, rich Mediterraneans or Arabs in the audience seemed to give a damn that, in many cases but by no means all, this envied Nordic quality was betrayed by an unashamedly coal-black bush bulging provocatively over the top of a minuscule piece of white fabric.

The seven Austrian girls from Reid's hotel were touring entertainers under the management of a shadowy Hindu sporting the unlikely moniker of Caesar, who had recruited them in Vienna and taken them on the Middle and Near Eastern circuit of fleshpots such as Baghdad, Damascus, Cairo and Nicosia. A good way to see the world, but it was a long, grinding tour, with wages negotiable around the fifteen Cyprus pounds a week mark, plus food and hotel accommodation, albeit in one-star jobs like the Parthenon. In addition, a girl could, and did—for that was why she was here—pick up much more money by renting herself out on a short-term lease. Between numbers she would come down and mingle with the business suits, encouraging them to purchase a bottle of whiskey at the alarming house rate. For every bottle thus sold the Crazy Horse would give her a two-pound commission, and who knew what to Indian Caesar of the sinister physiognomy. At the end of the evening each girl would almost inevitably go off with a suit, to his expensive hotel suite for the oui hours, and then back to the symbolic Parthenon for a day of rest. Whatever she made out of the whole thing was her affair, after, of course, rendering unto Caesar that which was Caesar's.

As another chorus of lovelies paraded on stage, a short, stout tuxedo approached Reid. There was a man inside it. He leaned over into Reid's ear.

"Excuse me," he whispered, shouting over the Beiruti belly-dance music. "There are three men who would like to talk to you, please."

Reid looked hard at the chubby Greek with the garlicky breath. Interesting. What now?

"Which three men?" He blew an imperfect smoke-ring into his visitor's dimpled chin, where it disappeared into the crevice.

The man nodded to a raised platform at the back of the room. There were several tables occupied by three men, but one trio in particular stood out. They oozed Levantine affluence. Besides, they were all staring at John Reid.

A soliciting blonde, flushed with momentary success at a neighboring table, glided among the three men, rising financial expectations throbbing between her thighs. One of the men put up four fingers, she trembled slightly, and then he ushered her away with a playful smack on the rump. You could hear her knees knocking from across the room.

They were obviously waiting for Reid to join them. He hated to disappoint total strangers, so he got up.

"Won't be long."

Vanessa smiled coyly, and said "See you soon." The Sudanese was riveted to the show and couldn't give a damn.

The gold teeth and diamond rings sparkled as the three Greek tycoons waved Reid into the fourth seat at the table.

"My name is Charalambides," volunteered the spokesman. "This is Velios, and this is Kyriakides."

The other two bowed silently in their seats, exuding warmth and bonhomie.

"Charalambides, eh? Possibly the Charalambides? Of the famous milk company?"

Mr. Charalambides returned the blatant probe with a most sensational smile, but no spoken word.

"Don't tell me," Reid joked, "Charalambides is a common name."

There was a trace of laughter from the trio, but it was a rehearsed movie script.

"And my name is John Reid, as you probably know. What can I do for you, gentlemen?"

The blonde reappeared with four bottles of whiskey and corresponding glasses. That's four bottles. Charalambides signed a chit. Reid, being a Scotch man, rapidly calculated that this came to 144 Cyprus pounds. The average Greek Cypriot wage was thirty-two pounds a week. Reid was dealing with fairly well-off gents here, to say the least. He might have a glass, but that would be all. He might also be dealing with pretty heavy drinkers too.

"You drink whiskey, Mr. Reid?," asked Charalambides, pouring. "You can see the show?"

"Sure, that's fine." He was rather touched that they were so anxious for his welfare. There was a silence broken only by the massive throb of the music as they watched the performance, all of them smoking and drinking, just like big boys. Well, the three Greeks were big boys. Reid was only pretending.

"We understand that you recently returned from Famagusta, Mr. Reid."

"That's right."

Charalambides quizzed Reid quite candidly about the cleanliness of the streets and about the strength of the Turkish army in the sector. He was astonished that Reid had been able to live in Famagusta for so many days without running into trouble. Reid was amused at their directness but, because he was sorry for their plight, which was the plight of most Greek Cypriots, he was glad to be of service. Any moment now, though, they might get to the point. This class of boy didn't go in for socializing with young foreign punks, just for the hell of it.

The Greek spokesman asked if the suburbs of Famagusta had changed much.

"Not at all," Reid replied. "In fact, they look very much as they did in 1963 when I lived there. I mean, aside from the inevitable changes. The houses are kept just as they were before the Invasion, I could see that. You see, Turkish Cypriots are living in a lot of them, and I get the feeling that they regard their occupancy as temporary, certainly as indecent. They're acting as caretakers, if you like, so that when the trouble ends, and the Greeks can go back to Famagusta, you'll find your houses exactly as you left them. I'm sure this is the case, and the Turkish Cypriots obviously hope you're looking after their property in the same way over here."

An enigmatic smile crossed the faces of the three Greeks simultaneously.

"Mr. Reid, we and many thousands of Greek Cypriots were forced to flee from what is now the Turkish zone when Turkey invaded in July 1974. We lost everything. Many of us took certain possessions with us, but there wasn't much time. Better to flee empty-handed and alive than be surrounded with one's valuables and dead, like an Egyptian mummy."

Charalambides pulled a piece of paper from his breast pocket and spread it on the table for his honored guest to look at.

"This is a partial map of Kato Varosha." He pointed to a spot in another diagram on the same page. "For instance, this is where I hid a very valuable cross."

Reid looked closer at the map.

"You want me to get the cross out for you?," he said. "That's it? How much is it worth?"

"A quarter of a million pounds, probably," replied Charalambides.

"What's my cut?" Reid demanded with a vigor which, upon immediate reflection, he felt was somewhat crass.

"Ten thousand pounds. Cyprus."

"Not enough," said Reid, with a solidity that, upon immediate reflection, he judged to be just right.

The three Greeks looked at each other. Serious.

"Ten percent," they countered through the milkman.

"Okay."

They all breathed a sigh of relief. So did Reid, it's just that they didn't hear it.

Charalambides continued in a lighter vein. "You are the only suitable person we have found who can do this."

The four of them leaned over the map in a conspiratorial huddle.

"My former home," said Charalambides. He took a long drink before he carried on. "I have written very detailed instructions here. How to find the cross once you gain access to the house."

Reid examined the notes curtly.

"Wait a minute. What if it's been discovered? I mean, by the present occupants. It's not exactly Fort Knox, is it?"

"Fort Knox?" It was clear from their expressions that Charalambides and the other two were suffering from an attack of linguistic constipation. It was almost uncanny how the expressions of all three matched one with the other, at all times, at all promptings. If one beamed, so did the other two. If Charalambides reacted with a glum look, then so did Velios and Kyriakides. It was as if they were Siamese triplets, attached to each other by the brain.

Reid spelled it out for them. "I mean, it'd be pretty easy to find. Pretty easy for the present occupants to stumble across it as they move furniture about. I reckon it's long gone. You can kiss your cross goodbye, Mr. Charalambides."

"I think not, Mr. Reid," the milkman said, and he explained about the secret, inner, safe that no one would suspect was there.

"Okay. I agree. It's worth a shot. What if it isn't there, though?"

"Then we have similar propositions for you, Mr. Reid."

Charalambides nodded to his partners, who half-produced maps of their own, hugging them to their chests like cheap Rumanian spies, and quickly replacing them.

"And more, Mr. Reid. Much more. We are only three. There are many other Greeks who have similar maps hidden away in a drawer, never really thinking that they may be used."

"Louis, this is the beginning of a beautiful friendship," Reid grinned.

"Yes, yes," enthused Charalambides, but you could see he'd missed the reference.

"Don't bogart this joint," Reid explained.

Charalambides looked astonished, but then his cheeks puffed out and his eyes sparkled. "Humphrey Bogart. Yes, Humphrey Bogart," and looked at his companions. Reid could hardly believe it when Velios and Kyriakides both raised their glasses, and ejaculated, of course in unison, and with some animation, "Here's lookin' at you, Kid."

It was so funny he burst out laughing, and then they did too. Several of the other Crazy Horse patrons looked around through the dense cigarette smoke and thick Arabic music, afraid they'd missed something as this was the point in the act where one of the Australian girls seemed to be giving birth to one of the Viennese babes from the Parthenon.

"I can trust you guys, right?," Reid smiled, after they'd gained control of themselves.

Charalambides looked firmly at the Scotsman from Aberfeldy. "Remember, Mr. Reid, we have to trust you too."

They all looked at each other tensely for a few seconds, guessing, assessing, relying heavily on intuition.

"Okay. I'll do it."

The faces of the three millionaires lit up as if one Christmas tree.

"I'll need tomorrow to get some stuff together. I'll go in Friday. Is that okay?"

The three nodded vigorously.

"Oh, I'd better take your map and the instructions. Wouldn't do to forget those, eh?"

Charalambides pushed an envelope across the table as Reid prepared to leave.

"What's this?"

"This is a small token of our good faith, which should adequately cover your expenses. It is not a down payment."

"That's very nice of you, Mr. Charalambides."

"Tsk!," he tsked, smiling. "Take it, please."

One of the Austrian girls was standing next to Mufid. She was wearing a skirt which was as short as a skirt could get and still be called a skirt. She was looking at Reid with interest. Perhaps he did have what it takes, after all. He would have pursued this opening immediately but for the fact that Vanessa was looking at him with equal interest. Possibly more.

The three of them who had come together left together, and returned to the Parthenon.

*   *   *

He didn't pivot on his heels and his eyes didn't exactly pop out of his head, but the manager of the Altun Tabya did actually do a double take as well as Cary Grant could ever have done. He said something— "Good God, I never thought I'd see you again" perhaps—but there was no problem, no problem at all, and Reid was able to secure a room at the normal rate. "Have you got one overlooking the rear of the hotel, you know, for quiet?"

The thousand quid that Charalambides had given him had been more than generous. No need for them to have done that really. Strange birds, the three of 'em.

He pulled a large, brown, leather money-bag from his grip, changed into a black tee-shirt and black trousers, both deliberately two sizes larger than his normal, laced up his running shoes and then studied the map Charalambides had given him. If this cross were still there and he could get it, if indeed the house still existed, and he could get in, and if he could make his way back to the Greek side with the cross, then this might be an interesting way to make a living. Better than hoein' corn, Preacher! With no passes needed anymore. That was a stroke of luck. It pays to cultivate the common bureaucratic suit, especially one with a human being inside.

He opened the window and looked out. It was dark. He put the money-bag around his neck and was out of the window and down the flaking drainpipe and into the alleyway below.

Lilliput Lane was evidently a garbage alley for the hotel. It ran along the side of the building, from the back to the front. Reid threaded his way carefully through it toward the street. In a trice he was ducking behind two large bins. A patrol of Turkish soldiers was standing by the hotel entrance, blocking his exit from the lane. It was unusual to see a knot of uniforms in the old city at night, just hanging around.

Suddenly they stopped chattering and stood to attention, saluting smartly. An old man emerged from the hotel, dressed completely in white. Immaculate frock coat, shirt and tie, trousers, spats. White from tip to toe. His thick hair was as white as his outfit. Limping slightly, and carrying a white cane, this old man seemed to command respect from the moment he appeared on the street. In a second he was gone, past the entrance to the lane, and down the street, followed by the gaggle of dog soldiers.

Who the hell was this dignitary? Why had he been in the hotel tonight, of all nights, just as Reid was setting out to do his job? Obviously he was someone of importance, one whom the soldiers feared, for they'd behaved as if he were royalty. Was it Reid's mission that had caused the old man to show up tonight? Couldn't be. The job hadn't been done yet, so there was nothing to fear. Anyway, the old man had seemed to be blind, with the cane and everything.

Come on, Reid! He dismissed his misgivings as paranoia, the suspicions of the guilty. He stood up and walked to the street and looked cautiously left. The little group had gone.

Strangely enough, it wasn't so much the idea of the authorities coming for him that had worried him; it was the old man himself. The picture of the spectral figure just wouldn't leave his mind, no matter how he tried to shrug it off. But then he'd seen the old dude for only a few seconds, and already the actual nitty gritty details of the image were beginning to fade from his memory. The cane was larger now, more prominent. The limp more accentuated. The hush which had fallen over the troops as the old man had emerged now became a courteous silence as a token of sympathy for a disabled veteran of some local war.

But perhaps the old man had been checking up on him after all. The thought kept creeping insidiously back into his mind. But there would be no reason. He hadn't done anything wrong, yet. So it must be coincidence.

He doubled back along the tiny lane, not wishing to tempt fate now by using the main thoroughfare. Heading past the rear of the hotel, he disappeared into the night.

*   *   *

They were copulating. You could hear them. She was giggling and he was cooing sweet everythings in her ear.

Reid looked gingerly around the doorway. The TV was on in the middle of the room, and, almost as if the main lights were burning bright above, he could make out quite clearly, in the flickering black and white of the set, a comfortable living room, elegant furniture. At the far end of the room, beyond the goggle box, was the main door to the house itself, or rather one of the probably two front doors, a house of this size. Taking up a good third of the floor was a luxurious white shag carpet, which, at the moment, was living up to its name.

He had to pass this doorway in order to get to the next room down the marble-tiled hall, a nice corridor, tasteful, obviously Greek-built. He peeked ever so slightly farther into the room in order to determine which of the many positions in the Kama Sutra they had adopted. This was critical for his timing. It was Missionary, just as he'd suspected. He could see them clearly, heads toward the front door. *The Magician* was playing on the box, with an inappropriately deep voice dubbing Bill Bixby into Turkish. It was fucking funny, in its own way. Reid stood in the corridor, the back of his head resting against the cool wall, as he waited for the inevitable male climax.

Missionary! Ah, the good old Victorian days, with those hot and hardy Christians carrying the banner deep into Black Africa, and coming across all those natives doing the Ubangi Stomp. Oh, dear, just like animals! "Man is not a beast!," they cried in horror. Beast was a big word in the 19th century. "Man is a higher order of being." And they would whack the offending native on the bum and pull him out of there. "Let me show you how to do it. How Jesus meant you to do it." Knowing from the bullshit they'd heard behind the kirk in Edinburgh that the first time is always the hardest, they would force themselves to take the plunge. Up and down, up and down. "For the sake of your souls, you heathen bastards!" There's nothing quite like a proselytizing Presbyterian newly on the job, far from the moral restraints of the satanic mills back home, and suddenly finding himself freed from the tyranny of his right hand. Out to impress with all that clumsy, undiminished ardor. Onward Christian Soldiers. Thousands of opportunities for conquest. An unlimited fund of new brides up and down the Dark Continent. Up and down, up and down, thaaaat's the way, up and down. No wonder there were so many fucking missionaries crawling all over each other to get into the tropical jungle and save those pagans from themselves. It's a hole, but someone's got to go in there. Hallelujah, Brother! "It was quite nice, wasn't it, Deirdre?"

The woman had stopped laughing and had begun to moan with an increasing passion. Evidently here was a lothario of a higher caliber. Nine-millimeter parabellum. 10-inch pom-pom, maybe. Christ, those things could blow a hole in a frigate from twenty miles, even in the fog. You don't even see it coming. Just the bang, and then, all of a sudden, you're going down. It's enough to make your head swim.

At the crucial moment, Reid stepped daintily past the doorway and in a second was in the next room, evidently a parlor, the ecstasy of the woman ringing in his ears. Like any man with a clear conscience and at least some experience of life, he always liked to hear that. Once again he adjusted his eyes to the dark, but this time the light from the television in the fun-room managed to find its way to a few feet inside the parlor, giving him a little leg up.

Crossing to a luxuriously-covered couch and, squatting behind it, he took a pencil flashlight and the map from his money-bag. After a few moments' study he stood up warily and stealthily paced across to the wall adjoining the living room.

He removed some glass and wooden objects from the cabinet that interested him, replacing them on a similar piece of furniture that stood against the adjacent wall. He was surprised that the cabinets marked on his diagram were still in exactly those positions, after all these years, and that the occupants hadn't shifted a single item. His hand groped behind the cabinet, in a sizable gap between the wood and the wall. Then he found it.

36 left, 24 right, 36 left. He twisted his hand to and fro behind the cabinet, bent over like a welder at a tight site. 36, 24, 36. Good figure.

Well, it looked as if the happy couple hadn't even discovered the safe. How they could have failed to was beyond Reid's comprehension. He could only put it down to the low level of Turkish curiosity, or the high level of Turkish courtesy. He pulled out a few small packages and thrust them into his money bag. He made sure he cleared the front portion of the safe and then his fingers were at work, running over the back plate, seeking the four tiny pressure points in the corners. One after the other. Not too hard. Just the right pressure. Hey presto! The miniature door sprang open.

In the next two seconds, John Reid was moving fast. Jab out flashlight. Jerk body backwards and melt rapidly and with a bit of luck gracefully into the darkness.

The voice of the woman in the next room had become audible, very audible, over the noise of the TV. She was coming his way. Possibly with the man. Had they heard him?

Reid crouched down behind a substantial wing-backed chair, looking out into the parlor through the crook in the base of its well-padded arm.

One good thing. The open safe door wouldn't be seen behind the cabinet. He should have reached just a little farther in while he was there. Stupid bastard! But maybe not. Even a second's delay would have cost him dearly. Naked lady framed in doorway. Coming into room. Reid prepared to duck if she switched on the light, but loyal to the mood of the evening she chose to remain in the soft, reflected light of the magical box. That, blended with the dull moonlight now pushing faintly in from outside, allowed Reid to watch voyeuristically as the woman crossed the room to the very cabinet he'd just raided.

The woman stooped down only a few feet from him, and opened up the body of the cabinet itself. He could smell her perfume; expensive, but he couldn't identify it. Years of experience of ladies thrusting a scented wrist under his nose had made him conscious and appreciative of these

85

things. It was pleasant, as all expensive perfumes are. A clinking of glass was heard and he could see quite plainly as she extracted a bottle and a couple of tumblers. He breathed a sigh of relief. She was only fetching drinks. They were going to get merry. Reid listened to the woman humming a tune. Perhaps the man was having trouble. Maybe the booze would help. Free him up a bit. Reid felt like a drink himself right now. In fact, he felt like rogering the woman. Suddenly he remembered the objets d'art that he'd removed to the other cabinet. That squashed any lewd thoughts for the moment. He crouched, tense, waiting for the naked lady to discover the transposition. If she did, the game would be up. He'd have to silence her, he knew that. And possibly the man too. Hopefully he could neutralize them harmlessly, or relatively so, anyway. He guessed he was ready.

She straightened up and crossed to the door, still humming.

The safe combination wouldn't fit her measurements. At least not the first 36. As she stood silhouetted in the doorway, calling out to the missionary, Reid observed with a surge of interest that there were a good eight inches between the two measurements, the safe's and hers. Perhaps it was the power implicit in the sheer size that was intimidating the man. One may not approve, but one could understand. After the initial awestruck gasp, it would take a certain natural confidence to be able to stare a pair of 44 Magnums in the face and still come up to scratch.

Reid heard the man reply above the noise of *The Magician*, and the woman returned to the cabinet, putting the bottle back in and plucking out another.

Must be bloody Courvoisier drinkers or something. The woman stood up, pausing as she did so. Reid stiffened as the woman, instead of going back toward the door, made her way carefully past the chair behind which he was crouching. He primed himself. There was nothing between them now. No cover. She turned his way. If she looked down she would certainly see him. He held his breath, not daring to move a muscle. The intimacy of the situation would have been greater only if she had known he was there.

She took one step to the window, pulled the curtain, and was at the door again, still humming her Ottoman melody. Then she was gone.

A hundred thousand quid'll pay for the operation after your heart attack, Reid. He stood up and went smartly to the cabinet. Soon his mitt was in the safe, reaching toward the back to the secret compartment behind. His fingers closed over a rough package. This was it. The cross, you lucky bastard! He removed the bundle delicately from the safe and, per instructions from Charalambides, sealed the false door by pulling it to, took the packages from his money bag and replaced them in the front part of the safe so that if, by chance, the current occupants of the house had already opened the safe, they wouldn't suspect a robbery. Then he closed the outer door.

He unfolded a loose chamois cover tied with a rubber band. Charalambides hadn't been lying; he had had to leave in a hurry. There it was. The cross. A jeweled Christian cross about ten inches long and seven wide at the cross bar. In the small beam from his torch Reid could see by the sparklers which lay embedded in the gold that it was indeed a prize worth rescuing. He had a sneaking feeling that its value was a lot more than the Greek millionaire had claimed, but what the hell!

In a few swift movements he put the cross into his money bag, tidied up the room, put away the torch, and made his way to the door.

He peered cautiously into the hallway. No one in sight. He could hear them at it again on the rug in the living room, drinks forgotten temporarily. A commercial was playing now, and Reid ventured a peek around the corner of their door. This time they were facing the window, her legs wrapped tightly around his neck. He was leaping up and down on her with fantastic determination.

This guy must be setting a world record for the fucking pole vault! Reid sidled neatly past the door, grinning hugely. Down the hallway to the kitchen. He found with alarm that the back door leading to the courtyard had not only been locked, but the key was nowhere in sight. He'd come in this way, totally unopposed; just walked in. Now what?

He looked around wildly, stabbing his flashlight into areas which might yield the lost key. How could it now be locked? His mind raced. The woman must have gone into the kitchen to do it before she'd come for the drinks. Yet he hadn't heard her do that. The noise of the box must have covered her movements. Good job she'd been talking as she'd come for the drinks, otherwise he'd have felt a right tit.

He couldn't find the key anywhere. The window. Only way to go. He flashed his light onto it. It was shut. Shit! A fly screen was letting in the air. No escape here. Too many pots and pans. Too many fiddly little articles on the work top. He didn't relish climbing through that lot.

Back into the passageway. The first door was locked. He'd tried that on his original trip down the hall. Must lead to the bedrooms. He tried it again anyway. It was still locked. Why the hell was it locked? Could the house be subdivided now? But no, where would the bedrooms of this section be then, in that case? Maybe it was some Turkish custom to lock the bedroom doors when you were screwing in the living room. Something religious maybe. Reid was beginning to feel trapped, and he didn't like that. Nothing for it but the parlor window.

He tiptoed down the cold floor, approaching the TV room again. It would have been neat if Charalambides's chart had made directions more explicit for the rest of the house, but the milkman had simply said, "The kitchen and the room with the cross. These are all you need to know in a diagram, Mr. Reid. The rest you will discover, if you need them. I do not think you will."

The game was still going on. Taking a deep breath, Reid simply entered the room and walked noiselessly across the carpet. His eyes were firmly on the humping couple as he stepped carefully past the TV. *The Magician* was coming to an end; the credits were rolling; and Reid was now behind the set, creeping toward the door. The lock turned easily. Silently, smoothly. He stood in the doorway, the most prurient of smirks on his face.

The man on the floor was approaching orgasm at last. You could tell that by the increased rate of breathing, the slowing down of the bodily movements into a more settled rhythm, and by the delicately encouraging expressions of the lady beneath.

There comes that fraction of a second between the irreversible commitment to a climax and the climax itself. It was at precisely this instant, when the Turk's testicles were in the first stage of explosion, and his head reared up, mouth open wide, lips pulled back, teeth bared, that he made eye contact with Reid over the top of the suddenly silent TV.

"Bottoms up!" Reid ejaculated in his best Oxford accent. And then came the roar. Reid was out of the door and beating a path to the gate as fast as his legs would carry him, the longest and most thunderous orgasm he'd ever heard ringing in his ears. And he was gone into the shadows.

*   *   *

"Vous parlez français, monsieur?"
The sinister, high-pitched voice came right out of the bloody blue,

yet at the same time nothing could have been more on cue. Reid pirou-etted, as elegantly as he could considering his weight was solely on the seat of his trousers, and saw the enigmatic white-clad figure of the previous evening standing there. He swallowed his mouthful of plain three-egg omelet in sheer surprise.

"Mais oui," he answered. The hairs stood up on the back of his neck, but he collected himself in a fraction of a second, and the hairs went back down as smoothly as had the nicely-yellowed omeletto.

The old man sprang into the chair across the table from Reid. He moved like an ancient cat, but a cat nonetheless. One of the big cats, although not a really big one, more like a lynx or a bobcat. Slight of build, but with a deceptive, latent power that his victims wouldn't see until it was too late.

"May I sit down?," he inquired after the fact, still speaking in French.

"Be my guest."

"I am the Professor."

"Of course you are."

The old man grinned, and his gleaming white teeth betrayed, by their extraordinary regularity, that they were well-fitting dentures. They matched in color and brilliance, but not in texture, the clothes he wore apparently as a uniform. He was not blind, as Reid had thought last night. His clear, ice-blue eyes pierced Reid's head like an X-ray. The trouble with X-ray equipment is that it malfunctions when the power goes off. He may or may not have known this. Reid did.

"And you are…?," asked the Professor, and in the same breath, "Do you mind if I smoke?" He pulled out a Rothman's and lit up.

"John Reid. Sure. Go ahead."

"Reid, eh. English, is this not so?"

"Scottish, actually. Do you want breakfast, Professor?"

"No, thank you. I had breakfast two hours ago. A small cup of coffee, perhaps."

He barked out instructions to the waiter who had been loitering without intent or expression on the other side of the otherwise empty dining room.

Well, this settled it. He had indeed been here to see Reid last night. But why? Perhaps he wanted Reid to go across the Green Line for him and pick up buried loot on the Greek side.

The Professor stared at Reid as the Scotsman tucked in to his watermelon. The aquiline nose, strong and well-constructed, both nostrils being of the same circumference and depth, and the modest, but forceful chin, gave Reid the feeling that he was truly in the presence of a ruthless old bugger.

"You had an adventure last night."

Reid almost choked on his grub. He didn't really, he just pretended to. You fake something, for the sake of it, just to see what happens. It's playing with people. It becomes second nature after a while. It has the advantage of propelling you forward into a situation where otherwise your natural coyness and reserve might hold you back and make the plunge all the longer to take. You get results. You get them, if you don't mind taking a risk.

"What do you mean?," Reid spluttered, a fake splutter of course, taking a gulp of coffee, real coffee.

"Calm yourself, calm yourself, please. Merely an innocent question," cooed the Professor slyly, studying Reid's features intensely, scrutinizing his brain. "A young man alone in a strange town should have an adventure every night, is this not so, John?"

It was interesting how he used the first name. A well-tried psychological ploy. And he pronounced it as Reid had done, and not in the French manner.

Reid eyed the Professor with extreme distrust, planning his next words carefully. He was beginning to regret his little antic of the night before. It had been irresponsible. He could have got clean away without anyone knowing he'd been there. But no. Had to be a smart bastard and show off. "Bottoms up?" What an asshole. Forget any future missions. He'd really screwed up. But then, the Professor would have queered his new career anyway, as he'd been at Reid's hotel the night before, before he'd even pulled off the job. So, Reid had been able to make his crack at no additional expense after all. At this moment the Professor probably had his men outside, waiting to take a dimwit prisoner. But if it came to a struggle, John Reid would have a lot of fun, even if the bastards did dispatch him to the pearly gates.

"No adventure, I'm afraid, Professor." Reid laughed with what he thought was cleverly simulated nervousness, making it look as if he were trying to regain his composure. He knew he had to winkle the old buzzard out if he was to find out what was going on. "I just stayed in my room last night and read a book."

"A good book, I trust. What was the title?"

"Teach Yourself Turkish in Ten Minutes."

The Professor looked puzzled.

"Best seller in Greece, I understand," said Reid.

"Are you sure you stayed in your room last night?," pumped the Professor, ever so softly, menacingly, like an overbearing headmaster to an eight-year-old truant who is guilty and they both know it.

Reid now knew what he'd only suspected before, that the old man had checked his room, but he had to stay one step ahead of the Professor if he were to survive this cross-examination.

"Now look here, old man, what business is it of yours what I did last night? Who are you anyway?"

The outraged citizen act usually works. Especially the voice rising half an octave.

"Calm yourself, John," soothed the Professor with oil. "I am merely an inquisitive retired teacher of French. I mean no harm. It is just that last night I heard you were staying at this hotel and I thought I would drop by for a chat. There are not many Europeans in this country, you know. When the manager knocked on your door, however, to convey my invitation to dinner, he received no reply. Not wishing to fail me—er, and worried for your health too, naturally—he entered, and found the room empty. What is strange, John, is that you had been seen going into your room, but not coming out. Do you not find that interesting?"

Reid really felt like grabbing the old bastard by the throat, his manner was so unctuous, but this was tricky territory, and he was a long way from the border. Besides, this Professor was obviously a big lad in the neighborhood.

He beckoned the Professor closer, taking him into his confidence. Now that he knew why the Professor had come by the previous night, or at least why he claimed he had, he had only to relieve the old man's suspicions and all would be well; should be well.

"As you probably know, Professor," he ventured, but this time in English, "I was here a few weeks ago."

"I do not speak English," the Professor replied hastily. "Please continue to speak, but in French, if you don't mind, John."

"Sorry, Professor, a slip. As I was saying, I was here a few weeks ago, in this hotel, another thing you're probably aware of. Well, I met a girl, you know." Reid winked.

"A Turkish woman?," asked the Professor, his face blank, inscrutable except that the mischief was fading from his eyes. That, of course, was a dead giveaway.

"Er, yes, of course," Reid answered rapidly, pretending to lose a little confidence. "It's a delicate situation, you see. The lady's, er, how shall I put this?—married. Do you see what I mean? That's why I returned to Famagusta yesterday. When you came to the hotel last night, I had slipped out of the window to see her."

The Professor stared at Reid more intently than ever.

"That's why you didn't find me here," Reid reiterated.

"I see," declared the Professor, leaning back in his chair, patently unconvinced. "I shall leave now, John."

As he stood up to go, the waiter came in with his coffee and water. The old man ushered him away curtly.

"A word of warning, John," he said as a parting gesture. "Be careful how you travel in these parts at night, alone. There is a criminal on the loose. It is quite probable that he is dangerous. Last night he broke into the home of one of our highest state officials. Fortunately he was disturbed before he could steal anything of importance."

A warm sensation went through Reid, the pleasant feeling that this was not a warning at all, but a threat.

"Hey, Professor, you don't think that was me, do you?," he shouted across the room.

"But of course not," answered the Professor. "You were with a Turkish woman last night. A married woman, is this not so?"

And he was out of the door.

Reid sipped his coffee and drew heavily on his Capstan, deep in thought. Chess is like that.

* * *

Charalambides nodded sadly.

"If you fear that your life may be in danger then, of course, you must not go back."

Velios and Kyriakides nodded their agreement fatalistically.

They all relaxed on the comfortable leaf-green and puce furniture in the Kennedy Hotel suite in the heart of Greek Nicosia.

Reid said, "I like your bodyguard theory, and I know Turkish soldiers get paid nothing at all, so it does stand to reason that some of them would want to take a job on the side. But I honestly can't imagine why he would need a bodyguard in Turkish Cyprus. I mean, he'd have nothing to fear if he is as he says, just a retired teacher of French."

"There must be crime in the Turkish zone," said Charalambides, "and I suppose that if he is rich, which he sounds, then he would be likely to pay for protection. And are you sure that he didn't mention his name at all during your conversation? We would know his name, you understand."

"Nope. He didn't mention it at all. The Professor. That's how he introduced himself. I'm sure he's a cop. A policeman, you know. Yet, he's in his early seventies, if he's a day. I don't know. Maybe I shouldn't have let him throw me like that."

"You are safe, Mr. Reid, that is the main thing."

Reid was preoccupied with his own train of thought. "I'll tell you something, though. Within two minutes I was out of that hotel and in a regular taxi. All along the Salamis Road back to Nicosia I kept expecting a road block. I had three plans worked out if there had been one."

The milk magnate said solemnly, "But you had no problem returning through the Turkish checkpoint?"

"No. None at all. Just walked through, as normal."

"Well, we shall probably never know if your Professor is who he says he is, or whether he is more. At least I have the cross you brought back for me, and you have 25,000 pounds more in your bank account. It has been profitable for both of us."

1957

EOKA hero Gregoris Afxentiou prepared to die. Twenty-eight years old, Grivas's second-in-command. The British Empire had pictures of him posted up all over the island. Underneath the not so flattering black and white image was a number, with a lot of zeroes after it, and the pound sign in front of it. Below that it said "Dead or alive." Money talks, even to the

93

faithful if there are enough zeroes. For Gregoris, now, there was no other way.

The patrol shouted to him to surrender. No reply. Afxentiou's four comrades looked to him for guidance.

"I shall fight, and I shall die," declared the young hero, his whole being taking on an aura of destiny that blinded his companions for a moment. They knew, they all knew.

He instructed the other guerrillas to get out of the hideout, which they did, reluctantly. They were not yet that committed. They scrambled out of the ground into the open air.

The troops called to him that unless he surrendered they would throw grenades in. Afxentiou responded with a burst of automatic gunfire, killing a British corporal.

A grenade was lobbed into the hole. The British troops called to him again. They were showing great patience and restraint. No reply.

"What's the point of shouting to him?," cried Avgoustis Efstathiou, one of the captured EOKA men. "He's dead."

A soldier grabbed Efstathiou and shoved him roughly toward the entrance to the hideout. "If he's dead, bring his body out."

"Don't shoot! Don't shoot!" shouted Efstathiou as he slithered back down into the hole. Once inside, he cried out to the British, "Now we are two." The explosion had injured Afxentiou's leg, but he was still fighting fit. "Come and get us!" Efstathiou, now, was committed.

For the next eight hours the two guerrillas held off the British party with gunfire and bombs, a microcosm of the major conflict taking place in Cyprus, where a few hundred guerrillas were successfully taking on the 40,000 man might of the Imperial Army.

At one point Afxentiou tried to make a break for it, throwing a smoke-grenade into the group of soldiers in order to mask his escape. But his gun jammed at the crucial moment, and by the time he cleared it the smoke had evaporated and he was a sitting duck. He barely managed to dive back into his hole.

In between the exchanges the British tried to figure out what to do. In the hide the two guerrillas discussed the past and the struggle to which they had dedicated their lives: To throw off colonial rule and become united with Greece in the long dreamed-of *Enosis*.

The troops of Her Majesty's Army were now becoming desperate.

They had not expected this kind of resistance. Crowds of reporters had come onto the scene now, and the entire battle had come under the scrutiny of the world.

The soldiers would not rush the hideout, as the furious resistance of the two fugitives would prove unnecessarily costly in terms of British lives. Finally they decided on their ploy. They poured hundreds of gallons of petrol down the hillside so that it ran into the hideout, almost drowning the two freedom fighters, and overwhelming them with the noxious fumes. Then the deluge was set alight, and in a flash the fire swept dramatically into the hole.

"Do not be afraid," screamed Afxentiou to his friend, and Efstathiou ran from the hideout, enveloped in flames. He was still not yet that committed. But he would live, to fight another day.

More grenades were thrown in and automatic gunfire poured into the hide, but Afxentiou remained where he was. Efstathiou's flames were extinguished, and hours later, when it had all died down, the troops attempted to enter the hole, but the heat and smoke were too much for them.

They shoved Efstathiou forward again, with orders to drag out the body of his comrade. He descended into the charred pit, but was overpowered by the thick smoke. It wasn't until the next morning that the troops got in, and in order to do so they had to tear off the roof of the subterranean hideout.

The grotesquely charred remains of Gregoris Afxentiou were finally brought out. A grenade had blown off one of his legs, and his head was barely attached to his neck.

Later Afxentiou's father was brought to identify his son. He couldn't. It is no longer Gregoris, he said, merely the black shell of a once human body. Afxentiou had gone to take his place among the heroes of Greek mythology.

1979

Reid hired a green Renault with a streak of yellow running down its back; a color scheme designed to nauseate any tailgating drivers who might take it into their heads to try to get up his arse on a lonely stretch of road.

He asked Vanessa if she wanted to come with him on a trip around the Greek side of the island for a couple of days. She said yes. They went up to the Troodos Mountains where Reid had frequently vacationed with his own family as a boy in the '50s, and where Colonel George Grivas had spent months on the run in the same period. The two had never met.

Baedekers' 1979 Guide to Cyprus. The village of Pano Panayia, birthplace of Archbishop Makarios. Dhekelia and Akrotiri, the British bases. An assortment of monasteries. The Larnaka salt lakes with their enormous congregations of flamingoes, and a curious and rather stupid trip to town to show Vanessa the old, now extinct, red-light area of Larnaka. That had never been in Baedeker. The rapidly growing city of Limassol farther along the coast. And cruises along the edges of the Green Line. The two of them became quite close.

There was only one moment that gave Reid a little concern. As he was negotiating a series of drastic bends on their way up a steep mountain road, he suddenly remembered that coming up immediately on the right was a breathtaking view, so for the dramatic effect it would have on his guest, he braked sharply, pulling over to the edge of the highway. Moments later a yellow Ford hurtled dangerously around the curve, only seconds behind them. Despite the angle of the road, Reid instantly recognized the two occupants of the Ford as his rather tough-looking breakfast companions the morning of his altercation with the plumber in Nicosia. He stored this away. He'd play with it when he had time.

Vanessa began to beg him to take her across the Green Line. To show her the sights there. I dunno, the Turkish side is too risky. Ah, come on, please. Pretty please. We'll be quite safe if we go alone. Just the two of us. Ah, but if there are two of us, we won't be alone. And then it might become really dangerous. It was one of those dialectics that's fun for thirty seconds and then becomes boring.

However, as the long summer Mediterranean days passed, the tinkle tinkle tinkle warning bell of danger tolled ever more remote.

1958

The war in Cyprus was hotting up. Captain Fletcher Reid had taken that particular time to trip gaily off to Calcutta for a couple of months to live with the lepers. Or so he said. He'd be gone for another four weeks or so. Mrs. Reid was in command, and the old man had left her his Webley, a huge—to young John Reid, anyway—black Army issue .38 caliber revolver. This was standard procedure. The soldier goes away. He leaves the gun with his wife. She has undergone the basic training in how to handle such a weapon, and to deal with any emergency. It was necessary, and good, Army practice. Who knew who might break into the house at night, especially if they knew the soldier was away? You didn't take chances.

Reid's mother had Mr. Webley with her at all times. She slept with him. When she and the two youngsters were in the living room, she'd have him lying on the side table by her right hand. She took her responsibilities seriously. Mary and John Reid, young as they were, knew not to touch Mr. Webley, and they didn't. They took their responsibilities seriously.

It was about seven o'clock one winter night, and dark outside. The four of them were playing a dictionary game. Mr. Webley wasn't participating but you knew he was there. It was your typical, cozy British 1950s family evening in the colonies. Tea and milk for the family. No booze, but Mr. Webley was loaded.

Young John was the first to notice the door handle. It was his turn at "okapi." His sister looked at him expectantly. But his eyes were glued to the closed living room door that led to the hallway. If you went through the door into the hallway and turned right, you'd get to the bedrooms. If you turned left, you'd be at the front door. The cream-colored living room door had one of those cream-colored levers that depressed in order to open the door. It was now depressing, ever so slowly. And John was staring at it, rigid.

Then Mary and Mrs. Reid, sensing that John's silence had nothing to do with ignorance of African fauna, both saw the door handle at the same time. Mary gasped. Someone was in the house. In the hallway. And they were coming into the living room.

John held his breath. He was only six. Mary gasped again. She was eight. Both children knew it was Grivas and his boys. This was it. Mrs. Reid knew it too. She would often threaten the kids with Grivas if they committed some misdemeanor, just as British mothers used to do with Bony back in the 19th century. The ultimate deterrent, worse than corporal punishment. The bogie man.

With no emotion, Mrs. Reid took up the Webley, hefted it in both hands and, still sitting, pointed it at the door, which began to open ever so slowly. Mrs. Reid pulled back the hammer and waited. You could hear their hearts beating. Then, Captain Fletcher Reid sprang into the room, arms akimbo, a big grin all over his face. "Surprise! Sur…"

Captain Reid took in the scene instantly and realized his joke had gone awry. He shouted, "All right, all right, it's only me, I'm home." Oh, shit!

Mrs. Reid kept the gun pointing at him, hammer still cocked, a strange look in her eyes. She didn't put the gun down.

"It's all right," Captain Reid said, in nervous soothing tones. "It's all right. I'm back early. I'm back early." Oh, shit!

Bloody right he was back early. Mary and John were still rigid, eyes wide open. Mrs. Reid was still pointing the Webley at the old man, the cold, frighteningly impassive look still on her face. This tableau remained for seconds but seemed like forever. The captain talked her down, and finally she made the hammer safe and lowered the gun. Then she put the revolver back on the table.

No one remembered what happened after that.

1979

Reid told Vanessa to hold fire a little while longer until he'd gone across first, to test the water.

The guards at both barriers welcomed him as an old friend. So did the ministers. He experienced no difficulty in passing once more into the Turkish zone. This completely relieved him about the Professor. If the old man had represented the authorities, Reid would have been bagged as soon as he'd crossed the line.

A long chat to Nearchos Papanicholaou about conditions on the Turkish side was followed by a long yarn to the Turkish minister about conditions on the Greek side. The more interesting details were carefully omitted.

*   *   *

The secretary's eyes were almond-shaped and black. Not brown, or blue, or chestnut, but black. Startlingly so, as if they had had the soul sucked out of them by one of the undead. They were alluring, at least to those who were not frightened off by them. Right now they blazed with a look of suspicion and amazement. Reid was a little astonished to find a woman in such a role. The westernization of Turkish Cypriot bureaucracy.

"Yes, President Denktash is in," she stated with uncalled for sullenness, almost a pout, "but he will not see anyone without an appointment."

Sure, she had a job to do, but there was no need for this attitude. She had bitch written all over her. The two under-secretaries, or whatever you call them, at the neighboring desks were staring at Reid. The waiting business suits, queuing patiently for their interviews with the President, gawked at him through a cigarette haze. He was on stage, and his fly was undone, so to speak.

"I'll be in Cyprus for a while. When can I have an appointment?"

"What is your name, and what is your business with President Denktash?"

She didn't take her eyes off Reid for a second.

"I'm an old friend of his. I'm sure he'll see me."

"You are English, not German," she realized aloud.

"Scottish, as a matter of fact." He broke into his well-tried smile.

"When did you arrive from Istanbul?" This was a non sequitur. She was mildly flustered. She knew what he was thinking.

"I didn't come in from Istanbul."

She looked at him with wonder, but not the sort where the mouth sags open and the body slumps forward. Her emotional upheavals were indicated by the raising and lowering of a well-attended eyebrow.

"I came across the Green Line."

"Impossible," she stated flatly.

"All right, it's impossible."

"But," she stuttered, "it … it is … illegal."

"No, it's not. It's all right. It's unusual, but it's all legal, don't worry."

She looked down, baffled. Then she re-grouped. "President Denktash leaves the country soon, and will not be back for four weeks. And he cannot see you today. You must leave now."

"Your English is excellent," he oozed. "Did you go to school in Britain?"

"You must go. President Denktash will not see you without an appointment."

"But how do you know?"

"I am his private secretary," answered the woman frostily. "If I say that President Denktash will not see you, he will not see you."

That seemed to be it, short of dashing by her, and gate-crashing Denktash's inner sanctum, but that would never do. Extraordinarily bad form.

"Do you have a pen and a piece of paper I could use?"

She reluctantly pushed a pad in front of him, and a ball-point pen, and he proceeded to write.

"Could you give this to Mr. Denktash, please?"

She took it gingerly between forefinger and thumb, as if it were a recently-used Trojan, and opened it.

"What is this? I cannot give this to President Denktash. It is meaningless rubbish."

Reid leaned across the desk until his face was within a few inches of hers. The other secretaries and the slowly growing audience of suits were following this interchange keenly. A fascinating soap opera episode.

"Possibly now, if you could take it in to him," he whispered, fixing her with an intense stare.

Her eyes, so close to his now, stared back, the mascara just starting to run. Before long she'd be a mess. They both knew this was a contest of will. This was the moment that would decide whether the secretary walked into Denktash's office or Reid left the building with the note in his hand and his tail between his legs.

He was no novice at this game; far from it. He'd discovered early in life the power of the eyes, especially over women, and that one can achieve startling results by using them in the right way.

After what felt like a never ending sensual wrestling match, where for moments at a time their minds became one, he felt her barriers fall, as if suddenly and all at the same time. Her eyes seemed to have become less dark, and he watched her pupils dilate. The muscles around her eyes twitched and then relaxed. He knew he had her, that she would take the message into Denktash, in fact that she would do anything for him. Her eyes were saying so as clearly as if she'd written it down on official paper.

Reid stood up straight, right hand going into his pocket, as little boys learn to do when they don't want the whole world to know they've got a bonk on. She was highly desirable all right, but any attempt to make this budding relationship any more physical would be fraught with difficulty. He knew this was the beginning, and at the same time the end, of their affair, but that it had been a good one while it lasted.

"I cannot take it in to him now," she said, with a last show of resistance, somewhat to Reid's surprise.

"Why not? Has he got someone in there at the moment?"

"No, but..."

"I'm sure President Denktash would be very annoyed if he found that he'd missed me. Do yourself a favor. Take it in to him, and don't worry about the message. He'll know what it means."

The lady had, without doubt, been softened up, and now this slightly veiled threat further weakened her resolve.

"Very well, but then you must go. He will not see you."

Her chair rolled back on its castors.

Women speak volumes, not only with words but by the way they occupy and leave a seat. Hundreds of years of conditioning can be wiped out in a flash by one woman who views a dress as a fun thing rather than as an embarrassing menace. Don't sit with your legs apart. Bad. When you cross your legs do it in one swift movement whereby the knees never visibly separate. And uncross them in the same way. You've got to wear a dress, but don't let the brutes see what you've got. The vast majority of women never even think about this process, consciously. But now and again a temptress will come along whose nerve ends tingle with power. Far more women wear, or would like to wear, far less underwear than most men think. This houri was wearing none at all. The secretary's eyes never left Reid's face. She wanted to savor and remember his every expression.

Slowly the long legs came together and the woman stood up, smoothing her tight, gray dress down. As she turned, Reid cleared his throat and fumbled for a Capstan. He glanced quickly around the room, emerging painfully into the real world again. Every suit in the place was leaning forward or backwards in an uncomfortable effort to gain the maximum benefit from the secretary's brief walk to Denktash's office. He saw the complete picture, and grinned. This would be a ritual, if the suits had any sense. Many of them came not so much to see the President but rather to win yet another glimpse of the chief private secretary's own hypnotic fantasy world. Admission free: members only.

She tapped gently on the door of the inner office, and went in, taking the message with her.

A few moments later she reappeared and coughed, a look of incredulity on her face.

"President Denktash will see you now."

*　*　*

"It's me, Sir," said Newcome down the phone.

"Ah, John, how go things east of Suez?"

"I don't think we are east of Suez, Sir."

"Oh, I think you may be, John. Check on a map one day; might be illuminating. How go things east of Suez, John?"

Newcome coughed.

"He's pal'd up with a girl, Sir."

"I would have expected no less."

"An American."

"That's good for international relations. Tourist?"

"I think so, but…"

"Come on, John, spit it out."

"Well, Sir, I've heard he's going across the Green Line again."

"Yes?"

"Thing is, Sir, I think she's going with him."

"Across the Green Line?"

"Yes, Sir."

"Is she indeed? What's her name, John, this American tourist."

"Riley. Vanessa Riley."

For one moment Newcome thought the phone had gone dead. When the tall man finally returned to active conversation, he said, "John, could you say that again? I didn't quite catch the name. Could you spell it for me?"

And Newcome did.

"Thank you, John. Height, if you please, and color of hair, and, if you know it, place of residence."

"Five eight, black hair, dark anyway, very pretty, Sir. Place of residence, Winston-Salem, North Carolina."

The tall man was very matter-of-fact, as he said, "Thank you, New-come. Keep me abreast."

And he hung up.

*   *   *

"Ah, Mr. Riley. Thank you for returning my call. Tell me, where is your daughter?"

"Paris."

"No she's not, Mr. Riley. She's in Nicosia, about to go over the Green Line into Turkish Cyprus with her new friend, John Reid."

This time the long silence was over the Carolinas.

"Tell me everything," Burt said.

And the tall man did, at least as much as he knew.

"I'm going to Cyprus," said Burt. "I don't know how the bastard got hold of her, but I'm going to take care of it. Just get your boys to keep their eyes open. I'll check in with you when I get there, okay?"

*   *   *

"Salamis," said Reid to the driver of the huge Itimat taxi as he and Vanessa jammed themselves in like salami between the several slices of Turkish sandwich bread who were also en route to Famagusta. Less than an hour later the car dropped them at the entrance to the old ruins, four miles north of Famagusta, and then continued on down the road into town.

The two of them walked along the dusty road toward the beach.

"This is still against my better judgment. If we get stopped, let me do the talking, okay?"

Vanessa nodded. Reid still felt uneasy about returning anywhere near the Famagusta area, the vague but unshakable image of the Professor still lurking in the back of his mind, no matter how hard he'd tried to exorcise it.

"If you don't take me over the Line, then I'm going alone." That had been the ultimatum. So, here they were. What the hell. It seemed safe enough. His recent trip to see Rauf Denktash had presaged nothing unto-ward, neither had his last excursion. The threat of any danger now seemed far away.

Getting Vanessa across the Green Line had required only a show of verbosity from Reid, a big smile and a bit of a bum wiggle here and there from Vanessa's designer jeans, and it had all been easy, peaceful.

The asphalt gave way to a sandy track. Suddenly Reid grabbed Vanessa's arm.

"What is it?," she asked in less alarm than she might have shown.

A fat black piece of hose slithered across the road in front of them. It was too hot to hiss.

"Harmless," Reid commented, as they resumed their tread. "Plenty of those little bastards in Salamis. But watch out. You never know. If you see the big ones—green, black spots—then run. They're the couplis. Only deadly snakes in Cyprus, so I'm told."

"You know where to catch the taxi back to Nicosia?," asked Vanessa, rapidly changing the subject.

"Don't worry, I'll get you back safely."

They turned right, crunching over the fallen pine needles on the track, and almost immediately saw the ancient Greco-Roman remains standing before them.

The site was completely deserted. Reid led Vanessa into what was left of the old Gymnasium overlooking the sea. No gym class today, though. She was impressed by the tall marble columns which once supported an enormous, decorated ceiling, but which now poked out of the ground like giant, fossilized penises.

"This is history, isn't it," she said as only an American can. She rubbed one of the pillars.

"Recent history," Reid specified. "These pillars were moved to this spot in the 1950s. From over there," and he pointed to a place a little farther down the track. They walked on.

"We're coming to the Amphitheatre now." They arrived at a magnificent semicircular auditorium made of stone. "They discovered this in 1959, I think it was, and began unearthing it. They say it was used as a theatre in the time of the Emperor Augustus."

"It's big. How many people?"

"Fifteen thousand, so they say. They had a grand opening night in 1963, and I was here. We watched Julius Caesar. Not the man himself, of course. The Shakespeare play. Fantastic experience. From the back row you can hear a whisper. Here, I'll show you," and he directed her to the top row of the colossal amphitheater, where she took a seat on one of the stone slabs serving as benches. Reid climbed down and stood in the center of the arena, his right hand in a declaiming position, and his left across his chest. He said, in a low voice, "Friends, Romans, Countrywomen, prick up your ears." He looked up at Vanessa in the top row. "Well, what d'ya think?"

"I heard something, John," Vanessa shouted down, "but I couldn't understand what you said. The only word I could make out was 'prick.'"

"It's better at night, with a lot of people," he yelled back, a deflated Antony, and bounded up one of the aisles to the top of the bowl to rejoin her. "Still, not bad builders, those Romans, eh?"

Vanessa laughed, bringing Reid's attention to several rows of stone cubicles set in the ground beyond the theater.

"Toilets," he grinned. "Bathrooms, as you Americans say."

They passed the remains of a Roman villa, and then left the track, cutting through the shrub and pine trees until they reached the Basilica of Saint Epiphanius, the ancient Archbishop of Constantia. Only the foundations remained. Reid pointed into the sun, to the far side of the track. "That's the famous Granite Forum. And do you see those columns? They're made from granite that came from Aswan in Egypt."

"This is fascinating," said Vanessa, taking it all in. "What a pity that the world can no longer see it. What a great amount of revenue lost for the Turkish government."

"They never charged for this, Vanessa. It was always free, at least it was in my day."

Shortly they came to a few more scattered ruins.

"They believe this was the Temple of Zeus." Reid was slightly surprised that he remembered so much so well after all these years.

"This track coming up. Let's turn right here, then go back on the main road. Then, if you don't mind the walk, we can cut across to the Tomb of the Kings, and the place where Barnabas is buried."

"Saint Barnabas?," exclaimed Vanessa with enthusiasm.

"You certainly know your Christian martyrs, all right," said Reid. "He came from Cyprus, as you probably know, and returned here with Saint Paul, forty-five years after the birth of Christ, to convert the Roman proconsul. He was stoned to death, here in Salamis, by his own people. They say you can never go back. And if that sort of thing can happen to you, then they're right, eh?" He laughed. Vanessa didn't. She said, "You should be a tour guide." But she soon picked up.

105

They stepped onto the road again, took another right, and then headed for the main Salamis Road, down which they had come in the Itimat taxi. Rounding a corner of dense shrubbery they stopped dead in their tracks. Directly ahead of them, thirty or forty yards along the track, was a platoon of Turkish soldiers approaching, looking from left to right.

A cry went up from one of the troops as he spotted the couple.

"Quick, back, back!," Reid shouted to Vanessa, pulling her behind the bushes. More yells were coming from the Turks as they broke into a run in pursuit. Whistles were being blown, and Reid knew, in that sinking moment of reality, that his worst suspicions had been confirmed. He should never have returned to Famagusta. What a prize jerk. They'd been waiting for him.

"Run. To the beach. This way!" They were off, haring along the track.

Glancing back, Reid saw that the soldiers had broken into view around the corner, and that he and the girl were now totally exposed.

"Faster! Faster!," he cried to Vanessa, as they approached a left curve, which led north in the direction of the ruins they had just explored.

"What the hell's happening?," yelled Vanessa, as he pulled her off the track. They began to plow through the loose pine-strewn sand toward the sea.

"Save it! Run!," he bellowed, and they came to a cluster of sand dunes on the approachway to the beach. Their four combined eyes swept the area frantically for cover of some sort.

"Over to the trees!" Reid prepared to swing right into the wood. A rifle crack punctuated the yelling of the soldiers as he rounded one of the dunes. He looked around to grab Vanessa, but she was hugging the dune, like a drunk hugs the porcelain.

"Oh, shit," he said.

He stopped dead. The screaming Turks were now about sixty yards away, and closing fast.

Gothically bemused, he stared at Vanessa in utter disbelief. Suddenly she looked up at him indignantly and gasped. "I fell," and she was up, and running with Reid. They were away, headed for the trees, hurtling over the sand littered with fallen branches and pine-cones.

To Reid's relief they reached the first of the Aleppo pines. They were now running like demons, feet pounding desperately through the soft fallen needles toward the beach.

Smashing their way through a clump of trees they hit soft sand. Fifteen years had seen little change in the area, and Reid had remembered right. They had only to gouge their way through this light brown stretch and they'd be on the hard, spotless, tanned sands of Salamis Beach. Then it was a short sprint to the first promontory. They would round that, probably get their feet somewhat wet, but by that time they'd be ahead of the pursuing soldiers. Sufficiently far in front to avoid all but the luckiest rifle bullet. But, as in the typical nightmare, the unexpected was lurking yet again. A soldier was standing on the beach, the hard beach, one boot in the water, his old nondescript rifle aimed right at the approaching pair, and blocking their avenue of escape.

With forty or so pursuers gaining on them as the belt of soft sand slowed them down, and with no other reasonable direction in which to go, Reid had little choice but to charge the lone sentry on the waterline.

"Let's get him." Vanessa's screech sounded like a pissed-off cockatoo on a New South Wales telephone pole. Reid's kind of bird. Rara avis rules, okay!

On the flat hard sand now the hundred yard dash toward the Turk looked like a mile to Reid. His legs were failing to transmit any idea of motion to his brain, just like a dream. On the other hand, Vanessa was moving fast, hair streaming, yelling obscenities, spit flying out of the side of her mouth.

They say your life flashes in front of you during those last few seconds on this planet, and that may be, but all they saw, as they barreled in tandem along the sand, was the enemy. They could make him out clearly now. A dark little fellow, young, almost too young to be wearing his ill-fitting uniform. But he was the enemy, and, in theory, he was there to stop John Reid and Vanessa Riley.

Twenty yards away, now, that was all. At thirty feet they could see the lad's sheer terror, his mouth gibbering inaudibly, but then nothing much could be heard above the sound of Vanessa yelling "bastard" over and over.

Somehow, though, the Turk managed to raise his rifle, pointing the ugly little weapon at Reid. As the report came, Reid and Vanessa launched themselves off the ground and hurled themselves through the air like big darts.

All three of them went down, sprawling on the sand and into the

107

shallow, gently-lapping water. The little soldier was no match for his opponents. And was it true that an Ottoman groin is three times more sensitive than its European counterpart? Anyone could have heard the thud as Vanessa's knee came up at a precise right angle. A swift and superfluous punch to the neck from John Reid, and the underfed private was prostrate.

Reid sprang to his feet. Vanessa was already up, reaching for him. This little tussle had slowed them down considerably. The group of pursuing soldiers was almost on them, and Reid and Vanessa could hear their footsteps louder and louder on the crunching sand.

In one of those brief seconds that seems to freeze time in the eye of the hurricane, Reid looked at Vanessa, grinned, and shouted, "You look pretty when you've got snot all over your face."

"Fuck you," she yelled, and then spun around to face the Turks. They actually stopped dead in their tracks, to a man. They'd never seen anything like it. It was the snot, yes, and somehow, from somewhere, she'd got blood all over her hands, probably from the Turkish kid on the ground. The snot was probably his too. But it was the noise, the demonic screaming, and the hair, the hair. She looked not just dangerous, but satanic. Like something out of a Goya painting. Scared the shit out of the soldiers for a moment.

Sweat was pouring from Reid's forehead as he tore away from the mangled dog-soldier, using the bullet-start he'd perfected as a youth after watching Bob Hayes win the 100 meters at Tokyo. And Vanessa was keeping pace. Silver medal, for sure, maybe gold the way she was going.

Because the Turks were running they couldn't aim their rifles. But why were they running at all? Why not just kneel down on the sand, take aim, and fire? There was much shouting, but they were amateurs, dressed as pros. However, the last thing Reid wanted was a lucky amateur trying his marksmanship, so they streaked around the hundred-foot high sandy promontory, a temporary lull, Reid knew only too well.

The stretch of beach that opened before them now led to Famagusta, interrupted only by a few promontories similar to the one they'd just passed. How little the coastline here had changed. They could swerve to the right and through the trees but they'd lose time. Besides, Reid couldn't be sure who, or what, lay there, waiting. Their best bet was a run along the shore, for he knew they could outdistance their pursuers. Knowing the Turks the way he did he was taking the gamble that the platoon wanted the glory of capturing the escaping couple, or killing them, all for themselves, and that they wouldn't radio ahead. But, radio to whom? It was a mass of confusion, and all Reid and Vanessa could do was run.

A hundred yards past the promontory, Reid looked back. He saw no soldiers, but what he did see sent a bolt of realization through him no less shocking than if he'd been hit by lightning. In an instant it forced him to accept the nasty truth which for the last several minutes he had been trying to deny to himself. The Professor was standing on top of the promontory, looking down on them. Suddenly a four-mile run along the beach seemed like suicide. The body of troops just rounding the promontory now may have been bungling incompetents, but there was a brain at the head of them, and he was up there, on the promontory, like a divine satyr, motionless, staring down onto the beach, his features too far away for Reid to make out. However, his expression, Reid just knew, was one of satisfaction.

Things were different now. Reid and Vanessa could no longer rely just on their track and field prowess. Reid had to use his head. But a plan was not forthcoming, except to dive for cover into the trees and hope to escape into the countryside. But, given the lay of the land, that had seemed crazy even before he'd seen the Professor. Now he knew that was exactly what the old man would expect them to do. Reid must keep his nerve, and continue running along the sand with Vanessa until a workable plan came to him.

He turned again, and sure enough, they were outpacing the ill-conditioned, weighted-down, booted soldiers. Reid also noted that the Professor had gone.

Their only chance was to get into the town of Famagusta itself, and throw off pursuit among the twisted little side streets of the walled city, or among the lesser known byways of the modern town. Reid decided on the latter, but his main concern now was the fact that they might not get there before their path along the beach became blocked by troops.

The only thoughts that were coming into his head were about the past, his own past, the past of the island itself.

They saw no one for the next few miles. Under more ideal circumstances this run would have been a breeze, just the sort of tonic Reid had often enjoyed on this very beach. Jogging in the heat of the afternoon sun, along the famous Cyprus beaches had been, in more peaceful times, an integral and pleasurable part of his day. But, dressed in Chino trousers and long-sleeved cord shirt, the experience was adulterated somewhat by a cold sweat and a prickly apprehension.

That apprehension was not unknown to him, not by a long way. It used to be fear in the old days, but not for too long. Fear is for the young, the inexperienced. The fear that turns the legs to jelly, that type. The paralyzing fear. That's no good, and he'd decided early that that kind of fear wasn't for him. What he substituted was an apprehension, a great apprehension sometimes, but it sure wasn't that old devil fear. He'd learned not to be incapacitated, either mentally or physically, for more than just a few seconds, the time it takes to overcome the fear. And you can learn, if you go about it the right way, if you can get into and live through the right sort of experiences.

A few black sea-urchins had been washed up on the beach and the tide was coming in quickly. The idle hydrological thought crossed his mind that if it weren't for the portal to the Atlantic at Gibraltar there wouldn't be a Mediterranean Sea at all. The amount of water this sea loses by evaporation is much greater than the volume discharged into it by its rivers. A more sobering thought also struck him. They might run out of beach before they could reach the Old City.

As they rounded the last of the promontories which punctuated this coastline like three giant verrucas, they could clearly see the old walled city. It was inside this walled city that Reid had stayed at the Altun Tabya Hotel, and from which he'd had to depart in such a hurry. Othello's Tower rose up from the wall nearest them, and he couldn't help wondering why it wasn't manned now, as it had been so magnificently in 1570. Perhaps he and Vanessa weren't that important. Perhaps the bastards had forgotten about them. Yet there remained the undeniable fact that they'd been shooting at them; to kill, what's more. Was it a trap? Were there soldiers waiting for them in the old, disused Customs sheds on the harbor front directly ahead?

Their run had been nerve-rackingly uneventful. Now they were at the end of the strip of beach, a beach narrowed drastically by the incoming tide. They jumped up onto the concrete of this once-busy harbor and weaved their way through the scores of Customs buildings that lay in the shadow of the fifty foot high Venetian walls. Without running into anyone they arrived safely at the base of the mighty Tower. They then traversed the first major section of the harbor, the old loading docks, by sprinting in and out of cover of the sheds and long metal huts that lay along the geometrically-shaped waterfront.

At last, ahead of them, was the long avenue once called Shakespeare Street, which ran the length of the final section. Somehow they had to pass through this avenue in order to get to the other side of the harbor. Scores of uniforms were floating about on the road so Reid quickly decided that their only option was the water. They would have to swim, tight up against the wall, right under the noses of the Turkish soldiers.

He checked his pockets. His cigarettes and lighter were still there and his passport was in his back trousers pocket, totally undisturbed by recent events. Stop for a smoke. Calm yourself. But no, time was of the essence. He didn't know if the soldiers on the harbor were waiting for them or whether they were simply stationed there as a matter of course. He and Vanessa couldn't take the chance of sauntering through Shakespeare Street, hoping the soldiers would take them for a couple of German tourists. Even Germans, although fairly common farther north in Kyrenia, would arouse attention here in Famagusta, as Reid had done himself on his previous visits to this town. So, now they had to get to the edge of the harbor wall, and that meant exposing themselves for a few seconds while they left the security of one of the large, rusty cranes nearby.

Casually they stepped out into the open, walked across the road and looked over the wall into the sea. The water was deep. Reid's passport would be ruined. Not to mention his cigarettes. But there seemed no other way. The water would always be deep. As they prepared to dive the twelve feet or so into the relatively calm water, Reid pulled back sharply. He had noticed that about fifty yards farther along the wall a series of bollards thrust their heads out of the water.

These bollards were attached to the wall itself and were evidently used as some sort of harbor facility. They appeared to be about three feet in diameter and made of stone, but of an older period than the wall itself. Perhaps the water had discolored them though. The bollards ran the length of the remaining wall as far as he could ascertain, and that was about five hundred yards. At the end of the wall, jutting out to sea like a chocolate éclair, was the southern mole. Beyond that was beach again.

The bollards looked as if they rose a foot above the level of the tide, and from where Reid stood they seemed to lie about four feet apart. Strange that he didn't remember these fixtures from the old days.

"You're not thinking what I think you're thinking," said Vanessa in a low tone.

"It's a stretch, I agree," he replied.

"You're out of your mind. Go ahead, but I'm walking."

This was no time for indecision. "On the other side of all this is the Constantia Hotel," and Reid pointed. "If you make it, be at the front door, and I'll come and get you. It's me they're after. They'll almost certainly leave you alone, especially as you're an American citizen. Good luck," and he slipped over the side of the harbor wall, grasping the edge with his fingers, and began to inch left along it toward the bollards.

If they spotted his clammy little fingers then they deserved to catch him as he dangled above the Mediterranean harbor, his feet a full two meters from the surface of the water.

He had traveled about twenty yards in this manner, and his arms were beginning to tire, when the dull commotion from Shakespeare Street suddenly took an excited turn. The voices came nearer and he heard footsteps coming toward the wall's edge, over which he was hanging like a gymnast on a chin-bar. He stopped moving and held his breath.

Someone was above him. Perhaps two of them. Yes, definitely two, they were talking now. How could they possibly miss seeing his fingers? He forced himself to keep breathing, and prepared to drop into the water at a moment's notice. For minutes on end he hung silently, motionless, from the wall, not daring to look up. The voices started to fade with the retreating footsteps, and Reid tried to pull his chin up to street level to see what was going on, but his arms were too tired to take the weight. He tried to find a foothold in which to take a break from the strain on his arms, but it was a modern stone wall, made slippery by the spray, with not a single crack in it that was of any use.

He deemed it wise to carry on shifting. After another twenty yards the pain had become agonizing. He could hear more voices now, and some seemed to be coming nearer again. He was just five feet from the nearest bollard. He was so tired he thought he was going to die; he just wanted to drop into the warm sea and put an end to it. Could he take the chance on shifting those last few handholds to get above the bollard before anyone saw the beast with five fingers? As a matter of fact, he had no choice. He simply couldn't hold on any longer. It's like when you need to pee, real bad. You get to a point when you do it in your pants and you don't give a damn, even if you're at a society ball. It was like that with Reid now. But he moved, and found himself over the first bollard.

He could see quite clearly now that the bollards were not, in fact, four feet apart, as he'd judged from a distance, but more like six, and their diameters were less than he'd figured; more like two feet. His plan, to drop onto the first one and then jump from bollard to bollard under the noses of the Turks until he reached the end of the harbor wall, now began to look distinctly unfeasible.

But he had to try it. There was no other way, unless he was prepared to get very wet and attract a lot of attention as the only breaststroke artist in the harbor. He glanced down quickly. Was the tide coming in or going out now? Hard to tell with that breakwater out there obscuring the more obvious manifestations of marine nature. A few minutes before it had been coming in, fast, but now it seemed to be on the way out. The bollards looked dry, and should remain that way. Gathering his nerve, he let go of the wall's edge, sliding bodily down the glistening face, and landed with a thud on the flat circle, hands flailing the wall for support until he got his balance.

Okay. Here he was, on Bollard Number One. Primo Bollard. Then something made him look to his left, out to the breakwater. About half a mile away was a ship, or more specifically a ferry, and it was coming toward the breakwater entrance. Reid knew too well what it was, it was the Mersin to Famagusta service, and there were people on board, lots of the bastards, having made the passage from Turkey. He could just make them out from where he stood on his merry bollard. There was no time to waste. Obviously the incoming ferry was the cause of all the excitement on the harbor, and soon people would be flocking en masse to the wall side to greet the boat as it docked. Not only that, Reid would become extremely visible to the ferry passengers as soon as their vessel pulled into the comparative calm of the harbor lagoon.

Six feet is a long way to jump without a run, and despite the fact that the standing long jump had been one of his specialties as a junior athlete, he doubted his ability to do it on the number of occasions that this situation demanded. Besides, the bollards were only two feet in diameter, far different to the luxury of a sand pit landing.

He launched himself into the air and a second later his right foot came to land on the bollard next in line. He swayed violently to his right, toward the wall, in an effort to prevent himself from pitching forward into the sea. More by luck than judgment he succeeded in remaining on the stonework.

He knew straight away that this was no good. Even if he mastered the technique of landing on each bollard without toppling over the edge, or without doing damage to himself as he landed each time, it would take him all day to get to the end of the wall. By that time, of course, he would have been discovered.

It was then he realized he'd been wrong about the tide. It was on its way in and seemed to be picking up speed as it did so. This meant that before he'd jumped many bollards they would become so slippery as to become untenable, and then they would disappear entirely beneath the surface of the now-threatening water. He looked up, half thinking that he should climb back up onto Shakespeare Street, but a quick study of the slimy wall reminded him of what he had already learned. No handholds.

But, hold on. Instead of jumping from one bollard to another, settling down to gather himself, then jumping again, he could sprint across from bollard to bollard without stopping, merely taking six-foot strides. But, could he do it without falling off into the sea? And could he complete the entire course in time? Most important, was he up to it?

His athlete's mind rapidly assessed the possibilities. It could be done, but he'd have to get into a rhythm immediately. At all costs he'd have to keep his right arm by his side, away from the treacherous harbor wall. One touch, one accidental knock of the elbow or fingers or shoulder, and he'd lose his balance and his rhythm. And that would be disastrous. It all depended on a smooth transition from one bollard to the next. He had to program into his mind the fact that the wall was there, mere inches to the right, but then he must forget it and concentrate his energies on the run and the timing. He quickly calculated the distance. At fifteen miles per hour, say, he should reach the end of the line in a little under a minute and a half. Yes. It looked feasible now. Definitely feasible.

Over. Next. Momentum. Next. Momentum. Next. More momentum. Soon he was in the rhythm of a six-foot stride, bounding from bollard to bollard in the most unusual and hazardous quarter-mile sprint of his career, and the 440 never had been his event.

His concentration was so intense that he didn't hear the shouts from the ferry as it drew closer, or the increasing hubbub of the throng above him on the waterfront. If he had taken notice, he would have seen everyone, soldiers and civilians, on land and at sea, watching him closely as he progressed with speed along the sea-line. The men above him were cheering and clapping by the time he reached the halfway bollard. Some of the ferry passengers, assuming that it was a show put on for them, a circus acrobat hired to drum up business for the ferry service, were also hooting and hollering and urging him on, but the majority, less worldly and unable to see the bollards, were just gawking, thunderstruck by the spectacle, the miracle perhaps. A few, those who had read and digested the Book of Matthew, could only conclude that it was the Second Coming, albeit a coming manifested in a rather strange way.

It must be Jesus Christ, Holmes. He's walking on water.

He's not walking, Watson. He's running. Running for his life.

Of great concern to Reid, however, were the bollards themselves. They were getting very wet. The tide was starting to lick at their very surface, and this would prove fatal. As he'd thoroughly mastered the six-foot rhythm and had convinced himself that he could handle the long sprint, it now became a race against the tide.

But disaster loomed, as all the spectators must have seen by now, at least those standing above him. One of the bollards was out. It simply wasn't there. If Reid had been able to reflect at this moment, he would have marveled that he'd had no problems of this kind before now. A chipped bollard. A lump eaten out of the middle. A smashed coke bottle lying on his very landing spot. A banana peel. But no, until now they had been perfect bollards, every one of them. But four bollards away was the gap. The cavity in the water left by a plucked giant's tooth.

When a runner runs, he sets his sights a certain number of yards ahead of him, depending on the length and type of race. Reid had settled on four bollards ahead, so it was with only a few short seconds to go that he found himself faced with the shocking dilemma. To give it all up, or to make the big jump.

Now, he wasn't a long jumper, never had been, not the long jump with a run type, anyway. Legs too short. But he'd often cleared twenty to twenty-one feet, and these days, at his age, could probably manage seventeen. But this was different. He'd been bollard-hopping for three hundred yards or more under the most trying pressures and he was tiring, fast. Added to that was the fact that if and when he landed he'd never be able to continue his run as he had been doing. He would come to a complete stop.

He knew he had no choice. A dilemma but no choice. That's how it was for the Reids. Always had been. Going back to Bonnie Prince Charlie. Even before that. Amid growing applause from the harbor and the ferry, he took off, fortunately with his left foot, his normal takeoff foot. He hung in the air for mesmerizing seconds, like Ralph Boston in the Rome Olympics, except that his right hand smacked painfully into the wall, throwing him off balance. He came down twelve feet farther on. His timing and judgment had been perfect, but the arm had screwed him. He should have considered the possibility of a missing bollard.

Oh, shit! The fucking banana peel. Not a real one, but it might as well have been. His heels made a passing acquaintance with the hard, wet stone and then shot forward into the water on the far side of the circle. How the hell he kept his upper body on the bollard he would never know. Maybe he lived right. Maybe someone up there was looking after him. Sir Isaac Newton. Lady Luck with a fallen apple in her mouth. With his hands acting as brakes, he managed to grind to a jarring halt on his undercarriage. A bolt of pain shot up his back and dissipated somewhere in the nerve endings of his shoulder blades, causing him to cry out, something he rarely did, even under trying circumstances. Only a supreme effort of will, and well-developed triceps, saved him from completely capsizing into the sea. Before he knew what was happening, he was sitting on the rim of the bollard, legs dangling over the side, and looking out like a spent prick toward the approaching ferry.

Now he became really aware of the crowd above him. The ferry, now only forty yards away and crawling with fascinated spectators, actually came as a shock. It had arrived far sooner than he'd thought possible. He was amazed at how all this public acclaim hadn't put him off his stride. He picked himself up, winded, dressed himself down, and prepared to surrender. He looked up again. There were stacks of soldiers there all right, but they weren't in any way threatening. They were merely enjoying the sport.

In a flash Reid got the picture. They were having a good time at his expense. Just waiting for him to slip into the water so they could fish him out and give him the appropriate welcome.

Fuck 'em, the bastards. He instantly hurled himself forward to the next bollard. Soon he was into the rhythm again: Space, bollard, space, bollard. A sharp pain shot through him every time he hit stone, but he did his best to ignore it. Simply dismissed it.

There was the mole ahead, the welcoming stone arm which formed the southern end of the harbor. Only a handful of bollards to go. The water was lapping furiously over their tops now, and Reid silently heaped gratitude upon the manufacturers of his excellent footwear.

He planted his left foot firmly on the last bollard. His right knee went up and he vaulted the four feet up onto the mole, no trouble.

Of all the known ways to survive a leap into the unknown, the most effective and least dangerous is to see, assess, decide and act in such rapid succession that the series of actions appears to be one swift, seamless movement. Reid saw that the drop on the far side of the mole was close to twenty feet. He assessed that because the surface was sand his landing would be fairly comfortable. He decided to jump. And he was gone, just as a shot rang out behind him from a Turkish rifle on Shakespeare Street.

If they wanted to get him they would have to jump too. But it was a big drop for encumbered troops with only sadly mundane dreams to protect them from a bad landing. One good thing, though. They weren't firing. Just running around, trying to find a place to get down to the sand. Reid streaked along the beach.

In the distance stood the Constantia Hotel, that magnificent Famagusta landmark that had gone up in the early '60s as the pioneer of the modern type of hotel, that architecturally sleek yet characterless sort of invention that had come to dominate tourist destinations all over the world, and to symbolize the soullessness of a great part of modern life in general. The old style George V was still there, farther along, past the Constantia, but, as with all splendid old colonial hotels, like Shepheard's in Cairo, it had been neglected in favor of its more modern counterparts such as the Constantia.

Reid had stayed at Shepheard's, but not the famous one, the one that had been burned down during the '53 revolution that had swept Naguib and Nasser to power. That had been before his time, but they'd rebuilt the hostelry in a different part of town, and he had stayed there often as a kid. But the new auberge had traded on the name of the old, and the romanticism had gone, even then. Anybody could sense that, even a child.

So, it's not a time thing, this romanticism, it's an idea thing. He wished he were back in Cairo now. Well, actually, only part of him did. Another segment of his brain was saying, "Go on, see it through. This is the real thing."

The giant Constantia was looming up. On the jagged rocks that led down to the sea from the hotel were the figures of soldiers. Not many, but enough to convince Reid that they were waiting for him.

He looked behind him and there, farther along Shakespeare Street, where the drop wasn't so great, jumping off the harbor wall onto the sand were a group of soldiers.

On Reid's right, running parallel to his own course, was the sandy, barren escarpment leading up to Delphi Street, the main highway that linked the old, Turkish, city with what had once been the modern, thriving Greek community of Varosha. Then, as Reid ran, the wasteland of the escarpment became a wooded area that extended the remaining half mile or so to the Constantia. What menace lurked in the woods? Waiting there, to pounce out on him as he drew level. Nothing happened. So, maybe that was the place to go. The woods.

He could hear faint shouts coming from the troops on the Constantia rocks. They were obviously getting ready to mow him down as he came within range, or possibly to capture him as he arrived at the rock barrier. It all depended on their orders, however, but chances were that they would use him as target practice. They bloody well needed it.

The small house was set back a little way in the woods. It looked quiet and empty, and Reid decided to make for it. Now you see him, now you don't. He veered sharply to his right and, moving into a higher gear, made for the woods.

The Turkish shouts became more distinct through the sound of the surf pounding against the shore. Reid was into the soft sand now, friendly brown pinecones littering his path, and then he was into the trees, rocketing toward the house.

It was a small red and white bungalow of whitewashed mud and brick. The typical flat roof had vanished into oblivion, for there was no one around to remember it the way it had been. A large, rust encrusted water tank survived as the main feature of what had evidently once been a beach garden. The place was deserted, had been for years. Immediately he saw the reason, an all too common sign in Turkish Cyprus. A gaping bombhole stared at him from the outer north wall, a legacy of the 1974 invasion.

He stopped short for the first time in half an hour, breathing hard, legs aching violently.

What he wouldn't do right now for the intimate companionship of his old friend Mr. Webley. Or, better still, an old MAT-49. That would frighten the bastards.

He looked rapidly about him. It was certainly the bedroom. Had been anyway. Only now it was a hotel suite for transient ants and swarms of little brown Mediterranean gecko lizards. Only the walls remained of the place which evidently had been a summer retreat, probably for a rich Nicosia Greek in the Good Old Days. Probably brought girls here, or boys. It had definitely never been anyone's full time home. Too small for that.

But he wasn't here for a property inspection. He was here to survive the menace that was growing ever more present. A quick look into the three other small rooms persuaded him that this building was not in any way a sanctuary. He had two choices, but not a dilemma. Either to press on through the woods and go inland, risking Delphi Street, which seemed a sure invitation to death, or to go back along the beach. Both options seemed crazy, and he cursed himself for not having gone into cover of the woods four miles earlier on in Salamis. At least that way he might have been able to go to ground. Wait until dark and pick them off individually. Acquire a gun with a bit of luck and blast a way out. That would have been tricky with Vanessa. It was all too late now. He was here, in this house, and he was hearing the excited voices of Turkish troops, rapidly closing in.

Reid was in a tiny room which had bits of light-hued tiled flooring still intact. A perfectly good Sheffield fork lay on the floor as a testimony to an age gone by, the stainless steel age. He stood up and looked through the small, glassless window. Instantly he recoiled. Not more than ten yards away three Turkish squaddies were standing, smoking and chatting amiably. He hadn't heard them because of the more distant hubbub, not to mention the deafening thud of his own heartbeat.

He couldn't believe that they hadn't heard him, but apparently they hadn't. He dropped to the ground, heart pounding even harder than before, limbs shaking a little, partly from fatigue but mostly from a combination of apprehension, adrenaline, and excitement. Now he knew his instincts had been right. If he'd made for Delphi Street he'd have run slap into the middle of the troops. His guess was that they had been placed

119

throughout these woods at intervals, probably of fifty yards, as this was typical Turkish Army dragnet procedure. But he still couldn't work out why hundreds of soldiers hadn't descended on the beach during his run and cut him down at their leisure.

He knew the Professor had something, if not everything, to do with it. But, what? The old man was surely, after all this, a policeman of some kind. That now went without saying. But, the extraordinary efforts to capture Reid or to kill him—he didn't know which yet—didn't seem to fit the crime he'd committed. Or did they? There was no way the Professor could know about the cross, so it had to be something else. Something more important than the cross. The Professor had mentioned a state official. Reid had broken into the home of one of Turkish Cyprus's highest state officials. Was that it? Was this the official's revenge for Reid's making him beat a hasty withdrawal? Had the official called the Professor in to track Reid down and capture or kill him?

No, this all seemed too wrong. The Professor had been on Reid's track before the official even knew of his existence. Also, the Professor could have had him arrested over breakfast that morning. Besides, even in a place as Byzantine as Turkish Cyprus a government official would have to have a damned brilliant reason to tie up such a large amount of manpower. And what reason could he give? No matter how monumentally pissed off at Reid's little prank he wouldn't go that far. He couldn't. It didn't seem to be making much sense to Reid at all. So, it had to be the Professor. His doing. But why? And, once again, the old man could have had him arrested over his watermelon and coffee. The whole thing was bizarre and perplexing.

Suddenly Reid heard what could only be a large number of troops entering the beach garden. But in the more immediate vicinity were the crunching footsteps of the three smoking soldiers coming toward the window he was crouching behind. He hoped that the sound of his pulse wouldn't give him away. Not daring to look up, he could almost feel the trio of Turks looking down on him from the window hole. What seemed like an eternity passed before he heard one of them, only inches behind the wall, say something in a loud, but unexcited guttural. Then the heavy footfalls moved off around the side of the house, but not before a lighted cigarette butt came hurtling over Reid's head, through the window, to land on the floor at his feet. It was a Philip Morris, unfiltered. Where the hell did this little Turkish soldier get a Philip Morris Unfiltered? Usually they smoked those disgusting Turkish brands, the cheap ones with the unpronounceable names, the sort provided as part of their army rations by a mainland Turkish government too tight to pay their soldiers any salary at all. Occasionally they might get a pack of ubiquitous and equally foul 555s or Rothmans Royals. Perhaps this boy was independently wealthy. And, to boot, he had smoked only three quarters of it.

As the name Philip Morris was slowly eaten away by the fire within the wee butt—the soldier had had the decency to smoke it from the right end, which is more than Reid could say for himself half the time—he listened to what was evidently a discussion. Then a whistle was blown.

This is it, Reid thought. And even as he thought it he heard cries and another whistle from some way off.

"Reinforcements," he grunted, putting his hand over his mouth as he realized he'd vocalized his own thoughts. Must be going loony with the strain.

He remembered his mother's oft-repeated words, "It's no use just sitting there." Under slightly less tense circumstances he would have smiled at the memory of this quaint phrase. But his mother was right. He stood up, extremely slowly and cautiously, looked right and left through the hole where the window used to be, and in an instant was pulling himself through it to drop silently onto the soft earth outside.

He edged around to the south wall of the house. There was no one there. On the north side, however, the activity was becoming intense. Reinforcements were, indeed, pouring into the garden in answer to the blown whistle. On the other side of the wall now, Reid could hear soldiers in the house, going through the rooms, including the very one he'd just been hiding in.

So far so good. But how the hell was he going to get out of this new situation? His back pressed up hard against the outer south wall of the building, he was totally at the mercy of anybody coming around to that side of the house, or of anyone coming through the woods from the direction of the hotel. Yet, if he hadn't got out of that room when he had, he would have been found, skulking among the ants and the lizards. At least, he was still in the game.

If you play the game enough times, you're bound to win occasionally, and more times than not if you play it long enough. You get good at it. It's

121

no longer just a question of chance. But you must still have luck on your side. And now Reid's luck kicked in. It was as if the man hadn't been there, and then he was. A Turkish soldier was lying on his back about twenty yards to the south, adjacent to a tree, his helmet on the ground by his side, but with no rifle in evidence. He was quite inert. There was something vaguely comical in the picture. Maybe he was asleep. No, that would be asking too much.

Reid had to venture over there. He had no choice. But he would have to break cover for a few seconds until he reached the trees.

It was now or never. The activity on the other side of the building was increasing. They'd be around to this side any minute. He sprinted across the topsoil, not taking his eyes off the prostrate Turk, and threw himself behind the tree, his hand raised to deliver a deadly blow to the little fellow on the ground.

The blow never fell. It didn't have to. Reid saw in an instant that the man was unconscious, breathing hard, a gash on his forehead. As the blood was flowing freely, it could only recently have happened. But why? And how?

Reid looked up at the tree. About five feet from the ground a piece of bark had been dislodged and a speck of blood was clearly visible on the ivory-colored surface. Reid smiled grimly.

An Ottoman Buster Keaton. Mustafa Chaplin. The young soldier, just like in those twenties Hollywood flickers, must have been trying to get to the scene and crashed into the tree. He'd obviously been carrying his helmet in his hand. If he'd been wearing it, Reid might have been dead by now. But what was this Turk doing here on his own like this? Why hadn't he been discovered by his colleagues? Perhaps he'd been for a personal visit behind a tree, had been left behind, and had tried to make up ground the best way he could. Yes, that seemed the likely answer.

From the time Reid left the cover of the wall to the time he made off toward the Constantia through the Aleppo and Mediterranean pines, no more than forty seconds could have elapsed. He silently thanked his mother as he glided through the woods, heading south, eyes darting from left to right, constantly on the lookout for uniforms. If these had been German troops his number would have been up long ago. But the Turkish soldiers on Cyprus, all fifty thousand of them, were, by and large, the dregs from mainland Turkey, too young and inexperienced, badly trained, ill-equipped and ill-fed, not paid a penny by their country, and with no incentive to succeed. They were simply cannon fodder. The lower ranks especially spent most of their waking hours tramping around the streets on Zombie Patrol. They were nice fellows, if given half the chance, but what the hell did they want to be in Cyprus for? As a consequence they were more of a danger to themselves than to an enemy in a combat situation, unless properly commanded.

Nevertheless, they had guns, and they were using them. And they shot to kill. There were also many of them, and they were looking for John Reid. He was concerned for Vanessa's safety, but the thing that worried him the most was the Professor. He was old, but he was a clever son of a bitch, very clever, and tenacious. He was certainly tenacious. Where was he? What was he doing? Reid cursed himself again for not having taken seriously his first instincts about the Professor. Those instincts had screamed at him that the old man was dangerous. You didn't have to have Mozart's IQ to figure that out. Why had he allowed himself to be persuaded that the Professor was harmless? Was he going soft? He'd been tough in similar situations before, stood his own ground, kept to his own instinctive beliefs no matter what.

Suddenly he found himself at the rock foundations of the Constantia. Towering directly overhead was the huge hotel.

Reid ran along the rock face toward the beach, but had only gone a few yards before he saw, through the trees, swarms of soldiers milling about on the water's edge. He returned silently to the base of the hotel. He was now in the classic situation that presented only one possible way out, and that relieved him. He couldn't go left, to the beach; he'd already tried that. He couldn't go right, through the woods, or back the way he'd come, for that would lead him smack into the patrols. The only option was to climb.

But it was a rock face. Solid. Smooth. Imposing. Rising to a height of fifty feet before the first visible handhold, a window ledge. He figured that it was a room on the first floor of the hotel itself, possibly a kitchen or utility room. But that was what he had to make for. And he didn't have much time to make the climb for it was almost certain that at any moment the soldiers would arrive in the area. If they appeared while he was on his way up he'd be pinned like a butterfly in a collection. But he had to risk it.

123

He began to climb. The sheer, vertical face presented little of assistance to a mountain climber, a finger hold here and there, the odd tuft of stubborn vegetation, and he struggled with the utmost difficulty to a height of about eight feet until he realized, with dismay, that even Sir Edmund Hillary couldn't have gone any higher. He dropped to the ground, and sat down glumly with his back to the wall.

This was it, man, truly it, unless he made off inland and braved the inevitable patrols. It was such a pity that he couldn't cross to the other side of the Constantia ,the south side ,because he knew that by doing so he had a much better chance of escape. There he could elude his pursuers in streets familiar to him yet probably unknown to the Turkish troops who were, after all, strangers here themselves. Yet, this seemed sadly irrelevant now.

He pulled out a Capstan, lit it, and thought. Certainly he'd take a couple of them before they got him. And get him they'd have to. He wouldn't be captured by the Turks. That would be worse than death. He knew the Turks too well to allow that to happen. He'd known them too long and too intimately as friends. Now he was the enemy, he'd be better off dead than alive in their barbaric hands.

He drew deeply on his cigarette, staring fixedly at a pine tree directly in front of him. A faint smile. An idea. A hope.

"Why walk when you can go by bike, Reid?," he said aloud. Immediately, he was on his feet, the cigarette stamped out in the dirt, and he was shimmying up the tree.

Easier this way. He progressed higher and higher up the branchless tree which, more from luck than convenience, had been planted, or had perhaps grown naturally, a mere ten feet from the rock face, rising up parallel to it.

Despite the painful irritation of the sharp little twigs which grow out of the trunks of pine trees in a halfhearted attempt to form branches, he moved upward with the speed of a fairly experienced coconut tree climber. Even his old friend Piri Poruto, the legendary Cook Islander, would have been hard pressed to match Reid in his ascent of this Mediterranean pine. The higher he went the more slender the trunk. The tree began to bow, with Reid coaxing it the way of the rock surface, until his back was virtually scraping the cliff itself. He was almost to the level of the window, but thought that to go any higher might cause the tree to snap at the very point where he was. Just a few feet farther, though, and he could grasp the ledge.

Then the soldiers appeared below. Four of them, jabbering away like fishwives. As Reid had forgotten most of his Turkish, he had no idea whether they were looking for him or discussing the state of the Ankara stock market. He suspected the former.

Meanwhile a white faced Scotchman was suspended like a fairy on a Christmas tree, fifty feet up, brushing with the breeze against the rock face, and staring down at an excited set of privates. He was amazed they hadn't looked heavenward yet and hoped they wouldn't have the brains to. The tree was now bent to an almost impossible degree, and he knew it was just a matter of time before 185 pounds snapped it at the point where he was hanging.

"It's no use just sitting there" came to him again. He would have to go higher, and right now, with not a moment to lose. But he knew that if he did, either the tree would snap or the troops would become aware of him, probably both. However, if he stayed where he was the same options presented themselves, with the additional one of certain failure.

A frightening daydream intruded upon the awful reality of his predicament. He saw himself falling to the soft earth fifty feet below—it looked far higher from up there than it had down on terra firma—and he could see himself breaking his back, yet being conscious and unable to move.

He inched slowly, carefully, upwards, hardly daring to breathe. One eye on the Turks below, and the other on the window ledge. He reached out, almost languidly, and grabbed the smooth marble with his left hand.

It was a critical moment, and one of enormous indecision, yet one which called for an enormous decision to be taken. When he let go, the tree would spring back into the vertical like a Roman catapult at a siege. This would give him away completely and expose him to the discretion of the soldiers below. He couldn't hang on much longer because of the strain on the tree and on himself.

His decision was made for him. The Turkish answer to Sherlock Holmes discovered the cigarette butt that Reid had thought he'd so carefully stomped into the dirt. The private looked up. He saw Reid instantly, and screamed hysterically, the way Turks do when they're frightened.

Reid let go of the tree with his right hand and grappled for the ledge.

As he did so, the force of the recoil tore his left hand from the ledge, and the vibration and the tug of the returning tree almost split him in two. For a horrifying instant he was airborne, between the wall and the returning pine, and only trained reflexes and his incalculable luck saved him from plunging. His arms waved frantically in the air, and the fingers of his right hand smashed into the cold stone of the building, immediately and instinctively forming a grip, despite the pain of the impact. His chin and left hand followed in short order. The sudden and shocking pain was almost enough to force him to release his hold, but his instinct for survival, and his early years as a self-driven athlete, assured that he would hang on, at least.

The alarming recoil of the tree also had the dramatic effect of frightening the Turks below into a confusion. All within the space of a few seconds they had been made aware of the enemy above them, not a good place to have an enemy known to be dangerous, and they had automatically prepared for battle, unaware of Reid's difficulty. The noise and speed of the recoiling tree had convinced them they were under attack, and that this was only the prelude to the main assault. They threw themselves to the ground, practically burying their heads in the sand. All of this was of little consolation to Reid, however. He was totally self-absorbed at the moment, in his life or death struggle fifty feet up in the air. He had no way of knowing the accidental effect his move had had on the Turks, only that he had to get into that window.

Using all his willpower, plus the desperate strength which adrenaline can lend, he pulled himself up onto the ledge. Fortunately it was wide enough to accommodate a man in a pinch.

As luck again would have it, the window was slightly open, and he was inside in a flash. It was a hotel room, a proper room for guests, with a king-size bed and all the stuff to be expected in such a room. But it was unoccupied.

He stood stock still, watching, listening, trying to control his labored breathing. At first he heard nothing except the pounding of the blood in his head, but then the sounds of shouting from outside drifted up to him. They would be in the hotel in a moment, looking for him.

* * *

At that very moment, of all possible times, there was someone at the bloody door, actually opening it with a key. He was in the room before

126

Reid could do anything about it. A bunch of keys in one hand, rifle in the other, and cigarette butt dangling wetly from his mouth. The second he realized the room was occupied, and that the occupier was the very man he was looking for, anxiety lit up his face like an electric lightbulb. He dropped the keys, fumbling for his weapon, but before you could say *Allegro non troppo*, Reid was performing one of the less complicated but most choreographically gratifying movements from Act I of Swan Lake, the one where the hero, looking a little twee perhaps in the execution, especially the bit where he does the *entrechat quatre*, seems to fly through the air, alights squarely in front of the enemy, grabs a handful of uniformed Turkish testicles, the man screams, and the hero drags him into the room with great speed and violence. The man's cigarette and rifle then fall noiselessly into the deep pile of the carpet. There are a few grunts in high tenor, but no struggle.

There aren't many guys who can comprehend, let alone defend themselves against, such a fast attack, especially by a much bigger, trained man, and this Turkish dog soldier was not a commando. His brain, clouded by fear, had not fully registered attack, therefore he hadn't yet had time to go into the defense mode. By then he was on his way out of the window, and Reid was headed toward the door.

Then he heard a muted but strangulated cry and turned. He leaped back to the window and looked down. He found himself staring into the brown eyes of the terrified youngster. Somehow the lad had managed to grasp the window ledge in a desperate last stab at survival. His eyes were pleading for mercy.

Reid knew that look well. Had seen it often in the ring. First when he was seven. The first time he'd boxed competitively. A new school. He'd only been there a week. They'd overmatched him with a bigger, heavier kid of ten, partly because Reid was bigger and heavier than all the other seven year olds, but also because they'd had a boring tourney so far, and wanted to see the shit knocked out of someone. Preferably someone they didn't know. To salve the conscience of failure. People are like that. The kid cut Reid's lip in the first round, and Reid went berserk. The terrified look in the kid's eyes as the teachers had finally pulled Reid off him. It took three of 'em. What they hadn't known was that Reid, even at seven, could be an extremely violent little son of a bitch. It didn't take much.

Later, in England, in the Southern Area amateurs. Reid was light-heavy then. Cruiser as the gym master called it. Three rounds of nonstop slugging. Then the opening that's bound to come if you stay in there long enough. One-two. Just the way any fighter likes it; if you're the one dishing it out, that is. His opponent on the canvas. Count of six. Then he was up, dazed. Reid could finish it now. The other kid's arms were down, the bloody face bobbing carelessly like one of those old Fred Flintstone punching bags. Same terrified, pleading look. Shit, he shouldn't have been in there if he couldn't take it. There was a song, popular back then, that contained the words "a crashing blow from a huge right hand sent a Louisiana fellow to the Promised Land." The fellow stayed down for half an hour. They thought he might die. Talk of Big Bad John being barred from the sport. Hysterical fuss from the wimpy antiboxing crowd, especially a large, very macho looking, pipe-smoking Swede who turned out to be a woman and much more violent than Sonny Liston. Some big cheese, who'd obviously never been in the ring in his life, called Reid a brainless idiot, an irresponsible fool who didn't know when to stop.

A split second of thought—not indecision—and Reid delivered the kayo punch. It was so hard that if he'd missed and hit the wall he'd have shattered his hand for good. However, it did assure that the little soldier would be unconscious as he hit the soil fifty feet below. He stood a chance, despite a nose that would never blow properly again.

Breathing hard, Reid recoiled into the room, and then was out into the corridor and running toward the elevator. Pulled up short as he came to the stairwell. Better option.

He got down to ground level and opened the door a fraction. There were millions of them outside. No go there. But he hadn't reached the end yet, the bottom of the stairs. There were still steps leading down. But to where? Hell, for all he knew. He took them, anyway, three at a time. Safer than the known way. There had to be something on the lower levels, like car parks or something. He arrived at a door one flight down, opened it and looked furtively through. A long, badly lit corridor stretched ahead, deserted save for a silent air conditioner, probably out of order, high on the left wall. He was in, then the heavy door clunked behind him. A subdued metal click followed. He tried the door. It was locked.

He set off down the narrow corridor, at the end of which, on the left, was another door, his only possible way out. He turned the handle. It wouldn't open.

This was bad. He couldn't stay in this corridor, and just wait for someone to come and find him. Yet what was the option? The door was heavy, but he had to get through it somehow. He tried the handle again, and gave it a charge with his shoulder. It opened immediately. He felt like a damned idiot. It had just been stiff, that's all.

Beyond was an antechamber, small, dark, evidently seldom used, and it led immediately to another door. There was a handwritten sign on this door, but he couldn't interpret it. Gingerly he pushed it open.

No sound was made or heard. He poked his head around the corner. Light shone through the high, frosted window on the far side, revealing a fair-sized room with another door beneath the window. Tiled floor and walls, and cubicles on the left which he recognized only too well. He was in a public toilet. Beyond the stalls on the left he could make out the far end of the urinal. All was quiet so he eased through onto the tiling, closing the door gently behind him.

One step at a time he approached the first cubicle. As quietly as he could, he dropped into a push-up position, looking underneath the doors of the three little compartments for desperate ankles with trousers bunched around them. All clear. He sprang up, and set his sights on the main door on the far side of the room.

He'd taken two steps forward when, from nowhere, a gigantic Mediterranean cough shattered the quietness of the room, followed by a horrendous spit into water. Reid froze in disbelief, not only at the magnificent execution of this typical Eastern custom, but at the fact that someone was in the room. Obviously a Turk was at the near end of the urinal, hidden from Reid's view by the cubicles.

Instinctively he pushed open the door of the convenience nearest him, one swift movement to avoid squeaking, and was inside, all breathing suspended. No lock on the door. Would have to wait it out. If it was a cleaner he might have done this cubicle already or he might be getting around to it. It was hard to tell. If the latter, then Reid would have to deal with him.

The Constantia was a building along western lines, and so had installed real toilets for its workers, not just holes in the ground. No more squatting for the peasants. But, almost inevitably, the standards had fallen since Johnny Turk had taken over the bowel business. In short, the bog hole stank, and Reid was strangely embarrassed to be here.

129

Evidently the man at the pissoir was doing what most people do at pissoirs, but he was doing it in spades. Either that, or it was a sound recording of Niagara Falls. Reid had once seen a rhinoceros peeing at Regents Park Zoo, and it had left an indelible impression on him. Maybe this wasn't a man, maybe it was a bloody rhino. Naturally assuming himself to be alone in this large chamber the rhino let out a fart, a truly wondrous fart, the Caruso of farts, a fart that could be measured only on the Richter Scale. A fart is funny, let's face it. The longer and louder and more unusual or unexpected a fart is, the funnier it is. Of all the farts Reid had ever heard this was certainly the loudest. It was, in fact, ear-splitting. A rhino fart. And it must have lasted seven seconds. On paper that doesn't sound like a long time, but try a seven-second fart sometime. You'd deflate like a balloon and disappear into the ionosphere. Truly, he'd never heard a fart like that. Hopefully, one day, medical science might get to examine the asshole that produced it. Reid felt himself on the point of cracking up, but then muffled footsteps began to cross the tiled floor. Reid peered through the crack. It wasn't a rhino after all. It was an elderly, unshaven man, a civilian, shuffling away from the urinoir, doing up his fly, and expelling one final cough as he went through the main door.

As the Prince of Wales used to say in the twenties, in answer to the question, Your Royal Highness, what do you consider the most important thing in life: "One should never fail to take the opportunity to relieve oneself." Although Reid was no fan of royalty as an institution, he never hesitated to take good, solid advice from his betters. After that, he was at the door.

Outside was a U-shaped courtyard, and his door was but one of many in the combined length of the three walls. Directly ahead of him, to the south, was his way out. There seemed to be no one about, yet he could hear a lot of shouting in the distance. He looked toward the horizon and saw the long row of hotels clustered along the right hand fringe of the famous Families Beach, which he had so many reasons to remember, some recent, some in the distant past. At least he'd got to the other side of the Constantia.

He rapidly assessed his assets. He knew the area, and he knew what he wanted to make for: The Green Line. He then strolled out into the courtyard, as carelessly as if he were a tourist, fully expecting to be shot in the back.

"Did you have a nice trip, Green Line Runner?"

The question came from a recessed doorway.

* * *

"Good, yeah, good. You?"

"Fine. I just strolled along the harbor road, as if I owned it. No one said a word. Then I cut up onto the main road, and, well, here I am."

She looked fresh, and pretty as a picture.

"You haven't been waiting long, I trust," he asked, solicitously.

She smiled again. "What do we do now, Batman?"

"I was about to ask you the same thing," Reid said, wondering what hell was about to break loose in the immediate future.

There was really only one answer he could think of. "Again, I think we'd better split up. You'll be okay, I'm sure. Just go into town, grab a cab and head for Nicosia. Once you're over the Green Line you'll be safe. I'll join you at the Parthenon when I can, okay? If I'm not back in a week you'd better go to the British Embassy, I guess."

"It seems it's our fate to be separated, doesn't it."

"It's only temporary. Once this is all over we can spend the rest of our lives together, if you want."

She looked distant for a moment. "The Parthenon, then. What are you going to do?"

* * *

Across the road, into the sand, and on to the beach. Still no disturbance, although more confused shouting was coming from the Constantia lobby itself. Obviously some of Reid's more recent exploits had been discovered, and were now being acted on. His main fear was that his clothing, which was rather distinctive in Turkish Cyprus, might be spotted, no matter how casual he pretended to be.

Fortunately the beach was still quite populated with sun bakers catching the last and least harmful rays of the Mediterranean sun. As he passed the George V, and came into Families proper, the number of persons became greater. Most were now packing to go home. Bikini-clad Turkish girls and their similarly dressed chaperones. The expectable swarm of beachfront Romeos and Adonises and Narcissuses. But no one scoring because of the chaperones, unless the chaperones were secretly making it

131

all the time and nobody knew. Not that anybody gave a damn anyway because this was 1979 and anything goes, man, at least it would if it hadn't been for the chaperones.

There were the stall holders, mostly flogging Bel-Cola as if it were the elixir of life which, through the heat of the day, it was. Finally there were the soldiers who were always to be seen on the Famagusta beaches anyway, little groups of them, very young fellows, perving at the girls, reading inane comics, and engaging in arm wrestling contests. But now who could predict the situation?

As Reid passed the string of hotels and buildings on his right he couldn't help noticing the differences between now and then, whenever "then" was. When he was a child here, Turkish women were not even seen on the beach. Now look at 'em. Only in Rio can you see briefer bikinis than these. And if these girls had ever contemplated a good pluck, it had never come off. Fifteen years makes that amount of difference.

The Palm Beach, that overly expensive, German-owned, Turkish-managed tourist trap for rich Turks from the mainland, was the last hotel on the beachfront before the Varosha barricade, which here was represented by an enormous wire fence that came down off the main coast road, across the beach itself, and jutted some twenty yards out into the sea, reaching to a height of around fifteen feet. This was the boundary of Varosha.

This barricade had nothing to do with the Green Line, which at this point on the island lay a little way to the south. In 1975, after the Green Line had been established and the Greeks and Turks had all done their refugee bit, the Turks started to come in from the mainland. First it was the troops, then all the garbage that Ankara wanted to get rid of. It became a Turkish Botany Bay. The Turkish side of the island soon fell into the Dark Ages and reports to the outside world, if they got out at all, were generally hopelessly inaccurate. No one really knew what was going on here; not even the Turkish Cypriots, and they're normally well informed about local items.

Shortly thereafter, the Turks decided to put up a separate barricade around the old commercial center of Varosha, a large area, the very heart of the modern town of Famagusta, including the world famous Golden Sands Beach. No one seems to know why the barricade was put up or what was going on inside. Someone knows, of course, but they're not telling. Certainly no one Reid had met knew anyone who'd ever been inside, not even officers in the Turkish Army. It was like a ghost town. Reid had managed to sneak a couple of looks over the tops of fences, and through holes in walls, but no one was ever to be seen inside. It was heavily patrolled on the outside, but on the inside there seemed to be nothing at all. He saw bomb holes everywhere though, but they'd been created during the invasion. It must have been for a good reason, but it was as if a whole town had ceased to exist.

His plan was to swing up behind the Plambitch, over the road and through the old park, near the zoo, into the trees, and then a little farther on he should come to the Green Line itself. Then it would just be a matter of finding a suitable place to get across, if he could. A Sunday afternoon stroll to church.

But the pleasant afternoon was over. Suddenly there was shouting behind him. A whistle was blown. He turned, and his heart sank. He'd been spotted.

He took off along the beach, weaving in and out of wide-eyed decamping sunbathers, a group of uniforms not far behind. There was still a chance, he thought. They won't shoot here . Too many people, too many of their own.

The barricade was looming up fast, and as he prepared to lunge to his right, to the south side of the Plambitch, his mouth went dry. Soldiers were sweeping down onto the beach through the weeds behind the hotel. For one second he thought he was trapped. In the next second he was running in the opposite direction, toward the sea, the high fence towering above him on his right.

As he plunged into the blood-warm Mediterranean so did one or two bullets from Turkish hardware. He kept going, and the water was up to his knees now. He was slowing drastically, but he reached the extent of the fence, and, plowing through the resisting sea, made desperately for the forbidden beach on the far side of the barricade. Suddenly the water was becoming shallower. His lungs were screeching at him for mercy, but only a little farther to go. It was almost a minute before he hit solid ground again, the luxury of the once idyllic Golden Sands. He was about thirty yards on the other side of the fence now, and sprinting hard across the sand toward a group of buildings. He'd just planted one foot in the soft sand leading to the refuge of these buildings when he felt a whack on the back of his head as if someone had dumped a blackjack on him.

His pace slowed immediately. A giant was swiftly sucking the energy from his battery. His arms and legs stopped working almost instantaneously. It was as if he'd been drugged. He stumbled, and fell on his face on the warm sand. He was so close to the buildings. He wasn't unconscious yet, but he was losing power. It felt like he'd been hit, but he couldn't believe it. There was nothing traumatic, no real pain, just a sickly, glowing feeling.

Must concentrate, Reid. Come on, you fool. Only a few yards. Don't black out. Not yet. Get your face off this nice, comfortable sand and get your ass into a safe place. His vision was blurred to the point of almost total blindness as he inched forward, an ever-narrowing tunnel was forming in front of his eyes, and his head was starting to throb wildly.

The next thing he knew he was pushing himself through a hole. It had to be a bomb-hole in one of the dilapidated buildings. It was all automatic pilot now. He'd done the programming. He knew where he must go. He just had to hope that he had the physical reserves to carry out the plan. Through another wall, across some dirt, through an open doorway into another building. He was crawling now, couldn't imagine how, and that amazed him at the time, but he could no longer see at all. It was all touch now. The dull pain in the back of his head was reaching the point of excruciation, and he was fading fast.

He fell to the ground again, but this time he couldn't get up. He really tried. "Must get a hideout before I black out. Must find somewhere safe." He was mumbling now, and was vaguely aware of sliding into a cool, small space, and then he was in another world. He heard a handle click behind him, but didn't know what it was. It must be a dream. Then full-color images of Fräulein Lise dominated his brain, and that was the last thing he remembered.

* * *

The buzz saw buzzed and buzzed in his head. He couldn't move. His whole body was squeezed into a ball and his legs and arms were numb. It was all dark, totally black. His last memory had been of Fräulein Lise on a revolving crucifix, except that Lise turned into Vanessa.

Was he dead? First thought, really. Was he blind? No. He raised his arm and struck something hard. Wood. A little door sprang open and light shone in. Where the hell was he? He struggled through the tiny doorway into a room. He'd been shut in a closet which formed part of this room. There were two old tables and a chair in the room, and that was all the furniture. Debris was scattered on the vinyl floor and a large bomb-hole gaped in the wall above the closet. It looked like an office of some sort.

He felt the side of his head. It was dull as shit, but not particularly painful. No red liquid on his hand. As the blood flowed back into his limbs, he stood up slowly and painfully. The pins and needles were devastating as the numbness began to retreat.

A tin can lay on the ground. He picked it up. As a mirror it wasn't much use, but he inspected his head as well as he could. He couldn't see the dried blood in his hair, but he could feel it. And no bullet hole, at least not immediately visible. That meant he was still alive. Must have been what the old thriller writers called a surface wound. Yes, as he sucked his fingers he tasted the chemicals hemo-this and hemo-that. So, they had managed to hit him. He placed the can back on the floor and walked groggily to the door and looked at the rest of the interior of the building. Nothing much, except a series of doorways into a series of rooms, the way it always is. Strolling through them, he came across the entrance from the beach through which he must have crawled.

As he eased back into more or less total awareness the thought came to him that perhaps there were soldiers out there looking for him. But, if so, how come he was still free? He could hear nothing and see nobody as he looked out onto the deserted, rubble ridden streets outside.

He looked at his watch. Just gone four o'clock. Four? It must be later. Had to be. The watch must have stopped then started again. No, not this watch. How long he'd been unconscious he didn't know, but it was still light. It could have been only a few minutes, half an hour at the most. Soon the patrols would be here. Better find a secure place for the night.

He went toward the large hole in the wall and looked out over Famagusta Bay. The sun was coming up over the horizon, and it looked peaceful. The cool, white, early morning Mediterranean. Unique. Half a mile out to sea he could make out the tiny geological hump he had swum to many times as a boy in the annual Camel Rock Race. On his third attempt he'd come in eighteenth, not bad for a thirteen-year-old kid competing against soldiers.

Early morning? The east? Suddenly it hit him. The sun was coming up. Well, whaddaya know! He was looking eastward and there was the sun on the horizon. That lucky old sun. It was the next day already. He'd been unconscious for the best part of twelve hours. His watch hadn't stopped, of course. A quick check of the date. Just like clockwork, it had rolled around heaven all day.

He rushed to the front of the building and scanned the street again with new hope, but at the same time with fresh concern. They must have been looking for him last night. Once again the question gnawed at him: Why was he still free? They should have had him by now.

He looked at his watch again. No sign, no sound, of anyone. They'd probably start again at six. That gave him a couple of hours then. But, for what? One thing for sure, it's no use just sitting there.

Outside on the street, the wreckage of the 1974 invasion remained as if time had frozen on an expensive mural. Buildings had collapsed and had been left as they'd fallen. Reid was unable to determine exactly what street he was on; it all looked so different from the once-thriving hub of activity it had been in the '60s. A thoroughly bombed town bears as little resemblance to its former self as a snowclad village does to itself in summer. All Reid knew was that he was stuck in the forbidden city of Varosha, or Marash as the Turks call it, that now mysterious, unknown area that had once been the heart of one of the busiest cities in the Near East.

Strange how closely he had so far managed to adhere to the plan he'd quickly formulated after the Salamis encounter with the soldiers, which had been to run into Famagusta, lose the Turk on his home ground, so to speak, and then make across country for the Green Line, eventually to cross into the British base of Dhekelia. He hoped Vanessa had made it. She should have done by now. She should be back at the Parthenon, asleep in her nice bed.

Reid couldn't understand how he was still alive, how the Turks had missed him with all those bullets, how absolutely lucky he'd been. Even the nick on the head wasn't bad, considering. Well, he was in Famagusta now. All he had to do was get the hell out of Varosha and into the countryside, and things should begin to get a lot easier.

Hungry suddenly. Very hungry. The dullness in his head was subsiding, however, as he moved around, and he finally stepped out of the relative security of this old office and ventured out into the unknown. He figured that if he headed west, and if he could get out of Varosha, he'd eventually strike the Green Line somewhere along the Larnaka Road. Then, hugging the Line until he could find a place to cross, he should find himself in the British base area by the end of the day. All it required was a little ingenuity, and a lot of luck.

Feeling more purposeful, he crossed the main road into a side street heading west. The stillness was eerie as he picked his way along the sides of buildings, such as Barclays Bank, which had once hummed with commerce. The ghosts of an age past were there with him on the streets as he walked, ghosts of businessmen, taxi drivers, stall keepers, street sweepers, the lot of them, including the ghost of John Reid himself from those happy days, lost souls all, wailing "Give us our town back." Reid, for one, couldn't give this old town back to anyone. It was beyond redemption. All he could do was press on to the end of the little street, to another crossing. To the right he could see the Plambitch behind the barricade. He was across the next main street and trotting silently and warily through a narrow lane when dead ahead of him he saw the barrier walls. Here they were high, with plaster peeling off them and debris forming a moraine at their base. A thin, open archway, which the Turks call a bab, led through into the outside world. Still a Turkish world, but, somehow, much saner than this place.

He tiptoed up to a green, nicely built wooden hut standing at the side of the bab, and listened carefully. Surely there was a guard, but where? Surely they must be swarming all over the place. He was puzzled and not a little unnerved by the quiet. After all, this was the gateway into and out of the Forbidden Area. One expects to see guards in such a strategic position.

As he listened he heard grunting coming from inside the little hut. Sounded like something trying to get out. Something evil, perhaps. There was a tiny window, festooned with a jungle of cobwebs inside and out, and it was dark inside. Couldn't see a thing. The grunting had stopped. A Turk is like any other human being, at least in one regard. There you are squatting on your hunkers over a hole in the floor, facing Mecca for inspiration, and praying that this time it's all going to come out all right, and suddenly there's this fucking asshole peering in the window at you like Tiny Tim with his nose pressed up against the frosted pane. You think he can see you. Of course he can't see a damned thing, but the effect is the same. However, this lad couldn't quit now. He'd passed the point of no return, had broken the pain barrier. He was entirely committed. Even if the Queen of England had walked in on him it would have made no difference. He grunted again, this time with passion. The first passionate grunt in a week. For a full minute Reid's nose made a fog on the glass as he mouthed over and over, "Come on, come on! What the hell's going on in there?" Finally his eyes grew accustomed to the dim light inside the hut, and at the very moment they did he recoiled, not so much from good manners as from sheer shock. The chubby round face was looking right at him. Seemed to be smiling.

It was still some seconds before a shout went up from inside the hut. He'd obviously thought initially that the spectator was one of his mates, but when Reid had failed to do something—don't know what exactly— the man put two and two together and came close to four, perhaps four on the nose. By that time Reid was walking carefully, almost daintily, through the barricade bab, out onto the wide avenue. Not a soul. He must now get to some sort of safety, in order to regroup.

The birds were singing. He hadn't heard that sound in what seemed like ages. The sun appeared brighter out here. It would feel a lot brighter still when he made it to the Green Line. He took one final look behind him at the ghost town, something to remember, always, and then stepped out of the shade of the high archway onto the street.

"Bonjour, John," whined the soft, high pitched, almost effeminate voice at Reid's shoulder.

*   *   *

Flesh can crawl. John Reid's did as he spun around.

There was the Professor, standing, smiling, at the head of a group of uniformed Turks, their arms pointed directly at Reid. At the end of their arms were hands, and those hands held rifles. They'd been waiting for him behind a bastion on the outside of the bab. Bastards.

Reid froze. Resistance was utterly useless. It was a fair cop.

"Remember me, John?," grinned the Professor, menacingly, his expert placing of words as punctuation marks having the desired effect of both annoying and intimidating his victim.

Reid couldn't answer. The saliva wouldn't form to get his voice working.

"Congratulations," continued the Professor, his non–Parisian accent coming across even more sinister than it ever had done before. "First of all, for being alive. One of my men swore that he hit you. Second, for selecting a hiding place that escaped the attention of my searchers. You have certainly been leading our troops a merry dance. Some of them are even saying that you are a devil. But they are brainless Turks from the mainland. Nevertheless, it is rather amusing, eh?"

Reid reached to his breast pocket for a cigarette. A soldier, possibly mistaking the intention, stepped forward before Reid could extract the pack and crashed the butt of his rifle into Reid's midsection. Reid did what the man wanted. He grunted and doubled over, winded.

The Professor said something in Turkish and another two guards grabbed their bent-over prisoner by the arms.

"Your little game is over, John," intoned the Professor, smiling sadistically.

"How come you were waiting for me in exactly the right spot?," Reid asked painfully, straightening up slowly. He was pushed violently forward and frog-marched back through the bab into the Forbidden Zone.

"There are not many places to choose from. Your blundering through the early morning streets was enough to alert even these fools. You have been under surveillance for several minutes, John. It just gave me time to get to the right exit, so that I could prepare my little welcome for you, that's all."

The Professor burst into a fit of high-pitched giggling.

"What are you after, exactly?," Reid asked.

"But you know what I am after, John. The question is, what are you after? And who are you?"

They turned into a main street and were walking hard in a southerly direction, accompanied by the swarm of mute goons.

"You know who I am," Reid answered, his mind racing.

"Yes, John. You are a British agent."

"Agent? You must be crazy. I'm just a tourist. Look, let me see someone in command here."

"I am in command here," uttered the Professor smugly, "and you can demand as much as you wish in your odious British imperialist tone, but it will do you no good. Even your friend Rauf Denktash cannot help you now."

139

At the mention of Denktash's name Reid glared at the Professor. But behind the glare was more than a modicum of worry.

"You see, I know almost everything, John. How could I fail to learn that a British agent had been to visit the leader of our country? It is what was discussed that I need to determine."

"I just dropped in," Reid protested. "I didn't know if he'd see me. I didn't even know if he was there. He could have been overseas at a conference or something. Anyway, I used to be his neighbor, that's all there is to it."

"But the coded message you passed to him through his secretary?," quizzed the Professor.

So that was it. The bitch. She'd had her revenge. Just the type to sit back in her comfortable armchair and enjoy watching a man being tortured. Reid made a mental note to fuck her if he saw her again, and then to give her a hard poke right on the point of the chin.

"That wasn't a coded message, damn it. It was an old Scottish poem."

"I see. You write poems to President Denktash. He will not see me, head of the Secret Service, without an appointment, yet he interrupts his busy schedule, just like that, to admit you, because you write him poetry."

Hell! The Secret Service. So the old man was admitting it quite freely. Reid was a little afraid now. He was in big enough trouble without finding himself in the hands of the head of the Turkish Cypriot Secret Service. That odd little voice exuded menace, and paranoia too. But Reid's main mental efforts were now geared toward survival and escape.

Finally they arrived at a large building on a side street, the appearance of which was a slight improvement on rubble. But, inside, another door led to an iron stairwell, and Reid was pushed up it to the floor above. Here were rooms in a reconditioned state, and the group of men marched into a small chamber dominated by a large walnut desk with papers arranged neatly on it. A plush, black leather chair sat behind it, and the Professor occupied it as if by divine right. A few cabinets were attached to the walls. A window smirked behind the Professor as if aware that the glass in it afforded it a rare distinction, and a humble fan hung on the ceiling, attractive but doing nothing. One of the guards pressed a button on the wall and the fan blades whirred painfully into motion, sending a gentle, well controlled message of air into the room.

"Sit down, John," instructed the Professor, and he made motions to the guards holding Reid. They forced him roughly onto a plain wooden chair by the desk, and two of them stood immediately behind him, holding his shoulders. The others stood around in watchful clusters, itching for a smoke.

"I am a peace-loving man, as you know, John," said the old man, lighting a cigarette and leaning back in his chair. His words managed to sound like a threat.

He then stared at Reid for a very long time without saying a word.

"May I have a cigarette?," Reid asked finally.

"Why, of course. Forgive me," and the Professor leaned forward over the desk. The guards relaxed their hold upon a silent command from the Professor's eyes, and Reid took a much-needed drag.

"Let us start from the beginning, John. Why did you come to Cyprus?"

"I've already told you. I'm a tourist."

Another interminable stare from the Professor.

"I came here as a tourist, to see the places I grew up in as a child."

"Ah yes, that was the explanation you gave to the checkpoint, John. I know that old—how do you say it?—chestnut? Chestnuts become boring very quickly. I am bored."

The Professor stared at his cigarette as he thought.

"But you overcame the difficulties placed in your way as if they did not exist. You are the first person ever to cross the Attila Line on your own and live. Yet it was so easy for you."

"I just wanted to get across, that's all. You still think I'm a bloody spy, don't you."

"Well, John, see it from my point of view. When I first heard that an Englishman had crossed through the checkpoint, alone, without an escort, and with no official reason, I was very suspicious. Why should anyone cross into the Turkish side, I wondered. You cannot blame me for that. When you came over soon afterwards, well, I was astonished, to say the least. I followed your activities very closely, John, as you suspected that morning at breakfast when your watermelon went down the wrong way. At first I thought you may be a lone individual spying for the Greeks, possibly for profit, but the ease with which you entered the Turkish zone caused me to reconsider. You see, John, if you had ventured into Turkish Cyprus only once and never again, then you would merely have gone down in history's footnotes under the classification "border jumpers." But you came back, John, not once but many times, and you came down to Famagusta, of all places, on two occasions, and went all over the Turkish side, traveling more freely than a native."

Reid was more than a little worried now. He suddenly felt very tired.

"It was your meeting with Denktash," continued the Professor, "which finally convinced me that you are a British agent. That, tied in with your little case of breaking and entering some weeks before. I have conclusive evidence that it was you, John. And your escape from Salamis, and from the Constantia Hotel. In short, you look like an agent, you act like an agent…"

"That's ridiculous. How can anyone look like an agent?" Reid retorted. "As for the so-called breaking and entering, you're bluffing, Professor. I already told you what I was doing that night. And I've explained the Denktash meeting too. In fact, if you're the head of the Secret Service, as you claim, you should know that what I'm saying is true, that Denktash and I both lived on the same street. Why don't you call him now and get the truth? He'll tell you that he taught me that poem in the '50s when I was a kid. It was his favorite poem. I knew that would get me into his office, if nothing else would."

"John, you are a very plausible young man. Moreover, you are an exquisite liar. You do it with such utter conviction. I do believe you when you tell me these lies. That is the fun of listening to you. However, what people say and what people mean are not always the same thing, are they? And things are not always what they seem." The Professor chuckled. "I strongly suspect that your little breaking and entering was done on behalf of Mr. Denktash. So, of course he is bound to agree with what you say. Am I not close to the truth, John?"

So, what it was beginning to look like to Reid was that the Turkish minister whose house he'd robbed was a traitor working with the Professor for the overthrow of the Denktash government. That was something worth remembering.

"You're off your fucking head, Professor," Reid yelled.

The grin disappeared from the old man's mouth. He barked a furious instruction to one of the guards, who raised the butt of his rifle and brought it down lightly on the back of Reid's head, not exactly where the bullet had creased it earlier but pretty damn close. Shit, that smarted. He slumped forward in his chair, groaning. Before he could lift a hand to soothe the injured spot, the two guards behind him grabbed his arms again and forced him into an upright position. One of them held Reid's chin roughly from behind, forcing him to look at the Professor.

The old man leaned forward in his chair, an aging bird of prey. "I took the trouble to have you checked out in London, John, and you prove to be a very interesting character, as I had suspected."

Reid's eyes widened through the pain. "What do you mean—'interesting character?'" he demanded as sternly as he could. The throbbing was beginning to subside slightly in the back of his neck.

The Professor beamed. "Your nation has underestimated the Cypriot mentality ever since Sir Garnet Wolseley landed on the island in 1878," complained the old man, "and since that time the world has seen Cyprus as only Greek. Those pathetic people whining constantly for union with Greece, and the ridiculous Greece kowtowing to the British government, afraid to take a stand against a bunch of effeminate London politicians. But all the time we Turkish Cypriots were building up our brains in the shade."

Another long pause as Reid glared at the Professor, and the Professor regarded Reid with an extraordinarily deceptive benignness.

"Your father was a British Army Officer here in Cyprus."

"So what!," Reid replied, sullenly. "That's hardly a secret."

"He was in Intelligence, I discovered," ventured the Professor, slyly.

"Uh? Well, you discovered wrong then."

"My apologies. That was you, John, wasn't it. Your father, of course, was a doctor. How stupid of me to confuse the two of you."

Reid just looked at him blankly.

"If you know so much, Professor, then you'll know that I'm a writer, living a routine, normal existence in London. You'll also have found no records at all that I was in British Intelligence."

"I admit that you have recently been living in Kensington High Street, London. Kensington. That is how it is said, isn't it. I can't quite remember. And that you landed in Cyprus three weeks ago. But it is the years before, when you were in British Intelligence, that interest me."

"That's absolute bullshit," Reid exploded. "Listen, Professor. If I were a spy, and that's what you're saying, does it make any sense that I would come into Turkish Cyprus across the Green Line, something that's never been done before, with no disguise, no pretense, when I could have done it so much more cleverly, if I were a spy? I don't even speak Turkish any more."

The Professor's eyes burned into Reid's head. "You forget, John, that I know the British intimately. I grew up with them. I went to school in England. I know your methods."

"Wait a minute, Professor. You told me you couldn't speak English."

"I said I do not speak English. That does not mean that I cannot speak it," said the Professor in perfect English. "I despise the British, and their language, that is all."

Good grief, how much the Professor sounded like Reid's grandfather. Different language, but the same sentiments.

"I see. Well, if you want to talk to me any more, it'll have to be in English."

"You are a difficult customer," said the Professor with a sigh, stubbing out another cigarette, and staring at Reid, a satanic grin on his face. "Now, John, the fun is over. To serious business. I know you are a spy. I have it on good authority. I want to know what you discussed with President Denktash, and I want you to tell me why you broke into the home of one of our state officials. I want to know what it was that Denktash sent you in there for. I want to know what he knows. But all in good time. First, I would like you to tell me why you came to Cyprus in the first place."

Reid thought it was about time to try a different approach, as it was quite obvious the Professor didn't buy the tourist story. "And if I do, Professor?"

"You will live, John, you will live."

"You mean, I'll be free to go, or what?"

"Oh dear, no, John," crowed the Professor. "By live I mean you will not die."

"Let me get this straight," Reid demanded. "I tell you, you throw me into jail. That's it, huh?"

"You put it crudely, John, but very accurately."

"And if I don't ... ?"

"I suggest, John, that you do not even explore that possibility. It would lead to unpleasant feelings between us."

"Well, I'm not saying any more. So lock me up, kill me, whatever you want. But if you do, the British government will hang you by the balls, Professor."

The old man emitted a laugh that would have made Bela Lugosi shudder. "How ironic that you should choose that most interesting expression, John, for how could you have known that...," and he broke off suddenly, as if he had gone too far. He lit another cigarette before he continued. "And your ridiculous British government does not frighten me, John. This is not the nineteenth century, and you do not have any Lord Palmerston to send in the gunboats any more. You have a puppet government which bows down to America and which cannot take any international action without going through years of futile United Nations discussions. Besides, John," and he continued in a calmer vein, "I cannot let you go now anyway, even if you are, as you claim, innocent of being a spy."

"Why the hell not?," Reid shouted.

"Murder, John. Remember? You are guilty of murder. Mass murder. Two Turkish soldiers already. It is you, John, who will be hung by the testicles, unless you tell me why you came to Cyprus," and the old man emitted an incredibly sinister cackle.

Reid's heart sank, for he sensed that the old man would live up to his promise.

The Professor stubbed out yet another cigarette. "John, when it comes to physical violence, I prefer others to do it for me. I do not even like to watch. But before that becomes necessary I would rather try to reason with you."

"Fuck off, Professor," Reid said, calmly.

The Professor's face hardened, and then turned purple. He screamed an order to one of the sentries, and the soldier stepped close to Reid, and struck him between the shoulder blades with his rifle butt.

Reid grunted and squirmed about in his chair. He felt it was the appropriate thing to do. Besides, it bloody well hurt.

"I thought you were averse to witnessing violence, Professor," he spluttered, as he strove to straighten himself in his seat.

"I do not call that violence, John. I hope you do not. If you do, then you must have led a very sheltered life, and later you will suffer greatly. Now, be sensible."

"Professor," said Reid, trying to be calm, "put yourself in my position..."

"No. Thank you, John. I would never do that. Just tell me why you are in Cyprus."

"Well, I'm not the old-fashioned British World War II flying hero type with a stiff upper lip and wooden nuts. I don't see any reason why I should undergo torture if I don't need to. It's just that these guards make me nervous."

The Professor laughed. "Ah, John. You are so transparent. These guards are necessary for my protection. You are a dangerous criminal."

"They put me off," Reid continued, struggling for credibility. "They just make me defensive."

The Professor stared at Reid, unsure of what exactly was afoot.

"All right, John. I shall place them outside the door. But I insist on leaving two in here."

"Okay, Professor, at least you're willing to compromise. That's better than nothing."

The old man grinned smugly. He was getting somewhere at last. He gave a command. All but two of the soldiers trooped out of the room, shutting the door behind them.

"Now, John, the information, if you please."

"Before we go on, one thing puzzles me," Reid said, "why you didn't have me arrested that morning at the Altun Tabya. You had the chance."

"Ah," replied the Professor, smiling. "You were too quick for me, John, on that occasion. However, the speed with which you departed removed any doubt from my mind about your real profession. By the time I returned to the hotel later that morning you had already crossed through the Ledra Palace checkpoint. I must admit to being very relieved when you returned a few weeks later. I thought I had lost you forever."

Suddenly he slapped the desk with the palm of his hand. "You will cooperate. Now. Do you understand?"

He was on his feet and his face was purple again. Spittle flew obliquely from his mouth in long, thin gobs.

"Go to hell, Professor," Reid said bravely.

"Very well." The Professor was calming down, but was still red in the face. "You will now be escorted to what I might term a place of interrogation. It is three floors below this one, a long way underground, so it will be fairly uncomfortable, I'm afraid. And don't think your screams will attract the attention of sympathetic passersby, because there are no passersby in this part of the city, as you may have gathered. We like to

146

keep the citizens out of this area, for many secret reasons. This is one of those reasons."

As the Professor stood up, stubbing out his cigarette and putting the confiscated British passport into his coat pocket, Reid wondered what form the interrogation would take. As if in answer to his thoughts, the Professor smiled maliciously and then signaled the two guards to close in on their prisoner.

"John, being an intelligence officer you have obviously been trained to resist the more modern, sophisticated methods of torture, such as brainwashing and deprivation. Well, I will not be conducting such pleasantries. You, John, will be subjected to the more basic instruments of pain."

Reid shuddered violently. Although he'd been truthful in his boast that death didn't worry him, he'd always doubted his ability to withstand real physical torture; the scientific form of sustained bestiality that you read about in Gestapo novels.

"I thought you didn't get involved in this physical violence," he grimaced, mouth dry, images of terror rushing through his head.

"It is not violence, John. Dear me, no. I would prefer to call it scientific exploration. My field of study has been, for many years, and for my own personal reasons, premature aging. I take great delight in operating on the human body, without anesthetic of course. And I am a specialist. My field of study is the genitals."

*   *   *

Reid didn't know whether it was the thought of losing his bollocks or the highly menacing tone of the Professor at that moment, but as the guard on his left reached for the door handle, Reid grabbed him around the waist and, using him as support, kicked his right leg back in mule-fashion so swiftly that the readied rifle of the second soldier was knocked clean out of his hands and was spinning up toward the ceiling before the Turks knew what was happening. Reid's right knee then shot forward, connecting with the coccyx of the unfortunate soldier whose torso Reid had just released. The sentry let out a shrill cry of enormous pain and crumpled to the floor, dropping his rifle as he did so. By the time the other, airborne, weapon had begun its descent, Reid had kicked his weight back into the room in a style reminiscent of a shot-putter as he shifts his body

147

to the front of the circle. He was actually behind the Professor as the rifle smashed to the ground.

Reid's left arm was around the Professor's neck, the old man's Adam's apple nestling into the crook of a Japanese stranglehold. The guard on Reid's right was actually standing still, his face contorted with pain, massaging the index finger which had been broken when the gun was kicked out of his grip. The door was flung open from the outside, crashing against the gasping Turk who lay prostrate clutching the bottom of his spine.

"Professor, you know what to do," Reid shouted, ferociously, his knee throbbing from the force of the blow given to the now whimpering soldier. As the others poured in from the hall outside, Reid backed up, dragging the Professor with him toward the desk like a rag doll.

The Professor choked out instructions to the soldiers. They slowly lowered their weapons and looked on, confused, awaiting guidance. Reid, now in a somewhat professorial mode, determined to give them that guidance.

"We're walking out of here, Professor. Now," he barked. The Professor, his body trembling, spoke some words in Turkish to the guards. Reid reached inside the Professor's coat with his right hand. "I'll take this, old man," and he replaced the passport in his own trouser pocket.

Reid reached backwards, his eyes glued to the sentries. "Tell your men to put their guns down on the floor, and to walk over there, by the window. Do it, Professor, or you're dead."

The Professor spelled out hoarse instructions to the men, who complied with little apparent reluctance. As they crossed to the window, Reid circled warily, keeping the Professor in front of him at all times.

"Believe me, Professor, I can kill you with one twist of my arm."

"Don't hurt me, please," choked the Professor, as Reid made his point by tightening the stranglehold.

"Hah. You can dish it out, but you can't take it, huh?"

The shoe was on the other foot now. Amazing how often in the movies the villain lets that happen. He reveals his evil scheme, down to the last detail, confident he's addressing a dead duck—who then turns the tables.

He opened the door and yanked the Professor after him through to the hallway, down the stairs and out through the ruined vestibule onto the street. The soldiers didn't seem to be following.

The brilliant sunshine was welcomed warmly. Reid took in a deep breath of fresh air, something he thought he might never again experience. As he marched the Professor in front of him, he looked up to the window of the room from which he'd just escaped. Leaning out were several of the soldiers, curiously surveying the scene below them.

"You'll never get away with this," snarled the Professor. Reid jerked cruelly on his stranglehold, causing the old man to retch.

"I can't believe you actually said that, Professor. Which movie did you get that out of? We're going to walk out of this ghost town. Through the gate, the way we came in, and if we run into any soldiers, and they give us trouble, you die before I do. I will not hesitate. Remember. One swift move, and you'll be on your way to hell. How do you like that for a line, eh?"

"They will finish you off. You're crazy," blurted the Professor in falsetto, frightened by his plight.

"Maybe, but you won't live to see it, old man," and Reid twisted savagely on the Professor's larynx.

The twist was done so unexpectedly that the Professor threw up. It wasn't all that much puke, comparatively speaking, and it splattered noiselessly on the ground, which was just as well because if any of it had landed on Reid he would have been mad as hell. The worst thing in the world is when someone throws up on you during a moment of crisis.

As they arrived at the first intersection Reid looked right and left. Left would take them to the bab. Right would bring them to the office building where Reid had spent the night curled up and blacked out in the little cubby hole. After a few seconds' hesitation he jerked the Professor to the left and headed off toward the bab. The old bastard was making continual clicking sounds that sounded quite pathetic, sort of like a kookaburra being roasted alive on a barbecue. Reid had evidently damaged the Professor's throat. They arrived at the bab.

"Not a word out of place, old man," hissed Reid, holding the Professor like a toy in front of him, and pushing his way through the arched gateway for the second time that morning.

The three guards outside on the avenue stared—startled—as the two men exited in their strange fashion.

"Tell them to throw down their rifles, Professor," Reid barked savagely. The Professor's Turkish command was obeyed instantly and they were across the street and walking down it toward the old park on their right.

The avenue seemed deserted as they swung right, into the park. This park, with its rich, brown, pine-needled earth, brought back countless memories again for Reid as they tramped over it toward the zoo.

A few weeks before, Reid had been lamenting the disappearance of the animals from this zoo, especially the peacocks. Errol, the Turkish Cypriot with whom he'd been engaged in conversation, had bitterly remarked, in bitingly good Anglo-Saxon, "Fuck the peacocks. What about the people?" It had seemed rather an apt reply, or rather a rap across the knuckles.

Reid and the Professor crossed through the former gardens to the street beyond.

With Reid pushing and dragging the old man up the hill they ran into two soldiers emerging from the other side of the incline. The squaddies snatched their rifles off their shoulders and aimed them immediately at Reid's head. The Professor wisely shouted out in Turkish, and they lowered their weapons. Reid pushed his captive past them to the top of the hill.

He was in unknown territory now. Many years before he would have known exactly what he would have seen on the other side of this hill, but it was 1979 now and the sight which greeted him was a poignant reminder of the tragedy of the Turkish invasion. Nevertheless, in its basics, the view was just what he'd anticipated and hoped for. Halfway down the hill lay the Green Line, stretching from left to right as far as one could see before trees and buildings blocked the view. At the bottom of the hill, beyond the Turkish barrier of barbed wire and oil drums piled on top of each other, was the deserted no-man's-land, which led directly to the Greek barrier, which complemented the Turkish line in its arrangement. The two enemy sides just stood there, facing each other across this deserted stretch of once-busy highway leading to the suburbs of Famagusta.

This peculiar linear setup sometimes led to a curious phenomenon. Two former friends would occasionally spot each other on opposite sides of the Green Line. They'd grown up together, in the same village. Now they were enemies, in different countries, but able to shout friendly greetings to each other across the Line. Although this practice was not encouraged by either side, it happened, and not infrequently, usually as the only form of communication between ordinary Greeks and Turks on the island—telephone service having been completely severed between the two sides. One side could not phone the other except by a complicated and costly (and bugged) intermediary process using international exchanges.

"We're going over, Professor," Reid said coolly, and gave the old man a shove down the hill. The guards, situated every twenty yards or so along the Line, turned to see this most unusual duo walking down the hill toward them. Two of them came forward. The Professor choked out something in Turkish again and once more resistance melted. Reid pushed the Professor through the sentries and oil drums, and continued down the road, walking sideways-on while he held the Professor, in order to try to cover both ends. He didn't want to get shot up the ass by the Turks.

They'd gone about twenty yards in this manner, about halfway to the Greek barrier, when, all of a sudden a shot rang out. This was something Reid had thought might happen, but he'd gambled against it. They were being sniped at from the Greek zone, his own side, as it were.

"Don't shoot! I'm British!," he hollered in Greek over his shoulder. "Don't shoot!"

He stepped back a few paces, trying to work out the safest position. He smiled as broadly as he could under the circumstances and waved at the Greeks with his free hand for all he was worth. A bullet tore up some tarmac in the road. The Professor was trembling violently and making small squeaking noises.

"Hey, don't shoot, fellas!," Reid shouted again, this time in English. By this time a few more rifles were singing. The Greeks evidently thought that two Turks were trying to cross into their zone, two Turks pretending to be British. An old trick, perhaps.

A hail of warning bullets poured into the area. Cursing the irony of the situation, Reid had no choice but to let go of the Professor, and run to cover back up the hill behind the Turkish lines, in order to save his own skin. Keeping a hold on the Professor under such trying circumstances would have quadrupled his chances of being hit, as the Greek projectiles now looked as if they were becoming a little more than just warnings.

Dodging between bullets, if that's possible, Reid dived behind a couple of oil drums, landing on his gut on the roadway, breathing hard. The Professor had been left to his own fate.

A guttural order in Turkish caused Reid to look up, and he got to his

151

feet at the beckoning of the armed uniforms in front of him. They were not amused. Just at this moment the Professor sprinted to safety at a speed incongruous with his age. As Reid watched the old man gasping for air he realized only too well that he'd failed in his bid to cross the Green Line. Not only was he now in deadly danger, he wasn't at all sure that he'd live through the next five minutes.

*   *   *

With astonishing symmetry, spittle was flying from both sides of the old man's mouth as he screamed Turkish abuse at Reid. Then, all of a sudden, his arms went to his sides, his tongue flopped out, and he gasped. Reid thought, for just a moment, that the Professor was going to keel over, but he didn't. He looked around him and then ordered the guards into action. Reid was struck repeatedly by several rifle butts, mostly to the body, and it was all he could do to fend off the more potentially damaging. He reeled forward, holding his kidneys.

"You will pay dearly for this," yelled the Professor, who now began panting wretchedly again, his oxygen-starved lungs grasping for the elusive air after his exertion. The soldiers from the Green Line had gathered around now, and more were coming from the top of the hill. Reid recognized a few of them from earlier in the day, proving that not all Turks look alike. The Professor, recovering slowly, very slowly, shouted instructions to them as they approached. One of them ran off the way he had come, and the others rallied around their chief. The old man was dictating orders continually, and looked about to explode with rage.

One of the soldiers stepped forward toward a perplexed, scared John Reid, and struck him on the temple with his rifle. Reid sagged to the ground, his vision clouding as he began to black out. He was certain to be killed here and now, on the Green Line.

But when he came around a few minutes later he saw the Professor, chest pumping in and out, standing over him, and the curious, startled faces of the young soldiers looking on. Reid made an attempt to get up, but they had tied his hands and feet.

"Now you will be unable to perform any of your little tricks in future." The head of the Turkish Cypriot Secret Service glowered between heavy breaths.

Reid's hands and feet had been tied with two army belts. He felt sure this was only a temporary measure until more secure fastenings could be obtained. He figured those were on their way now.

"You can't blame me for trying, Professor," he tried to joke. He felt physically very nauseated. The Professor failed to see the humor in Reid's comment and lunged at his prostrate captive, his foot connecting viciously with Reid's ribs.

"Shut up, you swine," screamed the Professor, his fury quite unabated. He kicked Reid again in the same place.

Reid rolled over, in great pain, his arms strapped behind him making things worse for him. He lay on his front, gasping and squirming.

"I am going to teach you a lesson you will never forget," exploded the Professor, a demonic look on his face. He sprang onto Reid's back, straddling him like a rider on a horse. He grasped Reid's belted wrists and pushed them up toward the shoulder blades.

"I am going to dislocate your shoulders, English pig," he screamed hysterically, as he struggled to push Reid's arms upward. The harder he did so the more Reid resisted, naturally. The fact that he shouted "Scotch, not English, you little shit," didn't help matters, but the old man didn't have the strength to accomplish his task, so, furiously and with great frustration, he yelled to a nearby soldier. The uniform put his gun on the ground and stepped over to the grim scene to become a participant instead of a mere spectator. He assumed a crouching position over Reid's head and faced the Professor as if the two of them were on a seesaw or in a rowboat. He then proceeded to assist the old man in his sadistic task, by pulling on Reid's arms while the Professor pushed.

The pain started to reach Reid's shoulders, an increasingly sharp pain racing throughout his back. He knew he couldn't resist much longer. And he could sense that the soldier was holding back, probably out of pity for the man upon whose head he was sitting. As the Professor screamed in exhortation, Reid frantically attempted to counter their combined efforts by summoning up all his strength and will power. But, lying on his front, with his hands tied behind him, was the worst possible position from which to try and match the power of two men engaged on such a mission.

Just as he thought his time was up, the soldier released his grip and stood up. There were no words, he just let go and stood up. For a moment the Professor just held Reid's hands, but it had all gone slack. Reid's arms sprang back to their original position, and the relief from the pressure caused a momentary dagger-like pain to shoot through his shoulders. He lay heavily, breathing hard, his teeth gradually unclenching, and his mind whirling.

Then the Professor got to his feet and as Reid glanced up he saw the old man kick the soldier in the balls. Reid thought the blow would knock the little uniform off his feet, and the man did, indeed, go down, with nary a grunt, and stayed there. At the same moment a black Mercedes shot over the crest of the hill from the direction of Varosha and slid to a halt in front of the grisly spectacle. The soldier who had been sent by the Professor some time before jumped neatly out from the front passenger side of the vehicle and ran over to the scene, exclaiming something in Turkish.

The old man appeared to think for a moment. Then three soldiers grabbed Reid and swung him to his feet. Two of them got hold of his torso, while the third man held his legs. Then they carried him like a sack of coal to the limousine. The Professor opened the rear door and they bundled him inside. There were three people in the car. The driver in the front, and in the huge back seat, by the far window, an armed soldier and, next to him, in the middle, much to Reid's surprise and alarm—Vanessa. She seemed to be completely unfettered.

He was placed next to Vanessa and an armed guard took up residence on his left. The Professor climbed into the front passenger seat, the driver jumped into his, and they were away. No further ado.

Down the other side of the hill, to the bottom, passing the old zoo on their left. All was silence within the car. They came to the Varosha barrier and a few sentries came forward from a bab new to Reid, but one of several which led into the deserted quarter.

The Professor leaned out, barking in Turkish, and the three guards let the car pass immediately into the Forbidden Zone, saluting stiffly as they faded back to their posts.

"This is it," thought Reid, his hands trying to work loose the belt that encompassed his wrists. "It's the torture chamber for sure."

On entering Varosha they turned left, and the car purred along the main avenue, hugging the barricade, until they arrived at the bab which Reid knew so well from recent events. They passed slowly out of it, out of Varosha again, and turned right, heading toward the old walled city of Famagusta.

Reid was puzzled and not a little frightened. Going in and out of the ghost town like that had confused him a little until he remembered there was no route more direct than the one they'd taken. Okay, but if they weren't going to the Forbidden Zone, and the torture chamber, then where the hell were they going?

The Professor was in an extremely emotional state of mind. Perhaps he was out for immediate revenge on Reid, as that same Reid had recently humiliated him in front of the Turkish soldiers. He couldn't just kill Reid like that, out in the open. Even the Professor couldn't get away with that. Perhaps he was taking him to a secluded spot. This could be serious trouble indeed. But Reid didn't feel like asking where they were going, and no one seemed about to volunteer the information.

They passed an ever growing number of troops. The Palm Beach Hotel flashed by, with glimpses of sand in between the bombed-out buildings. Then they were cruising down Delphi Street, with the Constantia Hotel towering over the Mediterranean rocks on their right. Soon they were at the old walled city, and swinging down the flower-lined avenue which formed the start of the Salamis Road, past the exterior of the Venetian walls of Old Famagusta, and then onto the country highway, heading north.

Reid couldn't begin to guess where they were being taken. The Professor's silence seemed to promise only ill. Reid looked wistfully at the countryside he remembered so well as the limousine sped along the almost deserted road.

Within a few minutes they were at the very entrance to the Salamis ruins where Reid had brought Vanessa the day before. He figured that for some oblique reason the Professor was going to take him back to this very scene. It did seem fitting perhaps. Maybe the old man was going to eradicate Reid in the Amphitheatre or offer him as a sacrifice to Zeus. But he guessed wrong. The car sped by on its northward course, heading toward Trikomo—birthplace of Colonel George Grivas—and Reid looked casually at the speedometer. 110. Reminiscent of the Greek taxi drivers in the old days. Those cabbies, like drivers in all hot climates, loved to get the most out of their cars, as they did with their women, with little regard for safety or a healthy lifespan. Just keep her lubricated and filled up, put your foot down hard, push her to the limit, and when the big-end goes, trade her in for a new model.

The driver slowed down and veered left at a fork, his tires screeching

155

as he took the corner at an insane 70. They were now on the Lefkoniko Road. Finally the Professor broke the silence. "You may think you are on your way to Nicosia, John. But I have to disappoint you. We are going to Kyrenia, far from the Attila Line and any temptation. You will not embarrass me again," and he turned back to survey the road ahead.

So that was it. Kyrenia. But then what? Was the old man going to imprison Reid in the castle there?

The Professor half turned again. "Oh, John, you will find Kyrenia has changed much since you last would have seen it. I am afraid I cannot offer you a sightseeing tour of the town, but you shall see some of it as we pass through. I shall order the driver to slow down to a respectable fifty miles per hour as we do so, so that you can observe the sights. But that is as slow as I intend this car to go, John, so please don't let any idea enter your head of trying to jump from the car, or 'bail out' as I believe you would say. That would only, er, endanger your health, so to speak. But then, you are not sitting in a window seat, are you." He cackled manically and turned back to face the road.

By now the car was slowing to a mere 50 or 60 in order to negotiate the worsening condition of the road's surface.

As the Professor turned around, smiling, Reid had already loosened the belts around his hands and feet to such an extent that he could slip them off at a moment's notice. At that instant he saw it coming. His right hand was in front of him, forming a cradle for his head. Everyone catapulted forward.

*　*　*

The driver of the limousine had as much chance of seeing the motorcyclist as Reid had—more—but his concentration hadn't been there. It should have been; the car was rounding the bend at close to sixty. The 50 c.c. Simpson was on the wrong side of the road anyway, the little yellow machine chugging away nonchalantly as if the rider had all the time in the world, which, of course, he did. He saw the big, black Mercedes only when it was on top of him, and despite a desperate veering to his left he was smashed violently and beyond all mortal hope as the driver of the limo naturally lost control and the car plunged into the ditch.

The six occupants of the car were jerked forward like marionettes in the hands of a crazed puppet-master as the car ground to a crunching halt in the ditch, its wheels whirring as the reliable engine kept running. The guard to Vanessa's right had evidently broken his puny little neck when his head had crashed into the seat in front of him. He was sitting in his place, his head lolling forward at a bizarre angle, his very pink tongue sticking out between rows of fascinatingly serrated teeth. His rifle, which had been waggling alternately at Reid and Vanessa throughout the whole trip, had managed to find its way underneath Reid's freed legs. Luckily it hadn't gone off. Reid was just about to go for it when the soldier on his left, who'd been projected over the top of the Professor's seat into the back of the old man himself, began to recover and struggle to get himself back into the rear. Reid grabbed the soldier's torso and pushed him further into the Professor, a move which took Reid right over to the left door.

As he grasped the silver handle and flung open the door he looked to the front of the car. The Professor was buried on the floor, almost entirely out of view, and the driver was patently dead, his head rammed through the steering-wheel.

Reid grabbed Vanessa, and they were out of the limo, into the ditch. They were shaken up, but both began sprinting south, by instinct, over the shrubby wasteland, jumping over several more ditches and down into a wadi. They were out of sight of the car now, and so they pulled up, breathing hard. It was beginning to get dark. Reid, for one, was so tired, he could hardly stand up. They climbed to the top of the other side of the valley and could just make out a roadway to the south, about five hundred yards in the distance. They made their way across to it, and cautiously set off down the road to their right, ready at any moment to dive into the ditch should they spot any headlights coming from either direction.

It wasn't long before they struck the village. It was quite dark now, and not a light shone from any of the buildings. As they drew level with the first of the houses, it became obvious that this tiny hamlet, consisting of a string of twenty or so old homes along the left of the road, was absolutely uninhabited.

Reid pushed open the door of the first shack and tried to make out what was inside. He poked his head in, and recoiled instantly from the fetid smell of decay. They walked rapidly to the next dwelling. This had possibly been a store of some sort at one time, but there were vast holes in the walls, so they passed to the next. Here they couldn't find the door, let alone get in. The fourth building offered a more satisfactory arrangement within its walls, for Reid's eyes, as they became accustomed to the dark, fell on an old bed frame.

Damned sight better than lying on the floor. He tested the old springs within the iron frame. Sleeping on bare springs is better than nothing.

He made sure the door was securely shut, and then they both eased ourselves carefully into position on the bed. It just about took their combined widths, provided they pressed together. Trying to ignore the slightly nauseating odor of must and dog shit, Reid fell asleep. He presumed Vanessa did the same.

* * *

Turkish voices pierced his dream like an alarm clock on a Monday morning. It took a few seconds to work out where he was but it was Vanessa standing right in the rays of sunlight pouring in through the chinks in the wooden door that brought him sharply back to the moment. He could see quite clearly the interior of the room in which they'd found refuge.

It had evidently been a Turkish village, probably deserted since the 1964 troubles, when so many Turks had first shifted around the island as refugees. It was a one room house, in the strictest sense of the word, but with an indoor toilet, the traditional hole in the corner, a luxury in those olden days of communal outdoor privies.

The wooden floor was rotten, demolished by ants over the years, large square areas of naked soil poking through. A small window in the wall had been boarded up and the remains of a big Oriental carpet stood as testimony to the persons, or probably one man and his wife, who had resided there. There was nothing else in the room save the old bed frame.

This archeological survey took only a moment. Far more pressing were the voices outside. The village had definitely been deserted, no question. Reid eased himself painfully off the bed, or rather, the springed surface enclosed in the unsympathetic metal frame, and Vanessa needlessly, but with good intentions, put her finger to her lips. Reid looked through a crack in the door. His eye became glued to the crack upon seeing what lay outside. Two Turkish soldiers were sitting in the front seat of a jeep, eating what was obviously breakfast, and chattering away like colobus monkeys in a zoo.

Could have been a routine patrol. But more than likely they were looking for company, the very same company they didn't yet know they had. Life is a surprise.

The more Reid stared at those bastards noshing on their damned breakfast the hungrier he became. It dawned on him that it had been exactly two days since either he or Vanessa had partaken of any food, before the Salamis trip, and then that had only been a light breakfast. Reid also felt desperately thirsty, and his mouth felt like a sewer, similar to the way one feels the morning after downing an entire bottle of Drambuie. Like the underneath of a kangaroo's balls after a good hop through the outback.

Through the chink in the door he could survey the whole street and the fronts of some of the neighboring shacks. He knew there couldn't be only two uniforms belonging to that jeep; Turkish motorized patrols usually traveled in sixes. Economy, if not strategy, prohibited a more generous allotment. He peered harder through the door, trying to increase the angle of his vision, but he couldn't see or hear a damn thing except the two soldiers in the vehicle.

He sat on the edge of the bed. He'd be enjoying this a lot more if he wasn't so hungry. There were only two of them in the jeep. The others had to be somewhere nearby. If he and Vanessa could divert the attention of the two in the jeep, maybe they could steal not only the food and water but also, hopefully, the vehicle itself. Reid knew he had to eat and drink something soon, Vanessa too, otherwise they were a couple of gone geese. But being hungry always did make Reid aggressive.

However, he knew that if they opened the door the Turks would spot them the moment they set foot outside. And then what? They were only twenty yards away. He and Vanessa would have to rush them. On the other hand, there may be a way to sneak up on them. But the question really remained, where were the others? That's what Reid needed to know. That, and where the hell was John Wayne?

His eyes fell on the boarded-up window again. He crossed the room, inspected it, and discovered that, although the planks had been nailed into the wooden frame from left to right, and neatly at that, they were now quite loosened with age. Gently, but firmly, he pulled one of them away. A mass of light streamed in. Reid blinked, like Anthony Quinn in *Barabbas* when he comes out of the salt mine after twenty years.

Directly ahead of him was the mud brick wall of the hovel next door, about two feet away. However, between the houses there was a tiny, bare alleyway running from the street through to the arid land behind the row of dwellings.

Hastily, but silently, Reid removed the remaining timbers and leaned bodily out of the window. He could hear the two breakfasters talking, but could see nothing except the alley beneath him and the wall facing him. Motioning to Vanessa to remain where she was, he pulled himself up and over the ledge, dropping noiselessly to the alley floor below.

Edging sideways through the narrow passage he came to the rear of the houses and looked out over the waste ground toward the South.

A few scattered outbuildings stood forlorn, but aside from these and a long, rusty water trough about fifty yards away, nothing jumped out. Then, slowly, he began to make out voices and laughter coming from the distance, beyond the horizon. Because of the way the land fell away into a valley some two or three hundred yards ahead, he couldn't make out exactly how many there were, or what they were doing. It was obviously the rest of the Turkish group.

No point crossing the wasteland. Back to the eaters. How to get them away from the jeep, so he and Vanessa could steal it, without getting their asses blown off.

He picked up a stone from the ground. If he were to throw it against one of the neighboring shacks, or perhaps onto a roof, would it attract their attention? Maybe. Maybe not. They might consider it to be one of their mates horsing around. Probably would, indeed. No, a better plan was coming.

Plans do come to you if you wait. It's like trying to get onto an expressway. You wait and the bastards won't let you on. Is there ever going to be a break in this stream of traffic? But, sure there is, sooner or later, it'll come to you, and you'll just merge right in, even if you have to wait all day. Now actual voices were coming to Reid from the far valley. They had suddenly risen to a startling new volume. He focused quickly. Four naked and seminaked dog soldiers appeared over the blue horizon from the dip beyond, laughing and shouting. They were in no hurry, picking their way carefully, barefooted, bare-assed, across the rocky, barren land, dicks waggling. It was a fair comic sight. Reid figured that this village must have been built just over the rim of the Pediaios River Valley, and this must be a rare section of that stream which was wet at this time of year. In short the Turks had been for a swim.

They were making their way slowly through a patch of sharp stones. In an instant Reid was out in the open, his back to the hovel wall, jumping up and down silently, waving his arms like a madman. Sure enough, it didn't take long before the swimmers spotted him, and then the shouting started.

Meanwhile he'd been walking slowly back down the alleyway. He looked in their open window, and told Vanessa in a whisper that as soon as the two squaddies disappeared from the jeep, and that it was safe for her to do so, she was to open the front door and make a run for it, and that he'd meet her at the jeep in just a few seconds. He reached the other end of the alley, and waited. If the two breakfasters chose his alley to come down, he'd retrace his steps rather smartly and wait behind the back wall, wait for them to overshoot and then beat them back to the jeep. He knew he wouldn't have much time, in fact it would be very hairy, especially if they brought their hardware with them. But he guessed that there were other alleyways, closer to the jeep, which would enable them to make a more direct run to their screaming companions. Reid was taking a gamble, but not a very big one.

At the back of the houses the swimmers were struggling into baggy white underpants, and struggling desperately and hopelessly to run over the unfriendly surface. At the front the two uniforms leaped out of the jeep, ran through another alleyway, and burst out into the wasteland three or four houses down.

Reid was across the street to the jeep in a matter of seconds, almost as fast as Bullet Bob got away from the blocks in the 100 meters final at Tokyo. Vanessa made it at the same time, and they vaulted over the front passenger door almost in tandem. Reid arrived on the driver's seat only a tenth of a second after Vanessa had swept up the food package that was lying on it, and thrown it in the back to join the six rifles that had been left there. Even before his bum hit the warm seat cover, Reid had turned the ignition key and released the hand brake. Now, if these boys had been Germans, say, he wouldn't have gotten away with all this, but they were Turks.

The engine spluttered into a form of primeval life—and died. His fingers twitched the key again. Nothing. Vanessa looked at him, tense. Reid was also tense at this stage, bloody tense. As he tried to excite interest in the motor again, the two uniformed Ottomans emerged onto the street between a house and what could, at one time, have been a sub–post office. The swimmers had apprised them of the approximate situation.

Reid had a choice now. Whether to go for a gun and let loose on the unarmed men rushing the jeep, or to keep at the ignition key. This time, as if in answer to a prayer, the engine coughed and immediately began to purr. He rammed his foot down on the clutch, shifting into second, and was off like a rocket, just as one of the Turks made a leap for the rear of the jeep. With the little soldier's hands clasped firmly over the metal edge, and his heels dug firmly into the roadway, Reid bullied his way through the transmission into top. The uniform continued to hold on.

Very soon they were doing about sixty. Only then did Reid look behind him, to see in the distance the outraged soldiers wriggling about on the road like tadpoles in a jar. He didn't notice, or even dream of looking for, the hands of the Turk who was holding on like grim death to the rear of the jeep, being dragged along. Towed along like a water-skier, the fellow was taking a fearful amount of punishment. What could have been going through his mind is anybody's guess, and how his boot-heels were standing up to the massive friction caused by the drag could only pay tribute to the West German footwear manufacturers who supplied the Turkish Army.

After four or five minutes had taken them as many miles, Reid slowed down and pulled into the side of the road. He jerked on the hand-brake but left the engine running.

"Vanessa, get the food, would you," he suggested rather urgently, and she complied, reaching into the back seat. She'd just picked up the bagged breakfast of one of the Turks when she froze. She'd finally seen the hands, gripping the back of the jeep like a vise. Then Reid looked and saw them too. Both of them were, for a moment, incapable of moving, so great was their surprise.

Nobody moved. It was like a painting. Vanessa had the bag in her left hand, and Reid was frozen in the motion of getting out of the jeep. The Turk was not forthcoming. Didn't take long for something to happen, though. Vanessa dropped the bag and Reid was up and over the back of the jeep and onto the roadside behind the Turk in a single bound, feet planted on the tarmac in a classic position of defense.

The little uniform was hanging grimly to the jeep, more dead than alive, and Reid wondered how the hell he'd managed to survive, let alone maintain a hold over that whole distance, at that speed. The soldier's face was black with dirt, and he seemed to be only faintly conscious as he continued to hang.

Reid stared at him, a little confused. The drag had, in actual fact, taken its toll of the soldier's boot-heels, for blood was oozing from beneath his olive-green trouser cuffs. The Turk wasn't moving now, not at all. Reid readied himself for a trick, knowing that at any moment the man could go for the guns in the back seat of the jeep.

But the move never came. He kicked the man gingerly, springing back immediately, ready. But no response. He shook him then, but the uniform remained still, glued to the side of the vehicle.

He carefully felt inside the man's collar, holding his hand on the man's carotid artery for several seconds.

Vanessa's voice to the side of Reid said, quite flatly, "He's dead, isn't he."

The drag had been too much for him. He'd simply expired, without a word, his grip on the metal as fierce as when he'd first put it there. Reid pried the hands from the jeep and dragged the body into a ditch a little way off the road. It was then that he noticed that not only had the Turk's boots been eroded by the drag, so had his actual heels and the soles of his feet. Not one toe remained on the dead Turk's stumps.

Reid wondered at man's endurance and determination, even in a little Turkish dog-soldier, and how one hangs on to life, resisting the alternative, until the end. He returned to the jeep, astonished and saddened by the experience. But hunger was digging into his gut. It's only human conditioning that says you can't eat after a thing like this. Reid's stomach said eat.

He and Vanessa climbed into their respective seats in the still-purring vehicle and she, then Reid, took a long swig of water from one of the canteens. It was better than an orgasm. They then started into the bag of grub, Vanessa desperately ripping open the paper to get to the contents. Reid had half expected to find all manner of weird Seljuk fare and was amazed to get an egg sandwich and a metal can full of baked beans. Cold baked beans. They were devoured rapidly by a ravenous man and an equally ravenous woman, and then another long draught of water.

Reid looked into the rear of the jeep again. On closer inspection, on the floor, he found several other bags of breakfast belonging to the swimmers. He took two of them, gave one to Vanessa, and they broke them

163

open, like savages. Another egg sandwich. But they were hungry beggars, and tucked in. A chocolate bar, in unmarked silver wrapping, was lurking at the bottom of each of the bags, and that went the same route. Pity there was no coffee. Reid reached into his pocket for a cigarette, then got out of the vehicle, and strolled over to the dead soldier. He looked curiously down on the little Turk, and lit his cigarette.

There had been something vaguely heroic about the way this fellow had died. Byron might have referred to it in one of his cantos. Reid wished that somehow the soldier's crazy feat could be recognized. Immortalized, perhaps. Even though this little soldier would have killed them with no hesitation. Forget it. Spit on him. I spit on your grave. Nevertheless, as he took his first drag, he looked at the soldier again. "This one's for you, pal."

Reid looked into the distance behind him. No way the other Turkish soldiers could attempt a pursuit. Reid could picture them in the roadway, hopping mad, castigating themselves and each other, preparing a story for their superiors.

Then they heard it. Something was coming. Up ahead. Reid stared down the road. Far away, a vehicle was on the road, coming their way, from the direction he and Vanessa were heading in. He rushed back to the jeep, jumped in, yelled to Vanessa to get in the back and lie down, released the hand brake, forced the engine into gear, and pulled off toward the fast approaching enemy. For that is who it was. He could see it now, clearly. A jeep full of Turkish uniforms.

Under these circumstances, instinct, based on experience, tells a man the choice he must make for the best chance at survival. Reid knew he couldn't return the way he'd come. Three reasons. One, it was taking him away from his objective, which was to escape. Two, it would also threaten the two of them with capture by known opponents, who may well have got their act together by now and be waiting for them back at the village. Three, it would lose him the advantage of surprise. So, his best bet was to plunge on. They would see him, for sure, anyway—but he hoped not Vanessa—as they drew closer.

But then, the old cogitation starts taking over from instinct. The more time you have to think, the more you think, and the more you think the more you steer away from instinct. Instinct is a primitive impulse. We're meant to be 20th century, and all that. Did the oncoming Turks know who was in the jeep? Had some radio contact been made? Had another jeep turned up at the village and rescued the swimmers? Were Reid and Vanessa going to be caught in the middle like a couple of knackwursts in a rye bread sandwich if another jeep were to roar up behind them, full of yelling, shooting dervishes?

He glanced quickly behind him. Nothing. But maybe these boys who were now approaching had been warned anyway. Maybe they would just open fire as they came nearer. Reid would just have to take the gamble. If he were to shoot off the road they'd be alerted for sure, no matter what. If he pressed on he couldn't fight it out with them. So, he'd have to play it cool, that's all. He was doing forty as the two vehicles came within two hundred yards of each other. All Reid could do now was sit tight and hope for the best. He wedged his cigarette firmly between his teeth with a determined gesture.

To his relief a few hands went up in greeting. It wasn't until they were on top of him that the Turks realized something was amiss. But by that time Reid had his twinkle toes down hard and was streaking away from them, leaving the Turks shouting in bewilderment as they slowly, but efficiently, turned their jeep around, and shot back down the road in pursuit.

Reid could only hope to outrace them now. He kept his foot flat to the floor, coaxing every bit of power out of the vehicle, and hoping to hell another enemy jeep wouldn't appear on the road ahead of him.

He hardly saw the town before he was in it. In an instant he knew where he was. The sleepy little town of Prastio, hardly deserving of the appellation "town," hadn't changed at all since he was a kid. He knew it well. He'd often cycled up the Larnaka–Lefkoniko Road to this point in the '60s. He suddenly realized that the road he'd just come down had also been one of his old cycling by-ways, but it had changed. The landscape seemed so different now. No, not the landscape, the atmosphere. As one can sometimes fail to recognize a face not seen for many years, one can similarly go through a stretch of countryside without remembering it. It had only been Prastio itself that had brought back everything so clearly.

He swung left so sharply in the middle of the tiny town that he almost killed an ancient Turk crossing the road.

Reid was now on the old familiar highway running down to Pergamos, and thus toward the outskirts of the British Sovereign Base Area. He rammed his foot down and was out of town and back into the countryside in a matter of moments.

Looking behind him, he saw that the pursuing jeep wasn't there.

"They must have missed the turn-off," he yelled to Vanessa, who had poked her head out.

"Can I come out now?," she shouted.

"No. Stay right there."

It was now a six-mile stretch to the Kouklia Crossroads, then another six into Pergamos. Reid didn't know what the Green Line was like at this point, what form it took. He hadn't visited this area during his return to Cyprus, but he figured it would be a lot easier to cross, as there would only be Turks manning the Line here, and no corresponding Greek troops on the other side to worry about; the other side being the British Base.

He rocketed past the Kouklia Reservoir on his left, overtook an old man on a donkey cart, and was stared at by three Turkish civilians on rickety bicycles, but aside from this the road was deserted.

Within five minutes he was in sight of the Kouklia Crossroads, and braking sharply. A roadblock lay before him, swarming with uniformed Turks.

"Down, Vanessa, down," he hissed, and she needed no bidding.

Once more a decision was called for. They could get out, taking a rifle or two, and head across country through the citrus groves which may or may not afford them cover for long. But then, they'd still have to cross the Lysi–Famagusta Road somewhere if they were to continue in their desired southerly direction, and that road was the very one that lay ahead, running east-west through the bloody roadblock. To try such a crossing on foot would be asking for trouble.

They couldn't go back. One swift look behind him made that clear. They were still being pursued. The jeep was now a dot at the end of the road, and growing in size each second. Reid had no real choice.

He grinned. He usually did in moments like this. It was better than crying, and Reid had always had a soft spot for Bulldog Drummond. Drummond would have grinned too. Old Bulldog may have been British Empire, an imperialist pig as they would call him these days, and he's despised because of it, but, damn it, Bulldog Drummond had his heart in the right place. So, Reid grinned. However, Bulldog would never have been so unsophisticated as to allow a tiny cigarette butt to burn his lips. John Reid threw the vehicle into gear.

It had only been a few seconds, but he'd forgotten Vanessa in all the excitement. He couldn't take her through what he planned to do now. Not a chance.

He reversed very smartly to a ditch by the side of the road, blocked from everyone's view but their own, and yelled, "Out, Vanessa!"

She jumped out, landing right on the side of the ditch, couldn't keep her balance, performed a neat pirouette, and fell in. It wasn't very far—only three feet, and she sprang up, her face a big question mark.

"Are you afraid?," Reid asked, talking to her from his seat, his arm resting on the side of the jeep.

"No," she replied, defiantly, and Read believed her.

"Good, because I can't take you with me."

"Why not?," she said, eyes brightening.

"No time for explanations. You've got to hide in this ditch until they've passed." Reid indicated with his hand the direction from which the pursuing jeep was traveling. "Then, somehow, you've got to get to Denktash in Nicosia, and warn him about the Professor."

"Warn him about what?," she asked.

Reid realized she didn't know what he knew. "The Professor's trying to effect a coup. Tell Denktash I sent you. Oh, shit. He's left the country. Look, do it, get to him, by phone, whatever you have to do. Can you do it?"

"Sure I can do it," she said, running her hand through her hair.

"That crossroads we passed not long ago?"

She nodded.

"Take a left, and try to get a lift. It'll take you to Nicosia. The Turkish for Nicosia is Lefkosha. Got it?"

"Got it."

"Get to the Parthenon. Stay there. If I get out of this, I'll call you there from the British base, okay?"

"Okay."

"And that poem I taught you a few days ago. That will get you to Denktash."

As he got ready to maneuver the vehicle back onto the road, Reid took one last look at her—black hair, beautiful as ever, tall, but foreshortened in the ditch.

"Watch out for Jap patrols." It was a joke.

"What do you mean?," she asked genuinely perplexed.

167

"Just a saying from World War II. My uncle used to say it all the time."

As Reid eased the jeep onto the tarmac, he heard her say, "I won't have any trouble there. I was born in Japan."

He was back on the road now. He could hear the engine of the jeep behind him, a couple of hundred yards now and closing fast, but the Turks in front of him, at the roadblock, appeared not to have seen him yet, and as he picked up speed heading toward them he hoped he could retain his anonymity until he was on top of the bastards. He was about three hundred yards from the crossroads when all hell broke loose. Guns began to open fire, and soldiers were running to position themselves in the middle of the road, obviously with one order only: Stop Bulldog Drummond.

Bullets were thudding into the fast-moving jeep with greater and greater frequency as Reid covered the remaining hundred yards at close to sixty-five miles an hour, which was as fast as this jeep could go. Then, when he was almost on them, his side of the windshield smashed into a million tiny fragments, as scores of bullets found their way to the target.

Instinct again. He had ducked down just before the first spray of glass covered him. Now he barreled toward the troops, his body arched out of the jeep in order better to protect himself from oncoming bullets, and in order to see where the hell he was going, his right hand propping open the door and his left on the wheel.

Over the roar of the engine he could hear the shouts of the frenzied Turks, as they scattered to all sides to avoid this kamikaze pilot. Reid swerved violently to the right to prepare to crash between the two parked Turkish jeeps that were touching nose to nose in the hope of blocking his path. By now he was sitting up straight, bracing himself and gritting the hell out of his teeth.

The impact was horrendous and the screech of metal deafening. He was jerked out of his seat like a puppet, his head smashing into the starry remains of the windshield, knocking the glass out onto the hood in one hit. How he managed to control the jeep was because the gods saw to it, that's all, for his feet had instantly left the floor. As the two parked jeeps splayed to left and right, he plowed through like an icebreaker punching its great fist through pack ice. His right door was ripped off its hinges. He bounced back into his seat and resumed his footing on the accelerator. How the machine had not stalled was beyond him. The gods up there on Olympus just shook their heads in wonderment, smiled at each other and muttered "Good lad" into their ambrosia. Reid stole a look behind him as he swerved over the debris-strewn road to the other side of the crossroads, and saw several troops running crazily around the smashed jeeps. In addition, the firing had started again. He ducked down and drove until he was out of range.

He couldn't quite believe he'd done it, that it had gone off so perfectly. Only a few miles to go now, to Pergamos, and he'd find a way to cross the Green Line when he got to it. He hoped to hell Vanessa was okay.

The engine stopped abruptly. He glided involuntarily to a halt. Shit! Bastard! He switched the ignition on and off frantically, trying to re-establish his relationship with the engine. He jumped out and ran to the back of the jeep. The number of bullet holes in the body of the vehicle was quite phenomenal. He looked back the way he'd come. A thin trail of black liquid told its own story.

He'd been lucky. One of the bullets could have brought with it enough heat to ignite the petrol, and the jeep could have exploded. Or maybe that was only in the movies.

Reid began his dash across the wasteland, heading for groves to the left of the road. A tiny windmill stood alone about halfway between the road and the trees, one of a thousand such windmills dotted about the island, and he veered toward it like a moth goes to a light bulb.

He'd covered only a few yards when he heard a jeep tearing down the highway from the direction of the roadblock. It could only be the jeep which had pursued Reid and Vanessa from Prastio. Reid sprinted faster across the dirt.

The orange groves were about four hundred yards away across this open stretch of land and as the Turkish jeep jumped off the road onto the wasteland Reid knew he'd never make it, no matter how fast he ran. Robbie Brightwell couldn't have made it. The troops would overtake him and cut him down as he ran.

One more quick look behind him to judge distance. Then he put his foot in it. "Oh, shit!," came the cry, long and loud. A tiny ditch reaching out for him. And he was over. Another bloody Bulldog Drummond story. But it's usually the heroine. But she wasn't here right now. Reid really, really hoped she was all right, and hadn't fallen into the wrong hands.

He lost several seconds, valuable seconds, just yelling "Shit," and then he was scrambling to his knees, the air knocked out of him. He turned.

169

The jeep was ninety yards away at the most, and boring in. The driver had selected Reid as the meal of the day. Forty yards and closing. The troops in the jeep were now yelling like devils, and Reid got ready to throw himself to one side, if he could.

He stood up bold, hurled the baseball full force at the driver, and then threw himself to his right. Of course the baseball was imaginary, but the driver didn't know that. Works every time. He swerved to his right, as they always do if the steering wheel is on the right, and blundered off his course. A ton and a half missed Reid by feet, and then he was back on his, up and running toward the windmill.

It must have been twenty seconds before the shooting started, but by that time Reid was nearly at the mill. He dashed around the flimsy metal framework and skidded to a halt. One look behind him told him all he needed to know. The jeep was still headed his way, but a number of uniforms were out of the vehicle already and running toward him.

Pity this mill wasn't the old Dutch type with its solid body to afford cover. A couple of shots ricocheted off the struts of the mill and Reid was on the move again, pounding over the loose earth toward the orange trees, trying desperately to keep the mill between himself and his pursuers.

He crashed into the groves, lungs bursting. The troops were almost at the windmill now, screaming at the top of their voices. Reid plunged through the thicket of small trees, trampling over fallen fruit, making instant orange juice and adding a new olfactory dimension to his socks. Using the sun as a guide he headed south. Soon he could hear only his own footsteps. He slowed down. He figured they'd already given up. Hopeless. Needle in a haystack job. They'd wait. Well two could play at that game. He decided to head east as well as south. They'd be expecting him to keep a straight course, that is if they thought about it at all. Might as well make it tough for the bastards. If these groves were as extensive as they'd looked from the road, he should, in a few miles or so, and barring accidents, arrive at the Green Line overlooking the British Base.

*   *   *

There was the Green Line. Half a mile away to the south across deserted, barren land. As Reid stood at the edge of the citrus grove, he wondered how the hell he was going to cross half a mile of no-man's-land without being seen. The groves of orange and lemon trees he'd just plowed

170

through had seemed to go on forever, which had been lucky for him, and he had hoped beyond hope that the bitter lemons might continue right up to the Green Line itself, affording him cover all the way. But it was not to be, and he could only thank Lady Luck that he was alive as far as this.

Nobody appeared to be pursuing him. The soldiers were probably hugging the roadway. Well, Reid was some miles away from there now. They may well have been expecting him to make for it in an attempt to cross directly into the British town of Pergamos. He had one unusual thing going for him: Most people in this modern world think "vehicle" and not "foot," and if they were to think "foot" it would only be after they'd thought "vehicle." The Turks, it might be supposed, were expecting him to try to appropriate another jeep in which to make his final attempt at the Line, so for this reason, among others, he was glad he was riding Shanks's Pony this time, even though the going was slower.

He had to admit that the thought of crossing this half mile of no-man's-land was an unenviable prospect. He knew well where he was, topographically, even though these citrus groves had been newly planted since his days there. The Green Line in this part of Cyprus had been set up on the ridge of a range of hills which led down on the other side to the British Base below. The ridge itself, dotted with hillocks, was manned intensively by Turkish soldiers, one every fifty yards it looked like from where Reid stood. He could see them clearly, some pacing, most standing still.

So this was where they all were. Reid had estimated about twenty thousand troops in Famagusta, ten maybe in Nicosia, and another five roaming the countryside. Despite apologists and so-called realists claiming that there were only fifteen thousand in Turkish Cyprus all told, most of the estimates Reid had had, from the civilian populations of both sides, was fifty. Judging by the concentration along the Line at this point, he was inclined to believe that fifty was more accurate. What a waste of bloody dogpower.

He looked to left and right. Scenery the same in both directions, half a mile of coverless wasteland separating the edge of the groves from the Green Line. He had to get to the ridge, then through the Line, and down the sloping hills which he knew lay immediately on the other side. But the first step was to cross this stretch of land without cover. And that would be suicide. He would stand out like a drinks fountain in the desert.

An hour went by. He was damned tired now, his sleep the previous night having been lengthy, but bloody uncomfortable, even though he'd been shacked up with a beautiful brunette. In addition a long run of danger wears you out and makes it difficult to sleep. Physically he felt wiped out. He pulled out a cigarette, his last, and smoked it gratefully. Capstan. Fine, fine cigarette for a man in a bind.

He wound up using most of the hour as a respite, shut his eyes for a while but didn't sleep. Just relaxed his limbs, one at a time, an old trick, and switched his mind off and thought about Reggae. He'd kind of decided to wait until nightfall. But the future was unilluminated.

The dark green, smooth body with the black triangular spots appeared as shocked as Reid. They both stared at each other, not moving a muscle. The coupli's head was within a foot of Reid's hand. He hoped it wouldn't be startled by the sudden outbreak of prickly sweat on his brow. One lunge from this fellow and he could forget all his troubles. He had no trouble whatever in recognizing it for what it was, and knew vaguely what to expect: The fangs going into the flesh, his flesh, that is, the venom glands activated, the poison shooting down the venom glands into the canal which runs down the middle of the serpent's tooth, the pain in the leg. Then it was only a matter of time before the blood-vessels started playing up, the vomiting started, and paralysis began. If the snake got him, how long should he hold out before rushing for help? That is, if he was capable of movement. Would the Turks have the anti-serum anyway? Fat bloody chance! Was this how it was going to end?

For an eternity man and snake looked fixedly at one other, and then, as suddenly as it had come, the mortal coil shuffled elegantly off into the trees.

Reid exhaled sharply. He had no time to wipe his brow, for footsteps, a lot of them, were approaching steadily from the right.

He stuck his head gingerly through a break in the grove, alert at the same time to the possibility of the coupli returning. He saw a file of soldiers coming his way. They were evidently patrolling the edge of the citrus grove.

Reid shrank back into cover as the troops filed by, a mere ten feet from him. A distance of about thirty feet separated each man. Reid crouched, waiting for them to pass.

The soldiers had no idea he was there. That was obvious. This was just a patrol, perhaps out looking for Reid, but more than likely simply part of the routine Green Line activities. They were silent and relaxed as they tramped by, the leading man with a rifle slung over his shoulder.

"Watch out for Jap patrols."

They had all passed now, eight of them, and he stood up warily, crossing to the very fringe of the trees again. He looked to his left and saw the troops filing away into the distance. Then he looked to his right.

He was down now, on all fours, ready to execute the plan that had come to him in only half a second. The straggler had evidently been for a brief visit in the grove, for he had been doing up his fly just as Reid had stuck his head out of cover.

The crunching footsteps were level with Reid now, and he waited, heart beating like a hammer, until the soldier passed. At that second he was out from behind cover, left hand around the Turk's mouth, and right hand pulling the soldier into the grove. It was all over in a very short space of time.

Not a loud sound had been made from the moment he'd plucked the loose Turk from his path to the time he laid him on the ground. The unlucky soldier was not as tall as Reid, but he was large, with a moon face and a fleshy body. Still, it was better than nothing. In this Turkish man's army, a private's uniform was not designed to fit properly. It was made specifically to irritate the poor bastard. Reid stripped the uniform from the body and put the clothes over his own. "Don't want to be shot as a bloody spy." Too many damned Gestapo novels.

Gestapo. World War II. "Watch out for Jap patrols." Then Vanessa came to him in the ditch, pretty as a princess in full, glorious Technicolor. For some reason she was waving a Samurai sword at him, and about to charge. "Won't have any trouble there. I was born in Japan."

He shook off the image, and tried to struggle into the boots, but this boy's feet were just too small, and Reid soon gave it up as a bad job. Running shoes would just have to do. The Turks wouldn't spot them anyway. Maybe.

Then he stepped out, bold as you like, onto the wasteland.

One foot gingerly after the other, step after step, yard after yard, trying his best to look and walk like a Turkish soldier. How does a Turkish private fart, he wondered. Probably like any other soldier.

Not a sign of trouble. All quiet on the western front. He looked to his left again. The patrol had disappeared around the circumference of the grove now, but what worried Reid was that sooner or later they'd discover the absence of the ninth man. That made speed important. Totally exposed, Reid crossed the wasteland toward the Green Line. Images of Japanese soldiers, but no really coherent thoughts, came into his mind as he approached the ridge. A few guards waved a friendly salute as he came within a hundred yards of the Line, and being a jolly sort of guy, Reid waved back. He felt very light, as if mildly drugged, and he was a little surprised that his brain seemed clear of negative processes; especially apprehension. He considered that, as he had come so far into the lions' den, and that because he was now way past the point of no return, and thus finally committed to success or death, the trepidation which normally accompanies danger had now given way to the acceptance which accompanies the inevitable. For inevitable it certainly was that he would either escape or die. There could be no surprises now.

He calmly selected a spot on the ridge in between two hillocks about eight feet high and shaped like little, malformed pyramids. This was where he would cross. There would be no second attempt.

Two Turks commanded the thirty-foot distance between the two hillocks. Each of them was leaning against his own hillock, facing inward toward the other, like two actors in opposite wings of the stage in a provincial playhouse.

Reid concluded that if he had waited for nightfall to make his break he may well have had a harder time of it. At this time of the morning, in broad daylight, far less suspicion would be cast on a lone Turkish soldier walking toward the Green Line, whereas in the dark probably everyone would be challenged. And who knew what the security measures were applied at night? He silently wished the best for the bladder of the dead Turk in the citrus grove.

The Turks were dozing, both of them, their rifles propped up by their sides, against the hillocks, as Reid drew almost level with the ridge. He could see beyond that ridge now, the steeply sloping hills rolling immediately down to the vast expanse of yet another no-man's-land some five hundred feet below, this new wasteland leading to the main serpentine road half a mile in the distance. That road represented the British Base. Okay, pretty much as he'd estimated.

He could see no one down there as he surveyed for miles the area of the base which had been one of the two granted to the British, by the

British themselves, coincidentally, in the 1960 Constitution, and the very base where he'd lived fourteen years before. It all looked the same down there as it had done when he'd been a kid. The main road leading to the RAF town of Pergamos, and the turn off leading through Rhine Camp to the principal part of the base at Dhekelia. This assessment took a mere few seconds, for his concentration was all but totally on the two Turks.

Reid stealthily approached the man on the left knoll. He was now out of sight of all but these two sleeping dog soldiers. Perhaps he could bypass them, slide quietly down the hill to the bottom, and then run like a bat out of hell across the no-man's-land to avoid any unlikely but possible stray bullets in the back.

With no sound at all in the area, except the Turk on his right snoring fitfully, Reid silently approached the ridge, and got down on his hunkers, preparing to take the leap. Right at that moment, the Turk five feet to his left stirred and awoke.

He stared at Reid. Reid, in a crouching position, stared at him. The Turk's eyes suddenly registered the truth and he glanced sideways at his rifle. He shouldn't have done. It was as far as he got. Reid came up from ground level with a Bolo punch that caught the good soldier's jaw like a hammer. As the victim sagged slowly, oh so slowly, to the base of the knoll, Reid was already facing the other sentry. The man had his rifle in his hand, and was aiming the weapon in Reid's general direction. More, in Reid's specific direction. The soldier let forth a massive shout as Reid took three rapid bounds forward and launched himself into the air with a flying kick, his foot connecting violently with the man's chest.

The Turk smashed against his own hillock and slid, badly winded, to the ground, as Reid landed on his own feet, almost toppling over the ridge as he did so.

At that very moment of imbalance, as he teetered on the edge, a third soldier appeared, rushing around the knoll, unarmed. He took in the scene, his eyes darting from left to right, as Reid struggled to regain his balance on the rim. Before the guard could work out that this was an impostor, Reid was in space.

He had perfected the trick as a kid in the wadis of Nicosia, those very wadis which now formed part of the no-man's-land in the Capital. You leap off a ridge, you sail several feet down through the air, and you land on your bum, hands behind you, in harmony with the descending slope, like a ski-jumper without skis. This little trick now stood him in good stead. It's a useful skill, but if your timing is off you'll never walk again. Reid's timing was spot on. It was a smooth escarpment and he'd dropped a good twenty feet before he thudded onto the grassy slope for a three-point landing, his hands acting as stabilizers. And then he was sliding, fast, but not fast enough. Fearing a bullet, he knew that somehow he had to speed up his descent, so he jerked his knees upwards, put his head between his legs and his arms around his knees, and became a snowball. Faster and faster he rolled down the slope, gaining extraordinary momentum with each second.

He could see absolutely nothing except the dark red blur of the blood pumping in his head. He could hear only the regular thuds of his own body as he barreled down the slope, and he could feel only the ever-worsening pain in his shoulders and coccyx as he was propelled farther and farther downward.

And then, all of a sudden, he was airborne, spinning over and over. He uncoiled swiftly and tried desperately to right himself and stop the spin. His mind spun as quickly as his body as he tried to make out where in the hell he was, and why he was spinning in mid-air. The blue sky alternated kaleidoscopically in his vision with the green-brown of the ground. He'd almost managed to straighten out when he felt a terrific jolt against his back, and he blacked out.

It was only a momentary blackout, and as his eyes focused he found that he was looking upwards. The mystery cleared itself up. He'd rolled right off the edge of the slope and shot out over the lip of a huge cave tucked into the base of the hills.

He lay breathless, smarting. He'd landed on soft soil, but had dropped a good thirty feet at a more than uncomfortable velocity. The Green Line ranged a long way above him and out of his line of vision. He could hear no shooting. It was quiet save for the deafening roar of his inner organs.

As he looked into the cave he recognized it as one he had, as a boy, occasionally explored for archeological remains, and not so archeological young ladies. One nice little bit of fluff named Davina. Fifteen she was. She'd let young Reid explore as far back in the cave as he cared to go. Fuck, he would still go for Davina today. What was she doing now? Who the hell knows? Did her husband and two-point-two kids know the secret of the cave? Maybe Reid had her all wrong. Maybe she was now a high-class call girl in Zurich, or something. Maybe she was okay, doing something constructive. He hoped so. He had admired Davina.

The cave ran a good fifty yards along the base of the hills. Reid wondered if the Turks would slide down after him. If so, he was in desperate trouble, for he found that his limbs were not working. Crowding out all other thoughts came the terrifying belief that he'd been paralyzed, and that his worst fear would become a reality; that of being taken alive by the Turks.

After several seconds of lying spread-eagled on his back, and trying to move his arms and legs, he began to feel a tingling sensation in them. A pins and needles cramp started to shoot through his arms and legs with alarming ferocity.

The sensation was exactly the same as when your leg goes to sleep and then, while coming back to life, goes through a de-cramping process that causes such discomfort that you don't know whether to laugh or cry. This was what was happening to Reid now. What with his roll down the hill, the sudden impact of landing on his back the way he had done, and with the tension of the situation as an aggravating factor, he'd simply seized up. Now he was going through the withdrawal and the pain was excruciating.

Instinctively he rolled over, gasping, arms and legs twitching. He took little comfort from the fact that he'd succeeded in moving, and twisted over again, rolling over and over sideways to try to relieve the violence of the pins and needles.

He could feel the blood rushing to his extremities, and he tried to stand, slowly, slowly. He groaned, and fell down on his back again. He started to shake his limbs wildly, and all the time he could feel a lessening of the pain, and an overall improvement.

As he looked up he saw the uniform on the lip of the cave. He almost jumped out of his skin. The Turk had obviously slithered down the hillside as far as he could without dropping off the edge. He now half stood, half lay on the slope, thirty feet above Reid, and he was fixing an aim. This boy was going for the grand prize at the fair.

Momentarily forgetting what he was going through, Reid sprang to his feet and dived headlong into the cave. He fully expected to hear a shot, but it didn't come.

As he stood panting in the entrance to the mammoth cave he squirmed about, shaking his arms and legs again to rid himself of the final sensations. He'd been lucky, extremely lucky, and as he looked out over the vast stretch of scrubby no-man's-land ahead of him, and to the road half a mile in the distance, he wondered what was going on thirty feet above his head on the slopes of the hills.

He could hear nothing. Was there only that one soldier, or was the hillside swarming with them? How far were they allowed to come into the British Base? In fact, where did the Turkish sector end and the British begin, exactly? Was it here, at the base of the hills, or was it at the road at the other side of the wasteland, or was it at the top of the ridge above Reid's head? Had he already crossed the Green Line in point of law, was he in the middle of it, or had he not yet come to it? These questions went quickly through his head, and he had a strong suspicion that the correct knowledge would prove vital. He clenched his fists to test that the cramp had gone.

He looked around him, taking in his surroundings. The sandstone cavern yawned back to a depth of thirty or forty feet across the soft dirt floor. It was as large as he'd remembered from many years ago, like the inside of Jonah's whale.

Peering gingerly out he could see nothing unusual. He looked upwards. Nothing but the lip of the cave.

He could make a dash for the road, but if he did he'd be picked off as target practice by who knows how many Turks. A real turkey-shoot. Even Reid's luck couldn't last that long. On the other hand, if he stayed where he was it would only be a matter of minutes, surely, before they found their way down and around to the cave and nailed him.

Reid ran to the other end of the cave and looked out again. Still nothing, and he could hear nothing either. But he knew the bastards were there, waiting.

By now they should have been down, and into the cave, if they were coming at all. Reid realized then that this was as far as they were prepared to go. Technically he must be in British territory now, or at least he was over the Green Line. That made sense. He could, once again, wait for nightfall to make a bolt for it, but then they might have flashlights, maybe even searchlights. Turkey-shoot again. Nighttime turkey. He tried to soothe himself with the idea that such illuminations would attract the

178

British from the road, that is if anyone were passing by, and because of that the Turks might not use such lights. It was in this state of half consolation that he hunkered down, going for a cigarette.

"Shit!" Took the last one back there. Could have used a strong cigarette right now.

*　*　*

Half an hour passed. Reid paced up and down the floor, looking out, trying to form a plan of action better than waiting until dark.

He had to divorce himself from the tiredness and pain that he still felt. He had to attempt to change into another person. To assume another identity for a while when the going was tough. Feeling pain and exhaustion now. So take on another skin. For a while. Until the pain goes.

"John!"

Reid jumped as he heard the thin, high-pitched voice shouting from above his head.

"John, we know you're in there."

He shrank back slightly into the cave, more from a reaction than anything else. The Professor was yelling out in English. How the hell had the bastard managed to arrive so quickly? How had he managed to clamber down that slope? But then, with assistance and all the time in the world, it wouldn't be too difficult. Besides, Reid remembered the speed that the old man was unexpectedly capable of.

"Come on out, John. Be a good fellow, come on out, and I will spare your life." Hell, he sounded like the villain in one of Oppenheim's old novels.

"Come on out, John," came the shrill order again.

An image of Edward G. Robinson as Little Caesar flashed through Reid's mind. He wanted to shout out, "If you want me, you'll have to come and get me!," but the words wouldn't come. Just as well. He decided on silence as his only weapon at this stage.

"John, we cannot come down to join you because we may be seen by the British to be violating neutral territory. You see, once we set foot on level ground, then we are breaking the law. And we would not wish to be law-breakers, would we, John?"

Good news, perhaps. If he stayed in the cave long enough, the Professor might give up and go away. But also bad news in that the Turk's

179

compliance with the rules dashed Reid's hopes that that there might be British patrols walking the area.

"The British do not worry about us as long as we stay in our territory. You see, John, look at the road."

Reid looked once more across the barren area. A British truck was trundling along the road toward Pergamos. He hoped that the sight of masses of Turks concentrated on the hillside would puzzle the occupants of the truck, and that they would come to investigate. Just in case that failed, Reid started jumping up and down at the mouth of the cave, waving his arms like a madman. It seemed unlikely that the British could miss seeing all this activity, but the vehicle carried on without a pause. Reid could only put that down to one of two things: Either the British were used to seeing a crowd of Turks on the hillside, or there were only a few of them up there, and not a big force, as he'd thought. But he couldn't take a chance on the latter. Besides, even if that were the case, the Turks would still pick him off as he made a dash for it, no matter how many there were up there.

"However, you are still in our territory, John, you are still in Turkish Cyprus. Inside the cave is Turkish, outside the cave is neutral ground. Crazy, isn't it, John?" And a loud burst of giggling came down from above. "Unfortunately, as I mentioned earlier, we cannot join you. Not yet, any-way. But, John, when night falls we cannot be seen. I now offer you the opportunity to surrender. If you choose not to accept my offer, we will come and get you tonight. And, John, there are many nice young men up here who are, er, dying to meet you, and to become better acquainted with you personally." The Professor's harsh laughter rang in Reid's ears, and then quiet fell.

This was worse than he'd expected. Worse than being shot as a spy, worse than the torture the Professor had previously promised.

"John, you will curse your mother for having given birth to you," shouted the Professor with emotion, again sounding like an Oppenheim villain. Then all was quiet again.

The minutes dragged by like hours, as Oppenheim would have said. Reid had finally decided on a daylight dash, risking the bullet up the ass rather than the objects the Professor had so strongly hinted at. Hell, if he was going to go he'd do it in style, trying. Suddenly he stiffened. He was alert again. Once more Lady Luck had come to favor him.

A dead man can win a fight! As he had been pondering the negatives of life, his eye had been following the course of a large, black dung beetle which had been threading its way diligently over the dirt floor at the entrance to the cave, and out into the open. On leaving the cave the insect had gone to its right and, running parallel to the hill, had disappeared slowly into the distance. The tumblebug itself was unremarkable, as was its journey. What struck Reid sharply was the critter's instinctive desire for shade. Rather than travel in the open it had selected a path under cover of a sandstone roof, a roof about a foot and a half above its head.

Almost not daring to hope, Reid crouched down on his hands and knees, then dropped to his stomach, eyes searching the path taken by the beetle. He hadn't noticed it before, being too preoccupied with other matters, but here was a possible avenue of escape, a slim chance, so slim that even if he had noticed it earlier he might well have dismissed it. Here was a way to get out of the cave, undetected from above.

At the mouth of the cave, where he now lay, the mouth gave way to the cheeks, if you like, a continuation of the hillside upon which the Turks were gathered. But a sheer drop of thirty feet, the nose, if you like, prevented them from dropping to the ground, not to mention the restraining illegality of such an action. So, on his right just outside the mouth of the cave was the vertical sandstone wall forming the base of the escarpment. At the bottom of this rugged wall a narrow ledge jutting out about two feet on the horizontal. Eighteen inches below this ledge was the dirt ground along which the beetle was now journeying.

Reid stared along this three-sided tunnel in the wake of the dung beetle. He knew that if this ledge continued along the wall for any distance he might be able to slide through, unseen from above. From the position the Turks occupied they would have no idea that this was, in fact, a ledge, its light-colored roof merging with the hue of the ground. A basic and excellent camouflage.

He stood up and looked cautiously to his right. The ledge seemed to go on for a long way, as far as he could see before the mild curvature of the hills blocked his view. He estimated fifty or sixty feet of clear crawl at least, and prepared to follow the dungy scarab into the unknown.

It was fairly easy going as he slid along on his gut. It certainly was shady in there. Wearing two sets of clothes, as it were, this was a welcome relief. He saw another British three-tonner go by on the distant road and he thanked the stars that the left side of his tunnel was open. The claustrophobic atmosphere was bad enough as it was, being added to somewhat by that faint, yet mysteriously pervading aroma of dogshit which had always seemed as much a part of the Levantine landscape as the juniper and the wattle. He recalled the old days when the dogs used to roam this area, thousands and thousands of strays throughout the Mesaoria Plain in central Cyprus, occasionally raiding villages in packs, and causing much bloody panic among the locals. He remembered too the many times he'd gone out to the plains with the Army in the '60s, and from behind a batch of sandbags, and under close supervision, had mowed them down with a Bren as they'd crossed the desert. Better off dead. He removed from his path a piece of rock-hard crap which must have been at least twenty years old, yet still, after all that time, giving off the hint of a smell.

He took great care to glue himself to the wall as he slithered along. Yet the problem remained of keeping his left shoulder from being spotted from above. Two feet of width is not great in these conditions, especially for a grown guy of Reid's size, but he was glad, at least, that he had eighteen inches of height to play with.

Still not a peep from the Turks. So far Reid had succeeded in breaking away from the cave.

He'd traveled about fifteen feet when he caught up with the young beetle as it wobbled in its ungainly fashion from side to side, its antennae probing, picking its way through terrain which to this small being must have seemed like landscape of the most Brobdingnagian proportions.

"Excuse me, Ringo," Reid whispered to the little fellow as he gently scooped him up, placing him cautiously to his left. Then he carried on, looking back to check on the welfare of his new friend. Ringo was now scurrying back into the shade of the tunnel, possibly wondering, as Gulliver had done, about the tricks the gods seem to play on all of us.

Reid had been traveling in his serpentine manner for about forty yards, and had been extremely pleased with the smooth, uncomplicated progress he'd made. His humor had improved the farther he'd gone, and he was feeling more and more positive that he'd effected his escape, when all of a sudden his hopes sank as drastically as the roof of the ledge.

The sandstone ceiling had become depressed to a mere nine or ten inches above ground level. Even if he were to reduce the height of his head by keeping his cheek pressed to the dirt, his shoulder blades would never make it through. He wondered if he were far enough away from the cave to make a break for it now. He hadn't even begun to round the curve of the hill yet. He'd have to slide out, get up, and then break out into a run after being holed up like this. No. Suicide. Sheer seppuku. Japanese again. Hell! Something was in the back of his mind, niggling like a worm. Irritating his brain. But then his spirits sank even lower as another dung beetle—it might even have been Ringo, they all look alike—crossed his path by his hand.

He lay face down in the desert sand, and idly flicked a piece of dirt in the direction of the bug. It immediately dug for cover, disappearing under the soil.

Lady Luck. She loves you, yeah, yeah, yeah. The insect world had provided him with yet another way out. He began to dig in front of him, with not a moment to lose, piling the loose, cool dirt up under his uniform and placing some of it to his left but still under the protective screen of the ledge. It proved relatively easy to create a narrow furrow and he slid his chest into it, his head scraping the stone ceiling above.

As he inched his way forward, digging handful after handful of dirt from in front of him, he carried it with extreme care around his side and dropped it between his legs behind him. It turned out to be a painfully slow process after a while, but at least the ledge remained at a constant height and didn't get any lower.

After two hours he wondered how long he could keep this up. He'd been digging like a mad mole to a depth of about four inches, perhaps a bit more at times, but he'd only covered a distance of ten feet. He was crushingly tired, and worried that time would run out on him. He couldn't keep digging forever. But he may have to, until nightfall, anyway. At that point he may still escape into the dark, as then the Turks would all be flocking to the cave. At least there was a ray of hope.

And then, as suddenly as it had dropped, the ledge rose again, this time to a height of three feet. One makes one's own luck. Reid rose to a crouching position and began stiffly shuffling along the much-enlarged tunnel.

He had gone about twenty yards in such a manner before he discovered that not only was the ceiling of the ledge rising but the width of it was diminishing at the same time, and at the same rate. Immediately in front of him the ledge disappeared totally, leaving him without any cover at all. The curve in the hillside, which coincided with his current position, had looked welcoming from a distance, but now he was actually there, it proved inadequate. Almost without any protection now, he leaned carefully out, and looked up. He could see the slope above the cave, could see it clearly, for the first time, and it was just as he'd suspected. Uniforms were crawling all over the place, some standing, some hugging the hill face, as they moved around the focal point—the man in white.

Reid could see him now, looking just as he'd left him the previous afternoon. The old man was perched immediately above the cave about sixty yards from where Reid now stood. Reid had been right in assuming that the Turks would be concentrated above the cave itself, vultures just waiting for a man to die. The ledge of the tunnel which had provided his escape was, as far as observers thirty feet above were concerned, simply rock ground. But it had come to an end now, and it was time for a decision.

Reid couldn't see the slope directly above him, but no one seemed to be there. Ten feet ahead of him was the slight curvature in the rock, and he knew that he must round it.

With his back to the wall, he glided slowly and smoothly toward the curve, and looked up. There, up on the far slope beyond the curve he saw scores of uniformed Turks edging their way along the hill face to join the Professor and his gang. Reid shrank back. If he stepped forward again he would be spotted. Only the lack of a hullabaloo told him that that hadn't already happened. However, if he stayed where he was any longer, hugging the wall like this, he would be espied sooner or later by someone. He was now blatantly exposed, like a prick sticking out of a pervert's raincoat. All they had to do was look his way and they'd see him.

"It's no use just sitting there," he smiled, grimly, and crouched down into imaginary starting blocks.

And he was off like Bob Hayes, always Hayes, forging his way across the barren stretch of land toward the road. Wearing two pairs of trousers and two shirts made the sprint difficult, but the running shoes aided his flight. And, no mere incidental this, he was running for his life. He covered the first hundred yards in fifteen seconds, the blood pounding in his head like nine-pound hammers.

He'd expected the bullets to fly but, although several rifles barked, and a lot of shouting took place, no lead bounced into the ground anywhere near him.

184

He pulled up, exhausted and shaking, hands on knees, Pheidippides after a race, a deadly race, panting. He stood up and surveyed the hills. Then he started walking slowly to his right. Soon he was on a level with the cave, and a good hundred yards away from it.

The Professor was standing on the lip of the cave, his fists clenched to his chest and gazing out onto the wasteland as Reid casually sauntered backwards. Reid, in turn, stared at the old man and the soldiers on the slopes. The Professor began gesticulating. Several rifles sang out, and Reid backed up further as a few bullets fell spent into the ground about ten feet in front of him.

Once he'd convinced himself that he was out of range, except perhaps from a sniper's bullet—and he didn't see why they should have one of those—he stood still.

"Hey, Professor," he yelled at the top of his voice. The old man signaled to his men to stop shooting. A broad smile broke out on Reid's face as it fully dawned on him that he'd finally made it, and that the Professor had lost the game.

Once he knew he had the old man's attention, and remembering how apoplectic the Professor had become when insulted with bad language, he cupped his hand to his mouth and shouted, "Take this, you fucking son of a bitch!," and gesticulated with crudity.

That the Professor had seen, heard and understood this message was obvious. Delighted, Reid broke into a slow jog across the wasteland toward the winding, welcoming road of the British Base.

*   *   *

The desert-brown Land Rover cut across the road and ground to a halt in front of John Reid.

"Good afternoon, Colonel. You seem to be going my way. Would you be kind enough to give me a lift to Dhekelia?"

A look of utter astonishment spread across the face of the officer sitting in the passenger seat, but it didn't prevent him from whipping out a large service revolver. His driver, a skinny, knotty-faced corporal, had his hands on the wheel and a large, toothy grin on his mug.

For a couple of seconds the scene was frozen, as if the gods had stilled the hands of time so that all of the participants in this game could savor the particular emotions which each of them was bringing to this play.

Reid looked at the black weapon pointed at him from the vehicle.

"Surely the suggestion wasn't that outrageous, Colonel," he quipped, unconcerned, but a trifle offended by the decidedly hostile reaction from this fellow Brit. However, the smile still on his face, he advanced toward the Land Rover.

"Where you are, Johnny!," cried the colonel in a fantastically loud voice. "Stay right where you are. One move and you're brown bread."

Reid stopped in his tracks. His smile didn't disappear altogether, for in the back of his mind he thought it might be a joke. Besides, he was in an amused frame of mind. If the colonel was serious, he was an asshole, and assholes are amusing when you've just escaped from great danger. But they can rapidly become tedious. This was one of those old farts who call everyone they don't like "Johnny." How appropriate.

"Look here, Colonel, I've just been through a rather trying few days."

The officer's large, round, florid face registered greater astonishment still.

"Corporal!," he shouted to his driver. "This one talks like a bloody Englishman."

"Yessir," grinned the wiry corp, who stared amiably at Reid, glad of the entertainment.

It was only then that Reid realized the reason for the gun. He was overdressed. And that was why he'd called him Johnny. Johnny Turk. He felt he owed the colonel an apology.

"But I am British. You can see that. Besides, I've got my ordinary togs on underneath this uniform. Look…" And his hand went to his belt.

"Get your hands over your head, Johnny!," barked the colonel in slow staccato. "Corporal, keep me covered while I search him."

The colonel climbed out of the Land Rover as the driver, still grinning, unclipped his khaki holster and pulled out his own revolver, pointing it nonchalantly somewhere in Reid's approximate direction. But then, it seemed to be in the colonel's direction too.

"Can't you hear I'm British? My name's John Reid."

The colonel put his gun in his holster and began the frisk.

"He's wearing other clothes, all right," he shouted to the driver. "All right, Johnny, off with 'em."

Reid proceeded to take off his Turkish uniform, and the officer gathered it up and slung it in the back of the Land Rover.

"How come your English is so good, Johnny?"

"Well, I have been speaking it for quite a long time, Colonel," Reid smiled, toying with the clown.

The driver laughed and the colonel shot him a glance which would have killed a lesser non-commissioned officer.

"Look, Colonel, I'm a British tourist…"

"If you're a tourist, then what the hell were you doing coming from the Green Line over there?"

He stuck his thumb backwards in the direction of the hills, not taking his eyes off his captive for a second. It was a good question. Reid realized he couldn't answer it convincingly without sitting down with this fellow for about an hour.

"Come on, Johnny. You're coming with us. You're no bloody tourist. You've defected. We'll only have to return you, you know. Now, into the bloody Landrover."

He pulled out his gun again and signaled for Reid to climb into the open back of the vehicle. He did and the colonel followed, his overblown posterior taking up most of the opposite bench. Reid was a little frustrated now.

"Let's get this chappie into detention as quickly as possible," the officer said to the corporal. "Slim Barracks, Corporal, as quick as you like."

The Rover pulled away. Reid looked to his right, over the wasteland.

"Colonel, do you see those troops on the hills over there, below the Green Line?"

"You think I'm blind?," replied the asshole tartly, his attention riveted on none other than his prisoner.

"Well, what are they doing there?," Reid demanded, somewhat authoritatively.

"They're probably extremely annoyed with you, Johnny. That's why they're hopping around on their collective one bloody leg. You're the third one this year, that I know about anyway. What is it, they don't give you chaps enough bordello leave or something?"

"Colonel," said Reid, seriously, "I've just escaped from the Turkish Zone after two days of being on the run over there."

"If you're a British tourist, as you claim, laddie," continued the rectum, unperturbed, "then how come you were in the Turkish Zone to begin with?"

187

"I crossed through the checkpoint in Nicosia, at the Ledra Palace."

"I see," said the colonel sarcastically, studying every inch of Reid's face. "You crossed over into the Turkish Zone in the first place. Deliberately. Then you escaped over the Green Line here. And in a Turk uniform to boot. That sounds just like a British tourist, doesn't it to you, Drive?"

"Yessir," shouted back the corporal over the roar of the speeding jeep. He couldn't have heard a word his superior had said.

"All right, Colonel. Ask me anything that could identify me as a British subject."

"Don't play games with me, Johnny," threatened the colonel. "I can't explain your knowledge of English. I must say I've never heard a Turk so word-perfect before, almost word-perfect anyway, unless…," and a wild look of realization came into his eyes.

Your time has finally come, Jason. You are on the brink of a major intelligence triumph which might rock nations.

He threw his head back and snorted a "Ha!," at the same time baring the inner parts of his rather carelessly depilated nostrils. "Corporal!," he yelled, "I think we've bagged a spy here, a bloody Turkish spy." He said this in a voice so incredibly loud that this time the corporal heard every word, even above the roar of the speeding Land Rover.

"Yessir," the driver shouted back, his vocabulary severely limited by tact rather than by poor education. It was apparently his view that you don't talk to assholes any more than you have to; you just get a lot of hot air back anyway.

"I knew it. Come clean, Johnny."

But Reid chose not to surprise the colonel.

As they passed through Pergamos, Reid looked to his right, up the road to the Green Line, the same road he'd come down from Prastio earlier in the day, except on the Turkish side. He couldn't see any troops manning the Line. They were obviously all with the Professor now, and probably about to fan back to their posts.

The Land Rover roared through the township, onto the Dhekelia Road, past Rhine Camp.

"Would a British passport convince you, Colonel?," Reid asked rather bitingly, having forgotten till now the trump card he held in his back pocket.

"No, it jolly well wouldn't," blared the officer, "not on your life. In fact, not a squeak out of you, me lad, until we arrive at base. Oh, Corporal, make that I–Corps. They'll soon get the truth out of him there."

"Yessir," shouted the driver again. Reid grinned at this. How frequent is irony. Intelligence Corps Headquarters was precisely the place he wanted to go.

It wasn't long before they arrived at the outskirts of Dhekelia. They swung right at the huge British Military Hospital at which Reid's father had been based for a while years before. When they reached I–Corps, he was hurried out by the pistol-packing colonel, through the door, to the desk.

"Who's in charge here?," yelled the colonel, the decibel level of his vocal delivery betraying the excitement he was experiencing at the thought of going into the history books as Marriott, Spycatcher.

"Major Bookless, Sir," replied the surprised duty sergeant, standing to immediate attention behind the counter.

"Get him for me, Sergeant, there's a good fellow."

"Right away, Sir."

A few moments later the sergeant emerged with a distinguished-looking officer, fortyish, graying hair, mustache neatly clipped. Light blue, friendly eyes. Nothing too serious, perhaps, although we all spend a lifetime building our own facade.

"Major Booker?," demanded the colonel, finally holstering his revolver with a flourish. Wyatt Earp, Frontier Tamer. The only thing he didn't do was spin it on his finger and say "Howdy, Pard."

"I'm Bookless, yes, Sir. What can I do for you?"

"Marriott. Harding Barracks. I've landed a right one for you here, Major. Thought I'd better bring him to I–Corps. Caught him coming over from the Turkish Zone, across the Line, Pergamos way. Says he's a British tourist, but he was wearing this…" With a gesture that would have done credit to Laurence Olivier, he signaled his driver who had followed in his wake carrying Reid's Turkish uniform. "I have every reason to believe he's a jolly spy. English is excellent, almost as good as mine. You can hardly tell, just by listening to him."

Major Bookless stared at Reid for a few long seconds.

"John Reid," said the prisoner, by way of introduction. "I must smell like a Bengali's armpit, Major, and would be greatly obliged if I could have a hot shower somewhere."

189

Bookless continued to stare at him, summing him up. "Thank you, Colonel Marriott. We'll take over now," he said briskly.

"Any time I can be of service to I–Corps, Major. Oh, and don't let the blighter fool you with the old passport routine. Says he has a British one on him. I didn't fall for that one, not for a moment," and the colonel wheeled left, and strutted to the door. "Don't forget, Major. Marriott's the name," and he was out on his heel.

"Passport, please," and the major extended his hand.

Reid dug into his pocket and handed it over.

"Is your name really John Reid?," Bookless asked, comparing the picture and details with his new visitor.

"Yes, really. R-E-I-D. Thistles and all that. Brigadoon. Heather on the hill."

The major laughed. "Frankly, even my grandmother wouldn't have taken you for a Turk, and she's in her eighties and has lived in Carlisle all her life. By the way, being a Scotsman, what's the first thing that comes to mind when you hear the name Carlisle?"

"Charles Edward Stuart." There was, of course, no hesitation. "But I did just come in over the Green Line. Listen, Major, the first order of the day, late as it is, has to be to get a message to Rauf Denktash. It is of extreme importance."

"Denktash?" Bookless looked vague but excited at the same time, a very interesting combination in a major. "I've never smelled a Bengali's armpit," he grinned, screwing up his eyes as if they were watering, "but I get the drift. Take a shower, compliments of the house, and then we can talk, all right? Oh, and I'll have some clean clothes for you when you're ready. We're about the same size, I think."

There was no point in pushing the Denktash thing right now. It wouldn't get Reid anywhere. There's a right time for everything.

"Oh, Major, could you rustle up a packet of Capstan cigarettes for me, full-strength. I'm dying for one."

While Bookless went into his office, a corporal showed Reid the way to the showers. The stream of hot water made him feel twenty pounds lighter, that's for sure, and the new clothes, he had to admit, fit like a work-glove.

Bookless's door was open and he saw Reid pass.

"Reid," he yelled from within.

"Yes, Sir," Reid responded automatically, and went in.

"Sorry," Bookless said, sheepishly. "I forgot you were a civilian."

Reid grinned. "So did I, Major."

The major passed across a pack of twenty Capstans, and a box of matches. The first cigarette tasted better than any Reid had ever had; with that and the cup of real coffee—not your instant crap—he began to feel very distinctly human again.

"My name's Alan, and I'd appreciate it if you'd call me that."

"John."

That was the way it was done. They shook hands across the desk.

"John, we've got some talking to do."

Reid held up his hand. "Alan, I'll tell you everything, but first this Denktash thing."

The major held up his hand. "Taken care of."

Reid looked blank, and he realized it.

Bookless was about to help him out. "Any moment now there'll be a..."

And there was. The major put his finger to his lips.

"This is Major Bookless," he said into the mouthpiece.

He listened intently, wrote something on a piece of paper, then he said, "Thank you very much," and hung up, and passed the paper across, Reid's side up so he could read it.

"That's a phone number in Rome," the major said, smiling. "Use this," and he swiveled the phone across the desk for Reid's use. "Just dial it as it's written."

As Reid was working his finger, Bookless said, "Oh, it's Denktash, by the way."

Reid's eyes registered some surprise as the President of Turkish Cyprus answered "Pronto" at the other end.

"Mr. President. This is John Reid. I'm in Dhekelia at British Army Intelligence headquarters."

And then he listened, for quite a long time.

"Thank you, Sir," he said, and the phone went dead.

He replaced the receiver and swung the phone over to an eagerly-awaiting Major Bookless.

"Well? Well?," he demanded, like a small child.

Reid took another sip of coffee. His mouth was unexpectedly dry, and he fished for another Capstan.

"He already knew about it. What I was going to tell him, I mean. I thought he might have done, but I didn't know for sure. I had to be sure. And he suspected I was going to call this evening."

"How did he know?," asked Bookless.

"A little bird told him."

Reid laughed aloud, longer than he should have done, perhaps, but he was dreadfully relieved. He drew on his cigarette. "First of all, Alan, I'd like to compliment you on your instincts and incredible speed of delivery. I've never seen anything quite like that."

Bookless smiled appreciatively. "Perhaps you might put in a word or two for me with one of the big boys in London. Get me out of this backwater."

Reid looked vague, but managed a nervous laugh. "I don't know any big boys, Alan."

He looked at Reid quizzically. "I had you checked out, John."

"While I was in the shower? No disrespect, Alan, but I don't see how you had the time, what with all the other surprises you've been planning."

"I had Sergeant Williams do it," he said. "He's very good at that."

"Ah. And?"

"Nothing. There's nothing on you at all."

"There you go, then," and Reid laughed.

Again, the quizzical look. "Yes. There you go, then."

There was a silence, then he continued, "If it's any consolation, I took the Denktash initiative as soon as you headed for the shower room."

"Tell me, how did you do it?"

"One phone call to London," Bookless answered, beaming. "I asked them to get me Denktash's phone number, I mean where he is right now."

"Sounds easy, the way you say it. Thanks, anyway."

"My pleasure," he laughed, looking out of the door. "Another coffee?"

"Yes, please. It's good stuff. By the way, Alan, one more thing if you don't mind. Could you have Sergeant Williams call the Parthenon Hotel in Nicosia. Sooner or later, with a bit of luck, one Vanessa Riley should be checking back in there. She may even be there already. I'd be much obliged if he could ask her, or leave word for her, to come here in the morning. And for him to leave his phone number. Would that be all right with you? I'd rather not do it myself."

That was taken care of. After the two coffee cups had been refreshed, Bookless said, "You'd better tell me everything, from the start. Are you up to it? I mean, you look all in. Would you rather hit the hay? We can put you up here for the night, you know. Actually, as long as you want, really. Single bed, but it'll be comfortable enough. We could continue this in the morning."

"Thanks. I'm a little whacked, but I'm fine."

So Reid settled back and told the major about meeting Billy Wackett on the tube.

When they'd finished the session, Bookless exhaled, "I'm exhausted just listening to it. Let me get one thing straight. You left Vanessa at the ditch. From that point on, as far as you're concerned, I'm clear. But Vanessa. Her story from then to now is—what, exactly? Did Denktash tell you?"

"Well," Reid replied, "he was speaking very fast, and I had to fill in between the lines a lot of the time. But, as I see it, Vanessa got a lift straightaway. She must have done, to have accomplished what she did so quickly. All the way to Nicosia, to Denktash's office. I got her to memorize the poem, but even so she must be very persuasive, because only a couple of hours after I left her she was talking personally on the phone to Denktash in Rome. She must have been, for it all to fit in. Anyway, Denktash did tell me that he arranged for her to get back over the Line, and she would have gone straight to the Parthenon, where I told her to go. We'll get the whole story when she arrives tomorrow morning. That is, if all goes well."

*   *   *

It wasn't enough that he couldn't get into first class, they had to go and sit him next to this fucking boring couple. God. Four hours of uninterrupted Bob and Kay Butler was more than a human being should be put through. Burt Zoffel was fuming. Had been since they left London.

The Butlers lived in Gravesend. They had been together twenty-two years. The last of their three children, Bill, had just rented a slum tenement with some mates in London and so, for the first time since they got married Mr. and Mrs. Butler were alone, just the two of them. It immediately felt uncomfortable, and it got worse, day by day.

Bob had done his National Service with the Catering Corps in Cyprus during the EOKA troubles in the '50s, fighting the enemy tirelessly from behind enormous ramparts of meat and veg. He had finally risen to the dizzying rank of corporal, and those two stripes would, for the rest of his life, represent the pinnacle of his achievement. It had been on his last leave back in Gravesend when, after all that bullshit talk with the other cooks in Cyprus, he had been worked up to a fever pitch about girls, and had landed his next-door neighbor's underage daughter in the family way. There had been hell to pay for that, but he did the right thing. Two minutes of rather disappointing heaven had sealed his fate forever. He hadn't been back to Cyprus since, and now was the perfect time for a summer vacation in an exotic part of the world. Better than watching bloody *Coronation Street* and *Crossroads* and Larry bloody Grayson, and doing the bloody Pools, and everything else they'd done for the last three bloody decades to avoid looking at each other, and themselves.

It wasn't the first time they'd been on holiday. Oh no, not by any means. Their virgin venture into the stunningly disheartening world of British beachfront lounging had taken the form of a disastrous week at Bognor bloody Regis. Why Bognor, for Christ's sake? Bob had asked his wife when she came up with the idea. No one could really remember why they went to Bognor, but they all remembered Bognor very well indeed. A bored little family, lying uncomfortably on the anemic sand, trying with quiet desperation to enjoy the weak mist coming in off the English Channel, when a lorry spun off the road, crashed down onto the beach and hit the eldest kid, Rob. Rob was five then. He was in hospital in London for a year. Not a good one, Bognor. Rob, now supposedly an adult, had moved to Tunbridge Wells last year, to take up a position as a bloody pen pusher in a legal firm there. The second child, Rosemary, named after Kay's mother, was a great-looking girl, now 18, and had been in London for ten months, working as a fashion model, she said. No one seemed to have seen any of her photos. She lived in the Barbican.

The plane landed, not a moment too soon, and after passing through Customs, Burt Zoffel picked up a public airport phone. The tall man, at the other end, said, "Mr. Riley. I'm glad to hear from you. Where are you?"

Burt was hot and angry. "It took me three fucking days to get here. I can't believe it. I'm in Larnaka Airport."

The tall man was comforting. "Your daughter is perfectly safe, Mr. Riley. She arrived not long ago at the Parthenon Hotel, in Nicosia, alone. My two men ascertained that a message was waiting for her there. The message instructed her to go to Army Intelligence Headquarters in Dhekelia. She has seen the message, has hired a green Renault—she was overheard specifying green, but I don't know if that has any significance—and will be leaving Nicosia early tomorrow morning. My men will follow her, Mr. Riley, just to observe."

"Why Intelligence Headquarters?"

"It's probably where our Mr. Reid is," replied the tall man.

Burt hung up and stared up at a departing airplane. Then he went to find a rental car. Bob and Kay Butler took a cab to the one of the new hotels right there on the water. The following morning the couple would acquire a car and go exploring in the hinterland.

*　*　*

Reid slept until eight that morning, which wasn't surprising. He put on a shirt and trousers and walked down the hallway to the shower room and pushed open the door. On his left was the long pink terracotta stall he'd used the late afternoon before, housing three shower-heads lined up next to each other in a row, so that, God forbid, lads so disposed could take a shower together if they wanted, and look at each other's willies. The stall had a beautifully arched entrance on either end. Beyond the showers were the toilets. Nicely appointed facilities in I–Corps.

The water was hot, and the pressure was extraordinary. You can't sustain a whistling tune for long when spray is constantly trickling into your mouth, but Reid was putting forth a manful effort with Johnny Mercer's old hit "You've Gotta Acc-en-tu-ate the Positive." He'd just got to the bit about "Have faith or pandemonium's liable to walk upon the scene" when he first became aware that someone else had come into the bathroom. On the shiny tiled walls beneath his shower-head he saw a vague reflection moving slowly. The man was probably coming in for a pee, which is why guys generally came in here. Reid glanced out of the stall. The man was indeed heading slowly toward the urinals. It was just a soldier. Reid had no reason to sense danger, but he sensed it anyway.

He reached out to cut off the shower, but decided against it. He moved along to the toilet end of the stall, grabbed a towel and dried off quickly, still whistling. His clothes were on a rack by his elbow. There's a time to be naked, and this wasn't it.

The man hadn't yet passed back along by the shower stall. Reid looked out again, and in a wall mirror above the wash basin saw the reflection of the soldier from the neck down; he couldn't get his face in the angle of the glass. He could see his form clearly, standing by the toilets, idly, loose, waiting. Not peeing at all. But, as Reid watched, the man dug into his trousers to pull something out. It wasn't quite what Reid had expected to see. He could make out quite clearly, and with enormous fascination, the object the soldier was retrieving from below his waist-band. It was bigger, more metallic, and much more dangerous than a penis. And it had a long silencer on the end of it.

The man started slowly walking toward the nearest entrance to the showers, gun extended. Reid cut off the flow of water, reached out for the slippery but still new and large bar of Pears soap on the shelf, placed his feet in position, and fixed his attention, with his arm ready. Just at that climactic moment where Johnny bears down on the end of the song with that wonderful refrain of "E-Lim-I–Nate the Negative," the soldier reached the shower stall and looked in, astonished to see a fully clothed gentleman in that position. The song faded at "Don't mess with Mr. In-Between" and Reid let it go. The bar of soap must have picked up a speed of 60 miles an hour in the short distance it traveled between shower stall and forehead, and then there was a sickening crack. Reid had expected him to drop like a felled ox, but he just stood there, stock still, looking at Reid with a pained expression on his face, gun still pointed. Reid dived for cover the length of the shower stall. He waited. Nothing. Then he heard the man fall, in a heap, and the gun clattered on the marble floor.

Reid stepped gingerly out of the other end of the stall, and there was the dirty bastard, face down, gun and soap by his side. Reid kicked the pistol away and felt the man's neck for a pulse. It had been a clean hit.

Reid walked out slowly and bumped into Major Bookless in the corridor.

"Alan, there's a dead cockroach on the floor in there. Wouldn't be nice for any of your lads to step on it."

Bookless opened the door, walked in, took one quick look, noticed the pistol on the floor, and said, "What's going on?"

"He slipped on a bar of soap."

The major knelt down, turned the body over, and felt the man's neck.

"Bit old to be a private, isn't he?," said Reid.

"You're right," replied the major, rummaging through the dead man's pockets to no avail. "He's not one of ours. Any ideas?"

"I think he's American. Look at the shoes. And the teeth. No Brit has teeth that good. And certainly no Russian. Has to be American."

Bookless removed one of the shoes and looked inside. "American, yes. Burt Zoffel, you think?"

"I don't know. It could be. He's be about the right age. I can't remember what Burt looked like, it's been twenty years since I've seen him. But it could be."

Bookless opened the door and yelled out, "Sarn't Williams."

The sergeant came in fast.

"Take care of this, would you, Sergeant. Lift his fingerprints and get them off to London as soon as you can. We're looking for a Burt Zoffel, American. CIA. Possibly a double agent. KGB. Zed-Oh-Double Eff-Ee-El."

*   *   *

"First things first," said Bookless, as Sergeant Williams brought in coffee, and another pack of Capstans, for which Reid was eternally grateful.

"Vanessa called this morning," said Bookless, his chin in the cup of his hand. "She's on her way down as we speak."

He grinned as he watched Reid's reaction. "She's got to you, hasn't she?"

"Maybe."

"We'll put her up here for a few days. The nurses have good guest quarters in what you used to call Area 1."

Sergeant Williams came back in. "It is Burt Zoffel, Sir. The Home Office had his prints. State Department, Washington, D.C. No more information. That's it."

As Williams went out, Reid said, "Gosh, that was quick. Sergeant Williams is very good."

"The best I've ever worked with. I would put him up for officer."

"Would?"

"He doesn't want it. Says he'd feel uncomfortable and besides, it would take him away from what he really enjoys."

"What's bothering me," said Reid, "is how Burt found me here, at I–Corps."

197

"Well, let's work it through. You and your writer friend were obviously right. Burt was a double agent. No CIA man would go to the lengths he went to unless he was a double agent. Of course, he couldn't run the risk of his family finding that out, so he would feed them some rubbish they'd buy. That first Zoffel you found, the one in Chicago, the old man. Suppose that was his father. He had been primed by Burt over the years. He calls Burt, lets him know someone is trying to find him. John Reid. From the Cyprus days. That in itself wouldn't have set Burt off on this mad mission. But then you found Burt's younger son, what's his name?"

"Joe."

"Right. It's obvious from your two calls to Joe that our scenario is close, if not spot on. Joe informs Burt of the two phone calls and he's now worried that you're something more than what you claim. Then you send that postcard with the Russian phrase at the end. That would have been the last straw. Remember, you'd left your phone number with Joe's wife, so all Burt had to do was get an address. That's easy enough. So he comes to London, and follows you from there to Cyprus. Anyone can do that. And, hey, presto."

Reid looked at Bookless as another thought that had been niggling him for days un-niggled itself and came right to the forefront of his brain. He almost yelled, "The two guys at the Parthenon."

"What's this?" asked Bookless, leaning forward.

"Sorry, Alan, I forgot to tell you about that."

And he told him about Newcome and Sandby, or at least his experience of them. He didn't even know their names.

Bookless reflected, stroking his chin, and murmuring, "Hmmm. How do you know they were following you? They might have been following Vanessa. It had to be one of you. After all, you didn't spot them at the hotel until after you'd met Vanessa. I've got the time sequence right, haven't I?"

"Yes, you do. Let me think."

After smoking furiously for a minute or so, Reid said, "No. I don't think so. Too much of a coincidence. These two men were British. Vanessa is American. They must have been following me. Let's say Burt hires someone in London. To follow me. Not to kill me, you understand, because those two men could have killed me a thousand times if they'd wanted to. They were very tough looking individuals. Not private detectives. No, no.

But they were at the Parthenon not long after I got there. How did they track me down? From London. I left London very quickly, in the dead of night, so to speak. I arrived in Larnaka, took a cab to my cousin's place…"

Reid jumped up, another evil thought, one piling on top of another. "Oh, no! Harry."

"Your cousin?"

"My cousin. How did those two guys find me at the Parthenon? Suddenly there they were. Alan, could you get Sergeant Williams in here at the double? I want him to hear this. Can't waste time."

Bookless yelled out, "Sarn't Williams!," and a few seconds later the good NCO hove into the room, on the triple.

"Sergeant Williams," said Reid. "My cousin, Harry Blaikie Brownlow, is the vicar at the Anglican Church in Larnaka. It is absolutely vital that you speak to him in person, as soon as you possibly can, to find out if he's all right. His mother's maiden name was Innes."

Reid looked at Bookless, and said, "With your permission, Major."

Bookless nodded, and the sergeant said, "I'm onto it, Sir," and disappeared.

"Alan, this may be over-reaction, but I don't think so. I don't believe those two lads actually tailed me to Cyprus, within sight of me, I mean. But there were ways they could have found out I'd gone there. And they could have done that quite soon afterwards. They fly to Larnaka, and find Mike the cabbie. They either threaten him, or, more likely, bribe him, and they get to the church. They don't find me because I've already gone to Nicosia, but they do find Harry. There's not a chance that Harry would have told them unless…"

"So, these two men, working for Burt Zoffel, track you down to the Parthenon in Nicosia. Their mission is not to kill you, but merely to observe and report back to Burt, to keep in him abreast of your progress, something like that."

"Right."

Bookless was looking hard at John Reid.

"John, I know you don't like coincidences, but doesn't it strike you as a coincidence that Vanessa should also appear suddenly at the Parthenon. And at the very time these two men appeared there. You yourself said that you were surprised she wasn't staying at a better-class hotel."

"What are you implying, Alan?"

"Vanessa is American, John. The late Burt Zoffel was American too."

"Do you realize how many Americans there are in this world, Alan?"

"Yes, I think so. But could she be CIA? I mean, I'm just throwing this out. After all, as you said yourself, she seemed strangely reluctant to talk about her past."

"Bit too young to be a secret agent, Alan. She's only twenty-one, you know. Born in Japan, that's what she told…"

And then he was rendered speechless, totally speechless.

"You all right, John?"

Reid looked at him a long time before answering. "I need a cigarette for this."

He was struggling for images and memories. Then, slowly, and with his mouth suddenly dry again, he continued, "Something else I left out of my narrative last night. Not deliberately. Just forgot to mention it."

Bookless was all ears, but still a little worried, you could tell.

Reid carried on, speaking slowly as in a dream "Just before I left London, a matter of a day or two, I can't really remember exactly, I was having my hair cut in Wac & Wave in my apartment block. I was sitting in, let's see, the middle chair; yeah, the middle chair of three, looking out of the big window onto the High Street. Jayne Mansfield was doing my hair."

"Jayne Mansfield?"

Reid laughed a little. "Yeah, Jayne Mansfield. That's not her real name, it's just what I call her."

Bookless had imagination as well as good instincts.

"I had a towel around my face. Jayne had just given me a shave and was asking me if she could perform any other services for me. I just happened to look out the window. Couldn't help it really, it was right there. Right there in front of me. Looking out onto the street. There was a girl. In the window. She was outside, on the street. Looking right at me. She had this look, you know. A tall brunette, very young, stunning. Sunglasses. A hat. I remember hoping she'd stay there until I got out of the chair, but by the time I did she'd gone. Hell! I can't believe it."

"Vanessa?"

Reid didn't need to nod, but he did, once, curtly. "I knew I'd seen her before. But, it gets worse, a whole lot worse. Jerry Heditsian's wife told me she'd got a postcard from the Zoffels in Tokyo in 1959. I told you that. That's twenty years ago. Well, twenty-one years ago, in 1958, the

Zoffels left Cyprus. I told you that too. We didn't know where they'd gone. Jerry's wife it was who told me. They'd gone to Tokyo, that's where they'd gone. It was obviously Burt Zoffel's next posting."

"And Tokyo is in Japan," Bookless said.

Reid took a deep drag of his Capstan. "It certainly is. Vanessa's twenty-one. In the ditch back there, where I left her, when we were in some considerable danger, I made some crack about the Japs and World War II. Told her to look out for Jap patrols, something like that. I was trying to lighten the situation. Then she told me not to worry, she was born in Japan. I forgot to tell you that. It was the last thing she said to me."

"Good God," exploded Bookless. "A Zoffel daughter you never knew about?"

"I'm afraid so. Born in Tokyo, after the Zoffels left Cyprus. Holy shit!"

"So what does this mean?"

"I dunno. Let's think about that for a second."

Reid was much more devastated than he would have thought possible. Bookless was right. She'd got to him, in more ways than one.

Bookless came in as a voice of reason. "If our scenario is correct about the two men, then why would Burt send Vanessa in as well? His own daughter. That makes no sense. As you yourself just said, she's too young to be a CIA agent. And surely the last thing Burt would want is the CIA getting involved in this. Just like the two men, she couldn't have been the hit squad. Burt himself was the hit squad. And if he had hired these two men as observers, then why employ Vanessa for the same purpose? It makes no sense."

"You're right. I suppose we'll just have to wait till Vanessa gets here."

*   *   *

It was on a twisting, turning and very lonely road near the village of Xylophagou that Bob Butler pulled over at a rare suitable place and stopped the car.

"No one'll know," he said. "It's not that big a deal out here. Not like bloody England."

On the surface the whole plan was absolutely insane. But Bob and Kay Butler were human beings, and human beings, all of us, have the unexpected character trait. With the Butlers it was danger. The flirting with danger. It had been that way in the late '60s, when they first heard of sado-masochism. They weren't really cut out for that sort of thing, but they tried it anyway. It was only the pain that made them move on to shoplifting and blue movies.

So Kay took the wheel. Over here they drove on the left too, so it wouldn't be so bad. Not like that bloody time when they'd taken that—well, vessel was the only word to describe it—across to Calais, full of the sense of foreign adventure, and motored down to Booloyn to lie on the boring bloody beach and enjoy just the same shitty weather they'd had at Bognor bloody Regis. Bloody foreigners, driving on the wrong side of the road. "We used to own France, you know." "No, tell me another, do." "You wouldn't know it now, though. Bloody frogs."

She'd been learning to drive all her adult life, and knew more about driving than Stirling Moss. But she'd managed to fail the test seventeen times, the most memorable being when she'd peed herself because a passing driver had honked at her while she was attempting a three-point turn in front of Safeways. Seventeen was not a British record, not by a long way, but it was still discouraging.

It was on this lonely road on an island in the Near East, with the shades of Crusaders and their chargers looming up in front of her, that Kay Butler sat in the driver's seat with an overwhelming sense of her own inadequacy. "Clutch, gear, clutch, gear," she kept saying to herself. But she was actually doing quite well, as they drove along at about 20 miles an hour, the rock cliffs rearing upward on their right and, on their left, the sheer, unobstructed plunge of a thousand feet.

"You could go a little faster," Bob ventured, and she shifted into third, too soon, and the car stalled, grinding to a halt right in the middle of the road, right between the tight double curves.

They both uttered the word "bugger" at the same time. That's what happens when you've been together too long. Two green peas imprisoned in a fucking pod.

How the Renault managed to pass them was anybody's guess, but it did, its left wheels practically swinging out over the edge of the precipice. The green car was going faster than Kay thought decent. Noting that there was a girl at the wheel, she yelled out something she had been yelling out for decades: "Women drivers!"

Then, a mere second later, as the woman driver hauled the wheel around to take the next bend, she glanced off the right side of the inevitable bus coming the other way and the Renault sailed over the edge of the ravine.

With Newcome driving, the two hit men came hurtling around the first bend in pursuit of the Renault, and there was the stalled car right in their path, the bus in front of it jerking to a halt, and the green car flying through the air. Sandby said "Oh, shit!" in an almost subdued voice, and Newcome swerved to the right. He made it. Just.

Newcome and Sandby immediately backed up, and with the aid of a cleft in the mountain did a U-turn in the road and disappeared up the hill the way they had come. During the police investigation that followed soon afterwards, their Ford was never mentioned. The Butlers would answer some questions. Bob said he was driving, and that the car had stalled. What could he do? It wasn't his fault. It was the bloody car, wasn't it. They would ultimately fly back to Gravesend and continue their lives, positively unenriched by their Levantine experience.

*   *   *

"Your cousin is alive, Sir," said Sergeant Williams. "He's in London, technically in a hospital bed. I personally spoke to him this morning, three o'clock his time, but he was up and about already. He asked me to tell you that he'd be in Scotland afore ye. They stuck him with a knife. Pretty bad. Sounds like he comes from tough stock."

"He does that," Reid replied.

"Oh, by the way, he told me to tell you they got Gobbo."

"Poor bastard."

Reid took a drag on a Capstan and stood up. "I think I'll wait in the lounge, Alan. I've got some thinking to do before Vanessa arrives. She should be here pretty soon."

And so he strolled to the front of the building and sat down, deep in thought, as he waited for the girl.